DCPL0700001703

KU-796-689

WITHDRAWN FROM STOCK
DUBLIN CITY PUBLIC LIBRARIES

The History of Things

NEW
ISLAND

THE HISTORY OF THINGS
First published 2007
by New Island
2 Brookside
Dundrum Road
Dublin 14

www.newisland.ie

Copyright © Sean Moncrieff 2007

The author has asserted his moral rights.

ISBN 978-1-905494-73-6

All rights reserved. The material in this publication is protected by copyright law.. Except as may be permitted by law, no part of the material may be reproduced (including by storage in a retrieval system) or transmitted in any form or by any means; adapted; rented or lent without the written permission of the copyright owner.

British Library Cataloguing Data. A CIP catalogue record for this book is available from the British Library.

Printed in the UK by Athenaeum Press Ltd., Gateshead, Tyne & Wear
Book design by Inka Hagen

10 9 8 7 6 5 4 3 2 1

SEAN
MONCRIEFF
The History of Things

for B

1

IT IS a banana-shaped road, closed at one end. Like spectators at a funeral, the cottages line up along either side, built in the early 1900s for employees of the now-defunct Northern Railways. About halfway down on the left sprouts the only two-storey structure, constructed some twenty years before the cottages and since then cunningly remodelled into a terrace of three houses. This terrace, and the land on which the cottages huddle, originally formed the estate of Doctor James Bass. Doctor Bass spent nearly two decades in India before moving to Dublin and constructing a lavish new home, from where he planned to run an import business.

However, Doctor Bass's lack of interest in business, combined with a consuming interest in brandy, soon dissolved this ambition. He sold the house and land to the railway and fled to his native York, where he was later caught up in a minor scandal involving the wife of a local magistrate and the theft of some expensive Burgundy. Doctor Bass was found dead soon after, in the company of several empty bottles of the missing wine.

But these events took place over a century ago; there have been many stories here since. Everyone has long forgotten how Bass Avenue earned its name.

*

THE SILVER car jerking up Bass Avenue was no threat, so they ignored it. They curled against the railings, occasionally whipping out an elbow or knee to maintain their portion of space. One produced a mobile phone and unenthusiastically pushed at the buttons, while the other two resumed a debate about game cheats for *High Jinx II* (specifically, ΔOXΔ), then moved on to how many flavours of chewing gum it is possible to have.

Inside the silver car, Tomas Dalton gripped the steering wheel like a strangler.

Bloodybloodybloody. Driving around like a bloody old fool. Why didn't you follow the removal van? Oh, no, you had to be cocky, like you'd be able to find your way by instinct, like the geographical knowledge was burned into your DNA. Bloody old fool.

Even the familiar buildings had seemed strange and slightly hostile, old friends offended that he hadn't called. The trip should have taken twenty minutes, but Tomas had spent well over an hour scurrying among the green-skinned graffiti-resistant cubes spreading out from the city centre like a fungus. He only found the Clontarf Road by accident and only recognised it because that gabbling estate agent had dragged him up to the corner of Bass Avenue to have a look. See? It's a major artery to Howth and Sutton and Malahide, none of your cheap cars passing through here. North inner city, yes, but a lot of professionals starting to look in this area, Mister Dalton, *a lot* of professionals. Prat.

Nothing but prats. Nightmare drive through Wales. Ghastly country. Ferry was like a slum, full of drunken tinkers and obese teenagers bulging out of mini-skirts, ratty underwear on show for everyone. And those removal men? For three hours? The fat swivel-eyed one anyway, man can't shut his mouth. Why are you moving back to Ireland? Why are you moving to *this* area? Are you a married man yourself? And where would Mrs Dalton be?

He'll be crowing now. Did you not follow us like I said? Did you get lost? Mind your own business, you hoggish vulgarian.

But he said none of these things out loud. Of course.

Calm down, man. Calm down. Tired. A long drive. Look, look – on the pavement, three boys. This implied three sets of parents, grandparents, friends, visiting cousins, drunken uncles. Tell your father dinner is ready. Dirty necks. Bash-dash. Older sisters sneaking smokes. Chewing gum. Yelling against the dusk, Hey, you spa-head.

Tomas summoned his vision of life here. The New Story: leaving on spring mornings, the tarmac freshly washed by a recent tumble of rain. Shot from a crane, wide and high above the road, to take it all in – Tomas exiting his home, children playing, neighbours chatting, washing windows and cars. Immediately, he would be waving at the cheeky lads playing football – these boys here – who would call him *Mister D*; at the old ladies across the road who loved to have him in for a cup of tea and a bikkie; at the black-haired widow with the shining, dimpled cheeks. The crane would descend into Bass Avenue as Tomas walked along it, finally ending close enough to pick out the broad smile lighting up his face.

Clichéd drivel, really. Dreadful.

Mister D grimly produced the content expression he would use in his new, happy life. He neatly parked the silver Saab in front of number 17, temporarily forgetting that he still wore a pair of pink, star-shaped sunglasses which Anna had left in the car months before and which he had worn only because he had none of his own and the glare had been terrible coming off the ferry. The glasses gave him an air of camp sadness, a female impersonator coming to the end of his career.

The boys watched the drag queen step onto the pavement, and said nothing.

Tomas smiled beneath his glam-rock shades. 'Hello. What are your names?'

One of the boys laughed, a plosive splutter which his hands failed to contain.

Mister D smiled, then frowned, then blushed, then pushed back his fringe.

'Oh, yes, of course,' he said, removing the sunglasses. 'They are my daughter's. It was sunny, you know.'

The boys began to move away. They shook their legs, rotated their shoulders and gently shoved each other, like boxers limbering up for a fight. They didn't look back. The middle one was tall, but Tomas estimated that they were no more than ten or eleven, not yet tortured by adulthood. The best age.

Across the street a short, blocky man stood on the pavement and watched, as if it was his job to monitor new arrivals. Occasional light winds dislodged the strands of hair carefully pasted across this man's otherwise naked head. The terraced cottage he stood outside had been recently plastered but was yet unpainted, giving it a grey, Stalinist feel. Most striking, however, were the two crimson wagon wheels attached to the railings in front.

Ranch-style. Not entirely convincing.

Tomas raised his arm to wave at the man, then thought better of it. He looked back at the boys. They were huddled together, playing a game which involved smacking each others' outstretched hands. Occasionally, one would dance away from the group, blowing on his reddened fingers.

'I'm from round here,' Tomas announced.

The boys ignored this.

He pointed. 'I grew up on the next street, you know, Beatha Road.'

They continued to ignore him.

'Would you like to make some money?'

They looked up.

The two smaller boys, Tomas realised, were twins – both chunky bodied, with short, carrot-coloured hair, round faces and ghostly pale skin. They wore matching baggy jeans and red hooded tops fraying at the collar. In response to Tomas's question, they said nothing, as if they didn't consider it their place to provide a reply. Instead they looked at each other, smirking, their green eyes perfectly round, and embarked on a short mutual chatter which sounded more like screeching than talk. Perhaps it wasn't English. Arabic? No – they look Irish, couldn't look more Irish. Abruptly, they stopped and smiled.

Obviously it was the role of the tall one to answer, though he took his time. He was dressed the same as his friends, except that his grubby top was a faded navy blue and sported the legend *Gangsta*. He breathed through his mouth, exposing the gaps in his teeth and an accumulation of some light brown substance at the corner of his lips. Through bloodhound eyelids and a lank fringe, he peered up at Tomas. Finally, in a quiet yet distinct voice he said, 'Story?'

They were all so *white*. Tomas felt foreign with his slightly stained skin, his squashed nose – a hint of the aboriginal.

'Beg your pardon?'

The twins, still looking at each other, giggled and gabbled some more.

'*Story?*'

Tomas stared at the boy in the hope that this might reveal his meaning. 'Sorry? Is that it?'

The twins' giggles transformed into snorts. The tall one whipped a tongue along his cracked lips.

'Story? Story? What's the story?'

'Oh, I see.' Another pause. Tomas glanced at his shoes. 'I'm Tomas Dalton. I've just moved into this house.'

The tall boy looked at the house, then back at Tomas. His mouth was still open, his breathing audible.

'You three are from round here?' Tomas asked.

The twins looked towards the tall boy. He moved his head slightly to one side.

'Spose.'

Dave, the quiet, pencil-thin removal man, climbed down from the truck, heaving a tea chest into his arms. Shoulder blades projected from his back like wings. The boys watched this with a professional-seeming interest.

'That's Dave,' said Tomas.

The three of them smiled now, as if it was obvious that this was Dave.

Smiling didn't make the tall one any better looking. It revealed how misshapen his teeth were. Should be seeing an orthodontist. Probably can't afford it. Shame.

Still, they *had* smiled. Encouraged, Tomas dug a hand into his trouser pocket and produced a ten euro note. Funny looking things.

'Would you do a little errand for me? A message? Children still do that, don't they?'

The twins exchanged more excited looks and made an *eek* sound. The tall boy closed one eye and studied Tomas.

'Whatcha want?'

'If you could just nip down to the shop for me, that would be fantastic.'

The boy swiped the note from Tomas's hand and shoved it in his pocket.

'Er, I want a box of five cigars.'

'Right.' They had already half-turned away.

'King Edwards. The fat ones, you know?'

'Right.'

Now they were walking off.

'You can keep the change.'

No answer.

'Thank you!'

Nothing.

'I'd keep an eye on *them*. Gowgers,' Alfie, the fat removal man, growled.

Tomas blinked, then slid his fingers through his slab of hair, grey now, but still somewhat boyish, he thought, in the way the fringe fell over his eyes.

'Not at all. They're just children.' Tomas looked back at the boys, then closed his eyes. 'There's a quote. Who said it? "What a melancholy world this would be without children, and what an inhuman world without the aged."'

Alfie grimaced. 'Yeah, well, *they're* nothing but little skangers. Look at the cut of them. It'll end badly.'

Tomas shrugged, then held up a finger. 'Coleridge. That's who it was.'

'Up to you.'

Stained grey trousers hung hazardously low from Alfie's hips. A formerly white shirt, heavily crusted around the collar, flapped in a light swirl of wind. Tomas had an urge to wrench the shirt straight, tuck it smartly into those trousers. Like Mother used to.

You are a very tidy person.

Nothing wrong with that.

Mother – she's here.

Alfie folded his arms. 'What did you say to them?'

'Not much. I've sent them on an errand to the shops.'

Alfie laughed. 'An errand? A message! I've heard it all now. The only message you'd get out of them would be a bloody...er, what do you call it...a ransom message. That's all you'll get.' The removal man looked around him, as if acknowledging an invisible audience. 'And where were you until now anyway? You were just behind us coming off the boat. Did you not follow us down the North Strand?'

'Best get the front door open,' said Tomas, striding towards the house.

Once inside, he nipped into the toilet under the stairs, then stomped from room to room, wrenching open windows as he went to release the oily smell of paint.

And where would Mrs Dalton be?

Marta had left him quietly and efficiently, as she did everything. Sitting small at the scrubbed kitchen table, scooping her mousy hair behind her ears. No, Tomas, there's nothing left for us any more, and there's no point making a fuss. I really wouldn't like that. It has died.

Just like that, she said it. Stood up and departed, her bag already packed. Tomas didn't leave the flat for three days afterwards, eating little, not sleeping at all. He walked around, feeling he should be searching for something, though he didn't know what.

A phone rang.

Tomas had to remind himself of who he was, what he was doing here, how his situation was changed. As he flipped open the mobile, he moved towards the window to try to recapture the feeling of optimism which he had embraced only minutes before. An orange sun was beginning its descent towards the rooftops. The display read *Eli*.

Eli Gadd would already be in a bar, taking part in one of his favourite parts of the film-making process: the pre-production piss-up.

The call, Tomas knew, would be to invite him along, meet the production staff, have a few drinks. Tomas would make some excuse and decline the invitation, as he always did. Then Eli would get to the real point – to remind Tomas that he had dinner tomorrow night with Karin Goldman, a disappointed-looking American actress and the star of their next film, *The Marrying Kind*, due to begin principle photography in Dublin in ten days' time.

How many films with Eli as producer? Six? No. This will be seven. Twenty years. All of it in north London. Until now. Because of me.

'Yesyesyes,' sighed Tomas. He clicked the phone shut.

Outside, Alfie and Dave were lumbering into the back of the truck, its sides wantonly splattered with mud from the trek through England and

Wales. The simple livery, *Swan Removals*, was barely legible. A cloud of rust around one of the rear lights gave the vehicle an exhausted air. Eventually, they extracted a large leather sofa. Seemed quite light, from the ease with which they carried it. Surprising, because he had paid £5,000 for it, and that was some years ago. Should be heavy for that money. Shop on Tottenham Court Road. They'd made love on it the first night it arrived. But that was the only time.

As if to escape this memory, Tomas walked outside. A woman had materialised in the doorway of the house next door, number 16. She was plain faced, wearing a shapeless cardigan over a grey, unflattering skirt. Her hair was wiry and stood out from her head. She stood bolt still, glaring at the removal truck.

'Hello,' said Tomas.

The woman didn't reply, didn't even flick her eyes in recognition.

'Just moving in,' he ventured.

Still no answer. As if she is in some sort of trance. Psychiatric problems, perhaps. Stuffed to the gills with lithium and valium.

Mammy, red-faced in the corner. Pills, pills, what do I want with pills? Poor thing.

'So did they get the message?' demanded Alfie.

Tomas shrugged. 'It's only been a few minutes.'

Alfie beamed. 'Ha! Did you hear?' he said to Dave, holding the other end of the couch. 'He's only after sending them on a message to the shops. They'll probably rob the shop when they're down there. When Mister Dalton told me, I turned around and I said to him, A message? All you'll get from them fellas is a ransom message.'

Dave nodded neutrally. Alfie chuckled.

'Ransom message,' he repeated, this time to the woman outside number 16. Still, she said nothing. She backed slowly into her house, all the while glaring at the three men.

*

DAVE WAS talking, a roll-up dangling from the corner of his mouth. Tomas watched closely, hoping the ash wouldn't fall on the table, then hoping it would so he'd have something to do.

Dave told them about a previous job, driving a van filled with washing machines. One foggy night, he had crashed into a horse.

They sat at the kitchen table, the last item to come into the house. Now they were working their way through the six-pack of Carlsberg which Tomas had supplied. Alfie and Dave would be going soon. Dave hadn't seen his kids in seventy-two hours. Yet they were gracious and comfortable with Tomas's suggestion of a couple of beers. He had nipped down to a shop on Clontarf Road to get the drink. Strange bunker of a place – strange road, mostly higgledy-piggledy red-brick. A tatty solicitor's office, citizens' advice bureau, doctor's surgery, two pubs (one, The Croppy Boy, seemed familiar), a chip shop, The Frying Tuck. BMW dealership, for the discerning drivers passing through, no doubt. Grey apartment blocks stacked up in both directions. Don't remember any of this.

No sign of the boys or the cigars. Dark now.

Even Alfie had become bored with asking about them.

I didn't realise what I'd crashed into, Dave told them. Not until he saw the horse's head, sheared from the rest of the body.

Not right having them here. Not now. *Inappropriate*. That's what. They move furniture, get paid, they go. Why didn't they just go? And the fat one sweating now, disgusting. Have to clean the seat after. Bet he'll be nosy again, want to know things, facts, dates, situations – knows enough already, too much. Life isn't currency, to be spent on strangers; could have given them the bottles and sent them on their way, they'd have been just as happy, happier, even.

Marta. It was the sort of patrician gesture she had been fond of – affording unlooked-for hospitality towards workmen. *Tomas, invite them in. Get them some beers, Tomas.*

Strange, anticipating what she'll never again have the chance to say.

Dave, his face half in shadow, took another suck on his cigarette, then dropped his voice so low they had to lean in to hear. He told them that the body of the horse was never found. The cops said that horses are like chickens that way. Even without a head, it would have kept running. It didn't know it was dead. Or didn't want to believe it.

Dave looked at the table. Tomas and Alfie said nothing. They looked at the table too.

'I killed a horse. Couldn't drive after that. Not long distances, anyway. I rang the cops the week after, but they never found the body. Said he probably fell into a bog hole. But he could have run for another couple of miles with no head on him. Can you imagine that?'

There was silence while they imagined.

A clock ticked.

Alfie slowly rolled his eyes.

'Jesus.'

The rasp of the doorbell startled them into laughter. Tomas put a hand on his chest, Dave wiped a snotty nostril with the back of his hand. Alfie yelled, 'That's the bleedin' horse, that is. Looking for Dave to get his head back. That's the horse!'

Still laughing – slightly drunk from the beer – Tomas walked down the dark hallway.

There was no one outside.

He glanced back at the kitchen, where Alfie was slapping Dave on the back and asking did that really happen? Really? He walked out to the front gate and looked up and down the street. It was empty. Doors shut and windows draped to keep in the precious light. Outside, the silver streetlamps struggled to illuminate the black shapes which populated Bass Avenue. A thick quiet blanketed everything, allowing in just the distant roar of the city. Tomas inhaled deeply. Dublin smelled like – what? Mixture of things. His olfactory memory of London was rubber – from the Underground, buses, taxis. Dublin smelled of vegetables, vegetables just about to go off. Mixed with concrete and petrol. Like an old-fashioned greengrocers shop with a builders providers on one side and a garage on the other. That was the smell.

Got to be those boys. How did they get away so quickly? Unless they're hiding somewhere, watching, hoping he would be annoyed. Cheeky brats.

Gently, Tomas closed the front gate, whistling loudly as he did so. Only then did he see the small box left behind on the doormat. Must have stepped right over it.

He moved back towards the door but an imperfection in the concrete caught his toe, causing him to suddenly lurch, then stagger like a jelly-limbed clown. Tomas righted himself, and presented an embarrassed smile to the desolate street.

*

TOMAS DROPPED the box on the table in front of Alfie.

'Now.'

'What's this?'

'King Edward's finest cigars. What I asked the boys to get for me.'

'Did you get your change?'

'I said they could keep the change.' Tomas sat down, flashing his even teeth.

'Where were they till now?'

'Now come on, Alfie.' Tomas swooped up the box. 'Admit it – they were fine children. Nothing wrong with them at all.'

Alfie offered a world-weary expression. Dave grinned and watched Tomas pick open the plastic wrapping.

'You don't have to smoke it now,' Tomas said, 'but take one of these with you.'

'Jesus, they're fairly big lads,' Dave said. 'Do you smoke many of them?'

'Just the occasional one.'

What Mother says about cigarettes. Tomas has no idea how many she smokes, only that she does, usually astride the wooden chair with the loose leg, the one beside the range. Untipped. Giving out about something. The unionists. The bishops. Wearing one of her long skirts so she could sit with her legs open like a man. Shouting at Daddy like he is personally responsible for the state the country is in, but him saying nothing, knowing she doesn't mean it that way.

Dave watched Tomas slip the first cigar from the pack. Lumps of dark tobacco showered from it, spreading across the table like a fall of black snow. The cigar drooped between Tomas's fingers as more pieces fell off. Within seconds, it had all but disintegrated.

Such was Dave, Alfie and Tomas's puzzlement that at first none of them mentioned the chunky smell now overwhelming the room, one which made them all think of school toilets. It was an odour which they were pro-grammed to find disgusting, even though this particular batch, being quite fresh, contained relatively few bacteria. Mostly water. Some urea. Trace elements of lead and mercury; the by-products of certain pesticides; some chemicals used in plastics, lubricants and solvents. A quantity of cotinine, a chemical derivative of nicotine.

The gush of urine spilled from the box and onto the kitchen table, sending splashes out against their clothes.

'Jesus!'

Chairs skidded backwards as they sprang up.

'That's fucking – that's piss!'

Alfie said nothing, a tongue lodged in his cheek. From his back pocket he extracted a cheap plastic biro and slid it into the cigar box. Like a cop exam-ining a murder weapon, he lifted the box from the table and studied it from all angles, careful not to touch. Finally he pointed, using his fat little finger to indicate a tiny hole.

'See there?'

Dave and Tomas leaned in.

'That must be where they got the piss into the box, though it's an awful small hole. I don't know – oh, a syringe, of course, that's how they did it – pissed into it and injected it into the packet.'

'That's sick,' said Dave.

Alfie threw the box and biro onto the table. 'I wouldn't like to think where they got the syringe from. Probably an old one off the ground some place. God knows what you might catch off that.'

He looked sympathetically at Tomas. 'If I was you, I'd get some heavy-duty bleach for all this. Scrub everything.'

Tomas shook his head like a bereaved parent.

'But why? I don't...'

Alfie shrugged. 'Told ya. They're skangers. Nothing but trouble. End of story.'

The urine had quickly formed into a narrow stream. It travelled towards the edge of the table and the helpless fall beyond.

2

'OH, I can't remember her name. But you know who I mean? The slutty one offa *Sex and the City*? Remember that show? She won a Golden Globe? Well, they're *all* sluts if you ask me. But the really, *really* slutty one. Eva looks like her. Well, Eva *right now* looks like how the slutty one used to look when they were making that show. Know what I mean? It's been a few years and, oh, it must be tough afterwards, you know? Glad I never did that. I have this friend in LA, Timmy? Gay guy, great trumpet player. Fabulous body, of course. And like, he doesn't *really* want to be an actor. Not really really. Anyway, he used to get regular work on *Friends*. As an extra, non-speaking. He'd be one of the crowd in that café they used to go to, I don't know the name. I actually hated that show. Was that just me? Anyway, Timmy would work most weeks on *Friends*. They put different clothes and wigs on him and moved him around and even though it's kinda boring being an extra, Timmy loved it, you know? So when the show ended, Timmy was really depressed. An extra, and he ends up going for therapy because *Friends* finished. And that sounds nuts, right? But when you think about it, it's just the same for Timmy as it is for Jennifer Aniston – who's a real B–I–T–C–H, by the way – you met her?'

Tomas had been keeping up, but a momentary lapse in concentration – a convoy of neat military trucks shuddering past the window – had caused him to lose track. Day in the Phoenix Park. Soldiers marching. Holding Daddy's hand. Why?

After that, there was no way back. Karin liked to jump from subject to subject, like a drunk looking for someone to dance with. Tomas erected an interested expression. Did this much drivel come out of her mouth all the time? Eli said she talked, but this is inhuman. Like demonic possession. She's talking *and* chewing. Don't show me the masticated bread on your lizardy tongue, woman, I don't want to see that. Met before. Few years back. Hope she doesn't ask. Can't remember a thing.

The dining room of the Shelbourne Hotel was still quite empty, with only one other couple on the far side. The light plunging in through the big windows was shimmering and impressionistic, falling like mist on the rows of empty tables, slightly sad in their stiff white tablecloths. She insisted on eating early, before the place filled up. Less chance of getting noticed. Not that anyone had.

'Hmm,' Tomas said.

Karin segued into a comparison of lifestyles between the east and west coasts. She had moved to New York two years previously, announcing that she was to return to her first love, the theatre. What they all say once the lead roles dry up – still too young or too proud to play the crazy grandmother parts. Did she ever work on stage? Thought she started in TV soaps.

She grabbed his hand and returned to an earlier story about how her friend's boyfriend had had a previous relationship where he had lived with a lesbian. As a result, the only way they could make love was if he dressed as a woman.

'So when he moves in with Eva, he can't do it in the normal way because he's been pretending to be a lesbian for years.'

'I see. And what happened?'

'Oh, they're still together.' Karin tore at a bread roll. 'But I'm not optimistic. And hey, don't take me up wrong with the word normal.'

'Sorry?'

'Normal. Normal. I said "do it in the normal way". That's not anything homophobic – I mean, I love gays. I just meant…you know what I meant, right?'

'Of course.'

'Oh no,' Karin grimaced. 'I'm so sorry. You think I'm weird or crazy or something for telling you that story, don't you?' She buried her face in her hands. Long pink fingernails sank into her stiff hair. 'I always say the wrong thing. Just blurt it out. Probably your mom or your sister or something is a lesbian and you're gonna hate me now.'

She looked up, regarding Tomas with a shocking vulnerability. He reached over and patted her fingers. Her hands looked old. Too old for the face, anyway. A delta of stringy green veins visible just underneath the slack, albino skin. What age? Could be fifty. The face, though – on a tight shot, she could get away with mid to late thirties. More than one lift, probably. Split the difference, say mid-forties. Hands always betray the plastic face. Why can't they do hands? What we touch with touches us, and can't be carved away. Anyway, trying to hide your obvious insanity, that's the real challenge.

'No, not at all. I had never heard of a lesbian man before. It was educational.'

'Thank you,' she said in a shrunken voice.

'And there are no lesbians in my family.'

None of your business.

The waitress arrived with their soup.

Tomas felt bereft of conversational ideas. They'd already discussed her flight, her hotel room, the driver they'd laid on and Karin's role in *The Marrying Kind*. She had demonstrated her Irish accent, which sounded Welsh, and then asked if he thought she was too old for the part – her love interest, the Irish actor Conor Hanley, was a good ten years her junior. No, no, no. Not at all, Tomas had assured her. No, no, no.

Have to keep her lighting diffuse, keep those ears out of close-ups. Suspiciously low on her head, dead give-away of all the work.

Already, Tomas felt a muddy gloom about the project. Why insist on working back here? Stupid reaction to the divorce. In London there had been a system, a permanent production office, people he knew, even the same actors a lot of the time. The divorce, a new film, the move here, those boys and their prank. Too much, far too much.

Why did they do that? Why go to all that trouble?

'Hmm.'

Karin slurped her soup and picked up a second bread roll. She ate in a frantic way, as if working against a deadline.

'So, Tomas, I understand you're living here now?'

'Yes. Moved in yesterday.'

Karin put down her spoon, having scooped up every visible drop of soup from the bowl. 'You're just divorced, aren't you? Don't tell me – she took everything so you don't have any furniture? Hey, I know women who took *his* clothes in the settlement, just for spite. Am I right?'

Tomas gave a crooked smile. He rocked his head from side to side. 'Well, yes and no.'

'Yes *and* no? How does that work?'

'You're right, I don't have much furniture. But I didn't want anything else. I wanted room for my, ah, collection, and that fills up most of the house.'

She arched an eyebrow, though not very much. Stuffed with botox. Disgusting.

'Uh-oh. *Collection?* What is it? Guns? Pornography?'

The waitress arrived with their main courses. Karin was having steak.

Bet those boys will disappear now. Bit vague about where they lived. Perhaps it's being an outsider, living in the big house. Would they still be considered posh? Hardly.

Karin sawed at her meat.

Shouldn't be that difficult to find out who they are, perhaps visit their parents. Don't complain, just let them know – from the area, a long time ago; might make a difference.

'So what do you collect?' demanded Karin.

'Well, old things, I suppose.'

'Like antiques?'

'Some. More like memorabilia, but connected with history. Especially Irish history. Letters, coins, that sort of thing. I've also hung on to some stuff from my own family. I'm a bit of a hoarder.'

'Oh.' Karin's voice trembled slightly. 'You're a history buff, then?'

'A little bit, I suppose. My mother got me interested.'

Chewing again, Karin nodded. She watched Tomas put down his knife and fork and hold up his hands, as if about to stage a puppet show.

'I started with four letters I inherited from my mother. They were written in 1918 by Harry Boland, who was a major figure here in the, er, War of Independence from the British.'

Nodding, Karin slugged on her wine.

'Harry Boland? Aidan Quinn played him in the film, right? I got it out before I came over here.'

'Yes, that's right. Well anyway, these letters are very rare.'

'Valuable?'

Tomas pursed his lips 'Don't know exactly. Perhaps.'

Karin made an impressed face. 'So where did your mom get them?' Karin was asking her questions in a clipped, business-like manner, her gaze directed to her dinner plate as she finished off the last of her steak.

'It's funny. She won them in a card game.'

Momentarily, Karin stopped chewing. 'Really? Sound likes the Old West.'

'It was, a bit. She loved cards. Bridge. Whist. Poker. She won the letters in a poker game from a local woman called...' He jammed his eyes shut. 'Doyle. Banana Doyle.'

'Banana?'

'That was her nickname. She had a stall that sold fruit and veg. Couldn't tell you what her real name was. That's just how she was known. Ma Banana, the kids called her, even her own children. Ma Banana.'

Tomas shrugged and smiled again. Karin finished off her wine.

'And these letters, what are they about? Politics?'

'Oh, no. They're love letters.'

Abruptly, Karin stopped drinking and put down her glass. She leaned forward on the table, turning her head slightly to give Tomas a quizzical look. Her slightly-too-full lips pinched into a smile.

'Ain't you a surprise? You're not really some boring history buff at all. You collect old love letters. Well, I like that.'

*

HE BROUGHT her to see the Spire, slightly appalled by how few options he could think of. Stephen's Green. Just a park. Trinity College. Bit too high-brow, perhaps. She linked him, occasionally squeezing his arm. She asked about his divorce and Tomas gave short, factual answers. It ended, just like that. Ran out of steam. Do I still love her? To be honest, I don't know.

Karin spoke about her two marriages, even though Tomas hadn't asked.

He eventually changed the subject, asked her how she managed to stay so slim. Worry, cigarettes and occasionally amphetamines, she told him. She launched into a detailed description of her body and its many flaws, then catalogued various failed keep-fit regimes. I wouldn't have surgery on my body. No: that's too much. Maybe a little bit of cosmetic on the face, sure, but having ribs removed and all that? Too weird.

Hmm, offered Tomas occasionally, content that Karin could indulge in a subject which didn't require him to say too much.

Don't get this prank out of proportion – may have been a bit disgusting, but boys that age are disgusting.

They halted at the southern side of O'Connell Bridge so Karin could have a good look.

'Oh,' she said, craning her head back. 'It's really nice.'

'Yes,' agreed Tomas. Of course you like it. Big and shiny and vulgar.

Going to their homes might only make it worse. Parents could get defensive, want to turn it into a row.

He felt a squeeze on his arm. 'There is something going on here?'

'Hmm,' said Tomas.

Get to know the neighbours, let them know the Dalton family history; then word gets around – locals, sort of. Go for a stroll, several strolls, on

Beatha Road – if anyone asks, looking at the house I grew up in. Word will get around.

He felt a tug.

'C'mon. Take me home.'

Outside the hotel she took his face in her hands, her long nails extended outwards. She kissed him gently on the lips, then in a soft voice said, 'I had a lovely time.'

'Good.'

'But I am genuinely tired. So I'm not going to invite you in. Not tonight, anyway.' She turned from him and walked away, waving one hand over her shoulder.

What?

What?

*

THE TAXI driver kept talking. Something about football.

Tomas wished the man would shut up, wished that he was the sort of person who told taxi drivers to shut up. It was nice that everyone made conversation here, but already it was intrusive – thousands of chattering voices, conspiring to rob him of enough time and quiet to think, to live his interior life, consider how to present himself.

Tomas nodded and made noises.

The woman wasn't? Seriously?

It was a given that actresses would be touchy-feely. Tomas had been linked and hugged and kissed, even had a buttock squeezed occasionally. It was flirtatious, yes, but no more than that – just the dynamics of a shoot.

'What number again?'

'Seventeen.'

Tomas began searching his pockets for cash. There was always camaraderie on a film, but without any real risk; it was friendship with an expiry date, which could, Tomas supposed, be continued on afterwards if anyone felt so inclined.

The driver pulled in, then peered upwards through the windscreen.

'You're right beside Croke Park here.'

'Yes.'

'You'll be watching the match on Sunday?'

Tomas handed over money. 'Yes, I might have a look.'

'And who'll win, do you think?'

Oh for God's sake. Not another *chat*.

'Who's playing? I knew there was a match on, but I'm not long back in the country.'

'Oh right, right, right.'

Daddy standing like a monument at the sideline, nodding when his son does well, creasing his face sympathetically when Tomas fumbles or lets a speedy forward streak past. On the way home he tells Tomas about man-marking, about keeping his body square between the ball and the other player. Shoves and small punches are a natural function of the game. Expect them. Never show fear. Watch everything around you.

The training is their calm and private dialogue, an endless series of twilight evenings, the cry of birds competing with the echoing clack of the *sloitar*. The smell of mud and sweat, the comfort of being in control in a simple, rectangular world of cause and effect.

Tomas got out without saying goodnight. Bass Avenue was empty, as usual, illuminated only by the feeble streetlamps and the shreds of light leaking from behind some of the curtains. Being a cul-de-sac must be what makes it so quiet. No reason to be here unless this is where you live, though he had noticed that during the day some people came through here and cut down the thin alleyway on the other side of the road. He looked at Croke Park, then back in the opposite direction where the city centre distantly glowed.

What did she say at the Spire? Something, wasn't listening – shouldn't have agreed. How can she think there's attraction – some sort of tactic? Nothing to be gained from it, nothing I can do for her career – she's here because she can't get work in Hollywood – genuine, then? The woman is completely bonkers.

As Tomas slipped his key into the front door, he felt a lick of anger.

How dare she make presumptions, just because of the divorce? Is the old crone that desperate? Her surgically enhanced bits drying up so fast she has to throw herself at anyone half-available. Sickening. And then to act as if I had given—

What?

Tomas couldn't finish the thought because the sudden cramps in his stomach were unbearable. It took all his resources just to wrench the front door open, to notice the thick brown smears around the handle and letterbox, to take a few steps inside, bend over and noisily vomit a gush of undigested salmon chunks, broccoli, bits of potato, a few flecks of it spattering his cosy suede shoes.

The stream of liquid burned the inside of his nostrils. He tried panting, but this only made him worse, brought on more retching, a greenish liquid this time which, as it splashed off the white banister, gave him a moment to realise that he had to get *out* of the house, it was the smell making him do this, the black pong of digested human decay, thickly coated on his front door.

Shit.

Tomas scrambled outside. He got as far as the gate, bent over, tried panting again, but even here he could smell it, as if the molecules had infested the inside of his nose, cursing him to detect nothing but rancid faeces forever more.

No, no, don't panic. Breathe.

He had to throw up one more time, his legs and shoes now covered with stains. But slowly he returned his breathing to normal, his mouth open like a man whose lungs have been withered by cancer. He stood.

The light from the hallway showed it was everywhere: around the knob, the keyhole, the letterbox, the doorbell. It was thick, but evenly coated – carefully applied with a brush and given time to dry.

They are clever.

He opened the gate and stepped onto the pavement.

They won't let a moment like this go unwitnessed. The planning, the preparation, the sheer *will* required to collect shit and daub it on a door. Must be a reason for going to all this trouble, must be. He put a hand on the gate to steady himself and peered towards the closed end of the street. Nothing except a ring of houses, low and squat, their façades resembling the faces of sad giants. At the other end there was some movement: the odd car sweeping past, wobbling light under a streetlamp, which could be a person. But it was too far away to tell, and Tomas was too exhausted now to go and look.

Not down there anyway.

That alleyway, just across the street, narrow and unpenetrated by light, that's them: quietly scuttling in the blackness, their little eyes unblinking.

He took a few steps into the road, then stopped. His head swam, and despite the strange sensation knotting in his limbs – something a like a sudden surge in blood pressure – despite his hungry desire to find these boys, he didn't want to move too far from his home, where at least there was a chance of safety. Patches of sweat formed along his back, sucking in his shirt.

So quiet.

Slowly, Tomas backed away.

Coming through the gate, he saw that the woman from number 16 had come out for a look. She stood rigid, arms at her side, hair erect. Dressed in the same dowdy clothes she had worn the day before. Tomas pointed at himself.

'Look,' he said in a voice that sounded like someone else's. 'Do you see?'

The woman remained silent.

'It's…you know. Faeces. On my house. Why? I…I…why?'

The woman went back into her house and shut the door.

3

ELI JABBED a thumb towards his pink-shirted sternum.

'Don't worry. The movie mogul will take care of it.'

'What are you going to do?'

'Have a word.'

'And say what, exactly? My friend doesn't like your friend?'

'Tomas! I'll just have a chat. How you doing, how's your hotel, all that. Then in the middle, I'll mention, casual-like, that you – Tomas – are just divorced and you're all vulnerable and that and we all need to help Tomas concentrate on the film so he can get over things. She'll get the hint.'

'In other words, you're going to tell her the truth.'

Shouldn't have said that. Not like you. Watch yourself.

Both men fell silent, allowing the clatter of the café to fill up the spaces around them. The café sold pancakes from behind a chrome counter to children and their tailored mothers, gaudily dressed students, Africans, Chinese, Malaysians, Eastern Europeans, all packed along low benches. Tomas didn't like it. Too warm. Not enough elbow room, smells invading from other people, the danger of spittle arcs ending up in tea, wafts of oriental halitosis. Eli bad enough, reeks of alcohol. Does the man wash?

Due to a strict philosophy of never denying himself anything, Eli Gadd often looked like someone abandoned. But he was a natty dresser – always a suit, usually pin-striped, a shirt and tie, often in competing shades of pink. He liked cufflinks, tie clips and chunky gold watches. Eli dressed and spoke and often acted like an East End gangster – Tomas had seen people genuinely scared of him – when in fact he was quite the opposite. It was moderately well-known within the industry that Eli Gadd had attended Cheltenham College and that his family were rich horse-breeders in Gloucestershire. That Eli adopted this pose, that he had done so for years, was usually a source of curiosity and mild amusement to Tomas. Today, though, he found it irksome. Why can't people tell the truth? Be who they are?

Be careful – listen to what you say and how you say it.

Usually, he found it easy to be Tomas Dalton. But not today; today there was a danger he could slip into someone else.

'Movie mogul,' Tomas eventually said. 'Did you know the word mogul actually drives from Mongol? The Mongols conquered India, oh, centuries back, but the word remained and eventually the emperors of Delhi were known as moguls by Europeans. The term was a bit patronising, of course, and became downright pejorative by the time it had arrived in the US. But now it means the direct opposite.'

'You finished in here?' Eli said. 'Smells making me sick.'

Tomas pointed towards the exit. Perhaps he should tell Eli about the boys. Might be the sort of problem he'd be good at solving. He could be quite subtle, despite all the wide boy bluster.

The night before had been lonely, disgusting work. He kept stopping to retch and afterwards had to burn his clothes in the living room fireplace. Should have called the police. Marta would have been on the phone straight away, her small voice thick with outrage, as if they should have known this would happen; as if she had warned them.

Instead he had sat on the couch, sipped tea and studied a framed poster for *Double Indemnity*, the blue-tinted version with Barbara Stanwyck sneering up at Fred MacMurray just as their lips are about to meet, *You can't kiss away a murder!* scrawled across their faces.

He had it all through college, though it wasn't framed then – it had spent most of those years blu-tacked to the bulging wallpaper of the bedsit on the Romford Road. He and Marta on a mattress beside the three-bar fire. She talking about her mind-crunching doctorate about the balance of female roles and phallic symbols in the films of Bergman. He didn't tell her that his favourite film was *Some Like It Hot*. Not for years.

Tomas had fallen asleep on the couch, then dreamed that he couldn't get to sleep, the clip-clop of hooves on concrete keeping him awake until eventually, intensely annoyed, he got up to confront the headless horse at the window. It wanted to come in.

Go away, Tomas barked.

Bollix, said the horse.

The History of Things

They left the café and headed for Grafton Street. During their years together, Tomas and Eli had developed a habit – as much superstitious as practical – known as the walkaround: a last-minute look at locations. All their films together had been successful, financially speaking, in no small part due to the fact they had essentially produced the same movie over and over, all romantic comedies set in London featuring an emotionally repressed man (he's been hurt before) who meets a feisty woman (she's hiding a secret). They don't get on at first but eventually they fall for each other. To keep it interesting, they would sometimes swap the gender roles (emotionally repressed women meets feisty man) and give the characters unusual jobs (artificial insemination operative was their proudest moment). But in its fundamentals, this was the same product, replayed in slightly different ways, hopefully improved with each visit. Neither Eli nor Tomas were perturbed by this repetition. Indeed, Tomas had secretly grown quite proud of their work – at least they were telling a *story*. A beginning, middle and end. So much else these days seemed to spurn narrative. All *bits* of information, flying around. Poses. Fashions which seemed to last for a week. Young people unable to read, unable concentrate on anything without an explosion or an obscenity.

As they walked, Eli sighed loudly. 'My bloody head hurts.'

'How was last night?'

'Fucking top notch. Got a good team. You shoulda come.'

Tomas didn't answer. He'd woken in a sweat and spent the morning busybusybusy: painting the front door, moving his tiny television into the lounge, hanging up dozens of pictures and placing some of his favourite pieces around the house. There was a World War I helmet; a non-working Bush wireless set; cameras in various stages of disassembly, some rusting, some giving off an otherworldly chrome sheen; movie posters; a bowl full of bolts; a brick; a first edition of *The Complete Works of P.H. Pearse*, set on a stand; framed letters and photographs; an intricate Persian rug for the floor of the lounge; a framed set of braces; yellowed newspapers; ancient pill bottles; a toilet bag almost completely devoured by mould. These things represented but a small percentage of Tomas's collection, forcing him to conclude that he would have to establish some sort of rotation system: display each piece for a few weeks, then put it back in one of the upstairs storage rooms. Place seems smaller now. Cosy.

He'd introduced himself to the neighbours in number 18, a grinning Nigerian family with a swarm of children. Mr and Mrs Kuku were small and identically plump and regarded Tomas with a tense wonder, waiting to see what he had to sell. They'd kept repeating a word, *trewicks, trewicks*, and Tomas had said yes, oh yes, trewicks. But this only made Mr Kuku even more insistent, pointing at the ground. Here, here, trewicks.

Yes, I know, Tomas had said, wishing he could leave now.

No, no, no. Here, here, in house only trewicks.

Oh. Three weeks?

Strangers too. But they had been left alone. Odd.

He tried the Staring Woman in number 16, but there was no answer.

'One concern,' said Tomas. 'Our leading lady is considerably older than our leading man. I mean, she *looks* older. It'll be tricky to hide that.'

The plot of *The Marrying Kind* involved a divorced, emotionally repressed woman (Karin Goldman) who works in a headstone factory. After winning the national lottery, she embarks on an enormous spending spree, in the course of which she meets a feisty, charming man (Conor Hanley) with a dark secret (he is a fraudster on the run from the police). The man plans to con the woman out of her money, but instead they fall in love.

Eli nodded slowly.

'Perhaps we could build it into the script?' offered Tomas.

'I dunno, mate. Old Bird with Young Guy: it won't sell. Not for a comedy. Not in the States. And I don't think Karin would be too thrilled with that suggestion anyway. No, just shoot her the best way you can and maybe we can tart her up a bit in post-production. Get rid of a few wrinkles.'

'Might be expensive.'

'Yeah?' Eli blew through his lips. 'We can't afford to muck around with the script or the schedule. Money's a bit tight on this one. Sorry, mate.'

Tomas shrugged his acceptance. Eli is realistic, practical. Tell him about these boys. Ask for advice, for once.

'And this money situation,' began Tomas.

'Yeah?'

'Is it because of making the film here? Because I...?'

Eli stopped walking. He turned to look up into Tomas's face, as if he'd never really studied it before. 'No,' he breathed. 'Course not.'

Tomas nodded, then looked away.

Eli held out his hands, as if holding an invisible plank of wood.

'Doing it in Dublin was a great idea. We couldn't keep shooting in Islington forever, could we? We've always made money, and we will this time. Don't you worry. Don't worry at all.' He reached up and plonked a hand on Tomas's shoulder, seemingly energised now. 'How's everything else? The new house. Any problems there?'

'No,' said Tomas. 'Everything's perfect.'

*

TOMAS IGNORED the phone at first. Has to be something. Out of the house for what? Two, three hours? More than enough time. Shouldn't have left at all. Filthy little rat boys watching, probably. In that alley, probably, waiting to see me rant and scream – already looked deranged outside, squinting at the gate like I'd never seen one before; that old woman thought so.

She had emerged from a cottage across the street. Her shrivelled face peeked out of an aquamarine plastic hat which matched her coat. In response to Tomas's greeting she had kept moving, but finally offered a hypnotic, skull-like grin which demanded his attention for far too long.

The Nigerian man sweeping in the front yard of number 18 had also jabbed a hand in the air. Already forgotten his name. Mister, mister, mister.

Memory such a useless thing.

The gate was fine, the hinges and handle still intact, no alien substances. Nothing in the front yard either – the front door shining from that morning's paint job, the windows without a mark.

Yet this left him more anxious than relieved, made him stop and look around again before he entered the house, Bass Avenue still quiet. A deliberate sort of quiet.

Bastards.

He had walked back to the gate and peered over at the alleyway, then rushed back to the house, suddenly gripped by the idea that this was where they *wanted* him to stand, to be distracted while God knows what went on inside. But the phone was ringing and Tomas knew it was beyond his powers to ignore it.

He halted, slapping his pockets for reading glasses which weren't there. Instead, he squinted. The display read *withheld*.

'Hello?'

A fidgeting sound, then, '*Bol-lix*.'

The small, squeaky voice delivered the word with a delicious relish. The line clicked off. Tomas stood still, eyes closed, aware of a slight shaking in his legs. He shovelled back his fringe, then looked again at the phone. He tried smiling. Prank calls were better than filth on the door. Proves you're not paranoid – they were watching, to know when to ring.

Tame, though, compared to before.

Ring me.

Marta is the first person to say this to him, a shoulder bag full of books thrown over her shoulder, slightly unsettling the line of her Mary Quant suit. Tomas stutters in response and she smiles, obviously pleased, unaware that he is startled not just by her boldness, but also by the realisation that he has never rung anyone before, hardly knows anyone with a phone. The priest. The doctor.

She sits beside him in the third lecture of the first day, when already he is enveloped by a howling loneliness, a certainty that he is too awkward and inarticulate to ever fit in here. But she sighs in exasperation a few times (what subject?) and he makes a bad joke about the lecturer's bow-tie and she giggles and whispers, Are you from Ireland? They continue the conversation by scribbling on each others' notebooks, their elbows pressed together, their hands circling.

They help each other gather friends around – Maurice from Bolton, Gideon from Staines, Jane from Kent. They catch each other sneaking looks during lectures, and by the end of the first Friday a humming tension has built between them.

Ring me.

How like her to be unafraid, to say what he could not. Tomas fumbles in his bag, but Marta already has a fountain pen ready, sliding her sweet, pink fingers around his wrist. Hold still, I don't want to smudge. Tell me if I'm hurting you. The nib digging in, his eyes watering. Delicious pressure.

Tomas found himself in the kitchen, decades later, the phone still in his hand.

It rang again.

There were numbers on the display this time, a long stream of them, though without his glasses Tomas couldn't see what they were. Still walking, he took a deep breath and answered, trying to sound fierce.

'Yes?'

'Hello?'

Anna always started phone conversations this way; at least all her conversations with Tomas – the opening word pursued by a question mark, as if she wasn't sure if her father wished to speak to her and would frankly be surprised if he did.

'Oh,' said Tomas.

'Oh?'

She did this too, copying his verbal mannerisms as if they were admissions.

It was just to bait him, or used to be – she had been doing it for such a long time she probably didn't even notice, and Tomas knew it would appear petty and defensive to point it out.

'Sorry. I was just on the phone. Thought you were someone else.'

'Sorry to disappoint you. Who did you think I was?'

'Oh, no one of any interest or importance. Work. Eli. The daily grind of show business. You know.'

'Oh,' said Anna for a third time, again infecting the sound with a heavy thud of judgment. Who – apart from Eli Gadd – *would* ring him in Dublin? Where he hadn't lived for decades, where he knew no one? Anna had been against the move. It was A Fantasy. It was Running Away.

Tomas was aware of these opinions, though now he didn't think of them. If they are watching, they must have done something. He moved into the kitchen and began checking windows. He tried to sound jaunty.

'So how are you?'

'Fine, fine.' She delivered the words wearily, as was her habit.

'Are you at work?'

'Yes, so I can't stay on long.'

'And how's that? How's work? How's the fight for social justice?'

He was at the back door now. Still bolted. He unlocked it and went out to the back yard. Anna paused for a moment, then sighed.

'The usual. Cutbacks. Bureaucracy. Ungrateful clients. This government, they're just…I can't begin to tell you.'

Anna was a case-worker for Camden Social Services, a job she believed in with an idolatrous intensity, but never seemed to enjoy.

'So,' she said, attempting to brighten up, 'how's your new house?'

'Great. Fantastic. Love it now. Absolutely love it.'

'Love it *now*?'

'Now that I've settled in, got myself a bit organised, you know.'

'And I suppose all your old friends from the neighbourhood have been around to welcome you back.'

'*Actually*, Anna, the people are *very* friendly here. I've been in with both of my neighbours, and they are lovely people. Really. There are kids who play on the road who do errands for me down to the shops. It's great. It's the way I remember it to be. Hardly changed at all.'

Yard seems fine.

Tomas went back inside and rebolted the door.

'Fantastic,' Anna said, without much enthusiasm. 'I can't wait to see it.'

Tomas headed for the stairs. 'I think you'll like it.'

She won't.

'Well, that's good, because I'll be over on Thursday. Have you got a pen?'

He halted. 'You're coming over?'

'Of course. I said I would, didn't I?'

'Well, yes, you did. I just didn't think it would be so soon. I'm delighted, of course. Really. That's wonderful, Anna.'

'So I've got my flight details here. Have you got a pen?'

'Yes. In my hand now.'

He recommended his ascent of the stairs. Should check the windows at the back. Could have climbed up the drainpipe.

Anna recited dates, times, flight numbers. 'Have you got that?'

Rooms seem fine. Nothing.

Tomas scrunched up his forehead. 'Yes, yes, Thursday, five o'clock.'

'Are you sure you've written this down?'

'Of course I have! See you Thursday. Bye bye.'

Tomas hung up.

They won't give in, just like that. Maybe unable to do anything – Monday, school day, what time? Nearly four. Be just out, only enough time for a prank call on the way home. Not watching, you old fool. Little boys, not master criminals.

Have to get this solved, don't want any episodes while Anna is staying, God no.

The phone rang again.

Squinting (where are those glasses?), Tomas could make out another long tumble of numbers. He said hello several times before recognising the featureless female tone as electronic: one new voice message. Tomas hung up, dialled and listened. The message had been left while he was speaking to Anna. The same jagged breathing, the same relish in the voice, and just one word: broken into two vowels to bring out its musicality.

'Ker-*weer*.'

*

HE SPENT a good hour considering, walking around the house hanging it up in various locations. Bedroom. No. Hallway, definitely not. Lounge, yes, but the sun too bright, might fade the fabric. Kitchen, absolutely not, all those smells and heat. Bedroom then, yes. No.

Eventually, Tomas opted for the kitchen. Seemed to fit here best, gave the room a comfortable, old-fashioned feel. Like home. Daddy, will you have a cup of tea?

Nearly dark now – been here for hours and failed to find anything wrong, just as his less hysterical self had predicted. Nothing. So he cleaned up the house, made an omelette, hung some pictures. The four Harry Boland letters he put at the top of the stairs, but the scapula deserved to be in the kitchen, at the centre of the home.

It's a *what?*

How many times in England had he been asked that? Even in Ireland the term had nearly died out. Tomas always took an academic, Marta-like pleasure in explaining that, as you can see, it's a sort of medal, made from cloth or canvas. Two medals, actually, both square, one carrying a picture, the other some text. They're connected by these two thin straps. The idea is that the head goes through the straps so that one of the medals rests on your chest, over your heart, while the other rests on your back, between the shoulder blades. Scapula.

Oh, they'd say as if fascinated but actually thinking, It looks a bit creepy.

Are scapulas rare? Is that why it's in a frame?

Not too common now. But I put it in the frame. It's mine. I wore it when I was a baby.

Oh.

Curious that he always fibbed about it. Did it to Karin, just the day before. The scapula was the first object he kept, long before the Boland letters. Pressed close to his warm heart, given to him for safekeeping by a proud mammy. My little man.

Embarrassment, perhaps; the religious connotations, all that. English always found it awkward. They never asked, Do you believe? Not once. They'd study the tiny illustration of Saint Brigid, her face in profile, eyes upward, a wooden cross squashed against her breast. The glowing halo and the tightly draped mantilla gave her the look of a comic book superhero.

What's that? they'd ask, pointing at the medal with the writing. Is it Latin?

Ni bu Sanct Brigid suanach
Ni bu huarach im sheire Dé,
Sech ni chiuir ni cossens
Ind nóeb dibad bethath che.

It's Irish, actually. You know, Gaelic.

And what does it say?

Oh, that Brigid spurned material possessions and loved God.

Can you speak Irish?

A little. In Ireland, I learned it at school.

Really?

Gluaisteán was a car.

Slan leat was goodbye.

Nollaig was Christmas.

It was all he remembered.

Queer. Was that just abuse, or do they really think it? Is that it?

The phone rang.

Grunting with irritation, Tomas reached one hand across the kitchen table to pick it up while with the other he flicked open his reading glasses (they'd been under the bed). There were numbers, though he didn't recognise the configuration.

'Top of the morning, though I guess it should be top of the evening.'

The voice was female, possibly Welsh.

'Hello?'

'Sorry,' Karin said, reverting to softened New Jersey. 'Dumb joke. So how are you this evening?'

Tomas rubbed his face. Good God, not again. Almost prefer another prank call. At least they appreciate the power of brevity.

'Fine, fine. Just pottering around the house.'

'Pottering.' Her voice had taken on a treacly, flirtatious quality. 'So what does that involve exactly?'

Tomas grimaced. 'Oh, just getting my stuff organised. Hanging up pictures, sorting through my collection, you know.'

'Must be very homey.'

'It's OK, it's coming along fine. I have far more things than I first assumed, of course.'

He heard her smile, and thought of his father's set of sturdy black rosary beads, kept hidden in the depths of those enormous trouser pockets from which sweets occasionally emerge. The beads are rarely produced, though. Tom Dalton isn't one for displays of piety. Yet they are always with him, gently chinking as he walks.

'You're funny,' Karin said.

A phone rang, Tomas's mobile this time. Karin said she'd hang on; insisted on it. He left the house phone on the kitchen table and jogged into the hallway.

'Tomas, mate. It's me. Just giving you a bell to warn you.'

'About Karin?'

'She on the blower already? Bloody hell. That woman is a *nutter.*'

Tomas hmmed. He straightened up some of the framed photographs in the hallway. One of a smooth-skinned Eli, ten years younger, hair springing from his head. He was squinting into the sunlight, grinning at a future he couldn't see.

'Look, I talked to her and she got the message, I reckon. I think your virtue is safe. She says she wants to be your friend. Think of her as your mum. Bye!'

He hung up. Tomas dutifully returned to the kitchen and sat.

'Sorry about that.'

'It's OK. Anything important?'

'No, just Eli. Film stuff.'

'I was speaking to him today, actually. I don't want to talk out of turn, but he is a weird little guy. That Cockney accent! I swear I only understood every third word he said, and that seemed to be "fuck" or "bloody". And *very* indiscreet. If I were you, babe, I wouldn't confide in him too much. We'll just leave it at that.'

Much to his own surprise, Tomas found himself smiling. He imagined Karin in her hotel room, bits of toilet paper wedged between her freshly painted toes, chewing gum and sipping on a whiskey sour. Split the screen to contrast with Tomas, sitting at his bare table, in his Spartan house. He stood and walked towards the lounge.

'So what have you been doing today?'

'Oh, the usual,' she hummed. 'Slept late, had an early lunch, then I walked around, went to see your spire again. Er, did a bit of shopping. Listened to the voices. On the street, I mean. Not in my head. You know what I was thinking? I don't know if I've got the accent quite right yet. What do you think?'

Tomas told her that she had the *Irish* accent off perfectly, but that now she was here she could perhaps work on refining it into a *Dublin* accent, which is quite pronounced when compared to other parts of the country. But he had no doubt she'd get it right. Another couple of days and you'll be chatting like a native.

'YesyesyesYES, that's just what I was thinking.' She tried out a few phrases in her target Dublinese accent. She still sounded Welsh.

'Anyway, then I came back here and I've just had some dinner – which was very nice – and then I thought about you, in that big old house all by yourself.'

'Well, it's not that big, actually.'

Tomas peered out the front window. All quiet on the street. Probably nothing else from them tonight, probably past their curfew. What's the curfew for an eleven-year-old? What time for bed? He tried to remember back to when Anna was that age, but couldn't.

'Yeah, but are you OK?' Karin said. 'Are you sure you're not lonely? Because – believe me, I know – it can get to feel *mighty* lonely after a divorce. There's no lonelier time. After my second – and everything was in the gossip rags because of his gambling and all – well, I would have, I dunno what I would have done if it wasn't for my sister, Faye. Of course, me having to go into hospital for a couple of months didn't help matters at all, but at least – thank *Gawd* – the tabloids didn't get a hold of that little titbit. And actually it was kinda good because they didn't know where to find me. I just disappeared. Pouf! And it gave me time to figure things out. To talk. You really need to talk to after a divorce, Tomas, you really need to talk it out.'

'Yes, yes.'

'Yes to which? Yes you agree? Yes you feel lonely? Yes you've talked it out? Tomas, who do you talk to?'

'Various people.' The smile rinsed from his face.

'That sounds a little bit vague to me. The thing is – and I'm only saying it because I've had all these feelings too – is that you go through some weird changes of emotion. First you hate your ex, then you feel guilty towards them, then you miss them. It's, it's…do you miss your ex?'

They arrange to meet in Soho Square on the first Saturday. Tomas pretends to know where it is, assuming a park will be easy to find. But he is nearly late because he has to go into a bookshop and look it up in an A to Z. They arrive at just the same time, and walk slowly towards each other, past earnest clumps of hairy young men sitting cross-legged on the grass. She wears a white blouse and an A-line skirt that swishes around her hips. She smells faintly of jasmine.

Karin was still talking.

'Dumb question, sorry, because it doesn't really matter. The important thing, like I say, is the talk. Gotta talk. So who did you talk to after you were divorced from…what was her name?'

Tomas looked at the couch. The clock ticked.

'Marta.'

He assumes she'll want to go for a walk or to the pictures, but Marta quickly relieves him of this anxiety by squatting down on the parched grass and indicating he do the same. They talk about the new friends they have collected, about Dublin, her home in Muswell Hill. She tells him she thinks she is a communist, though she hasn't joined any group yet. She wants to do some more reading first. Tomas says this is probably wise. They exchange a deep smirk, like they were both far older and enjoying this chance to act like teenagers.

I like you, Tomas says; just like that. She leans back, the early autumn sun emerging from behind her sparkling hair. It blinds him, yet he knows she is smiling.

'So who did you talk to about Marta?'

'Well, I have a daughter.'

'I don't buy that for a second. You can't talk to kids about this kind of thing. They don't want to hear it.'

'Various friends.'

'Not Eli. Don't tell me you talk to Eli.'

'Not about personal matters, no.'

There was a pause, during which Tomas heard a clinking sound. He peered out the window again. Across the street, a scrawny dog was sniffing a dust-bin.

'Look, Karin.'

'You know, you can be very formal, for an Irishman. A little stiff. But don't worry, I think I like that.'

The hammering on the front door caused Tomas to drop the phone, then catch it as it was halfway to the floor. And his first impulse after that was to back away from the noise rather than investigate further. It reminded him of his dream about the headless horse, a wild tumble of thumps, without any design or authorial intelligence; a fat man falling down the stairs.

Just as abruptly, the pounding stopped, then started again, though less randomly now. It seemed to be against the lower part of the door, and was cross-faded with another sound, a murmuring. Tomas looked around him.

'Tomas, what's going on there? What's that noise?'

The unused brass poker leaned against the fireplace. Tomas picked it up, tested its weight. He told Karin he'd ring her back, threw the phone on the couch. A third deluge of thumping shook the front of the house. Tomas could hear a number of clocks ticking, could feel blood washing through his veins.

He stood, legs apart, poker up, and wrenched open the front door.

There was nothing.

'I…I…'

The man was on the ground, his legs buckled, his right arm folded against his chest. His face was close to purple and his teeth were bared.

'I think,' he panted. 'Having a heart attack.'

4

GARDA NORBERT Clarke probed his pink, bald head with both hands, like he was searching for infestation. He glumly regarded Tomas's Persian rug.

'It is quite embarrassing. It's just that, well, I am a bit overweight and Anne – my wife – has been getting on to me about it a lot lately. Just this morning before I left the house, actually. She wants to start a family, you know, and she's worried because my father died from heart disease and he was only in his fifties. Didn't smoke or anything. So I suppose, when I felt the pain shoot up my arm…I assumed. Oh, it's silly. But I don't know anything about electricity.'

Tomas sipped his tea. Don't know about electricity. Bloody fool.

'Not silly at all. Perfectly understandable.'

The two men exchanged a smile and wished they could be elsewhere. Garda Norbert Clarke hoped Tomas wasn't going to tell anyone about this, especially the station. Never live it down. He seemed like a nice chap, though. Laid back.

Tomas wondered who he would tell first. Not embarrassing, ridiculous – a garda, a policeman who's *supposed* to be able to deal with pressure, in hysterics on the doorstep, and quite obviously *not* having a heart attack. Tomas had to calm him down – encourage deep, raspy breaths, talk softly, pat on the back – and only then had a chance to fetch a phase tester and jam it into the doorbell. It lit up.

Tomas had felt a shot of pride and admiration, almost flattered that they would go to this much trouble for him.

Don't be silly.

'Actually, Norbert – and I don't mean to sound callous – but in a way it's good that this has happened. Well, not *good*, naturally. But useful in the sense that you've witnessed what these boys are capable of. You see, I was going to ring the guards, obviously. But to be perfectly frank I didn't know if I'd be believed.'

Garda Clarke nodded eagerly. 'Well, it is pretty extraordinary for eleven-year-old boys to know about electrical things like that. As I say, they are a complete mystery to me.'

Stop making excuses. You're pathetic enough.

Are you being cruel?

With exquisite care and some gaffer tape, the boys had replaced the old Bakelite button with a metal one, then attached the live wire to the new button, ensuring that anyone who called to Tomas's house would receive a rather hefty electric shock – enough to convince Garda Norbert Clarke that his struggling heart muscle was finally overwhelmed.

Yet this breathless man was right – what would children know of the sub-atomic menace of electricity and circuits, copper wiring and plastic insulation? Perhaps they had been told. Instructed. Or watched as older hands did the work.

'It's a good thing that you are a bit of an expert in these matters. As for those other pranks…with the faeces and the cigars. They are just…' Norbert shivered, his clothed blubber ridged by unseen winds. 'All in all, it's fortunate I called in.'

'Well, not for you.'

The garda half-smiled and rubbed his head again, as if he had just realised the absence of hair. Baldness looked somewhat tragic on a man so young. Was he even thirty? Tom Dalton, Sr. had been bald – all his adult life, as far as Tomas knew – yet on his father it seemed not a deficiency, but an attribute, part of the comforting solidity he projected, like an old scar.

Norbert Clarke wasn't solid. He wasn't that fat, but there was a fleshy, un-formed quality to his body – Tomas could imagine it wobbling with each movement underneath the navy uniform, and for a moment felt a rush of pity for Anne, the wife so keen to conceive, to pretend at eroticism with this jelly of a man. This? A garda? In Tomas's youth they were an order of thick-necked giants, glowering disapproval from under peaked caps.

Norbert had explained – Call me Norbert, please – that he was the com-munity policeman for the area, here to introduce himself. Not a real cop at all, then. A PR man, a spinner of half-truths, hand-picked for his genius at being inoffensive.

You're being harsh?

No.

'So do you know these boys? Know their families?' Tomas asked.

Norbert reached for a briefcase stuffed with pamphlets.

'Oh yes, the twins and that tall boy with the buck teeth. All related to each other, I think. Well known round here. The local scallywags. They live…' he gestured vaguely, 'across the way.'

'Do they get in trouble a lot?'

Norbert shrugged. The soft skin around his neck multiplied.

'Nothing comes to mind. Nothing serious, anyway. Odd bit of mischief. I wouldn't worry about it, Mister Dalton. There's worse. Much, much worse than them.'

He glanced around the room, as if embarrassed.

'It's a working-class area, you know. There's some poverty, all the problems that go with that. But these kids aren't the worst, really. And they're young. I'll make sure this gets nipped in the bud.'

Norbert Clarke had a slight lisp. Ths getsh.

'Well, have they done this sort of thing to anyone else?'

The garda made a thoughtful face as he extracted some leaflets from his briefcase and left them discreetly on the coffee table, the way a bribe might be delivered to a corrupt politician.

'I'll look into it, though to be honest, I don't think so. I've been here about four years, and I know everybody, pretty much. I think I would have heard if there was any trouble like this before. Leave it with me, I'll ask around.' Athsk around. Tomas leaned forward.

'I would like to understand why they have picked on *me*. Is it something I've done or said or…?'

Norbert's cheeks ballooned with air. 'Oh, take your pick, could be anything. Boredom, most likely. You've just moved in. They don't know you, you don't know them, so I suppose – in their minds – that would make you a little more vulnerable.'

Tomas made a tent with his fingers. 'Yes. The funny thing is that I'm actually from around here.'

Norbert Clarke cocked his head sideways. 'Really?' There was a tremor of doubt in his voice. 'From whereabouts?'

'I grew up on Beatha Road, number 5. My mother was born there.'

'Really?' Norbert Clarke muttered the name Dalton, Dalton, Dalton and looked towards the living room window. The icy evening sunshine gave Bass

Avenue a super-real aspect, as if it was a film set for an old western, a cunning portrait of Tomas Dalton's past, rendered from cheap wood.

Norbert shook his head. 'Em, I don't know anyone around here with that name. Do you have any family left? And I *think* number 5 on Beatha is empty now. There was a Romanian family living there, but they were deported. I think they had bought the house too. Probably been repossessed by the bank.'

'My God,' Tomas said. 'That's terrible.' Meaning the house.

'Yes. Shame. Family didn't have a visa, and we have to be strict about that sort of thing now. Not pleasant. Luckily, it's not my department. You haven't been around for a look?'

'Not yet. Too busy with everything.'

'Yes.' The tone of doubt was gone, but had been replaced by something Tomas couldn't quite identify.

'Well, it has been over thirty years. That's why a young chap like yourself wouldn't have heard of the Daltons. I doubt if there's anyone left who has. But there was a time, when I was a child, everybody here knew my parents. Especially my mother, who was quite a fearsome character.'

Norbert smiled and nodded indulgently. 'Place must have changed a lot.'

Tomas began to laugh, then pulled up short. He looked out the window. 'I'm not sure. I really can't remember what it was like.' He shrugged, as if apologising for this answer. Norbert Clarke set about trying to close his bulging briefcase. The effort made him blow through his nostrils and grow red in the face. After a few attempted squeezes, he gave up.

'Right. Better be off. Thanks very much for the tea and, er, rescuing me. Lucky thing you understand electrics. Do you think I'll have to get myself checked out? Go to hospital? In your experience, is that necessary?'

Tomas smiled. 'No, I don't think so. But I'm not an expert. Really.'

Norbert made a world-weary face. Never kid a kidder.

They walked to the front door, then shook hands. Norbert dropped his voice to a low, even tone. He stood up straight and seemed to become more solid, an impressive switch of persona.

'As for your little problem. My advice is do nothing. If you retaliate or go to the parents, that can get their backs up. I know who they are, I know the families, so leave it with me. I'll have a little chat and I'd say you should have no more problems.' He was staring directly at Tomas now. His eyes were the colour of the sky. 'OK?'

'Yes. Fine.'

'My number is on those leaflets if you need me. See you soon.'

Norbert Clarke shut the front door behind him, leaving Tomas to stand in the shadowy hallway with a frown lining his face. For a few moments, he didn't move.

'Hospital.'

He laughed lightly and headed back to the living room. Hospital for an electric shock? Don't know. No, not much of a charge in that doorbell. Probably do his podgy heart some good. Tomas began gathering up the teapot and cups he had set out for Norbert Clarke.

Hospital.

Tomas sat back onto the couch. *Me having to go into hospital for a couple of months didn't help matters at all,* Karin had said.

Two months?

She is awfully thin.

*

TOMAS STUDIED Bass Avenue. Empty. He shut the door behind him and headed for the alley across the street. Halfway along, it spread into a small open area scattered with black smudges left behind by bonfires. There were empty Coke cans, crisp bags, cigarette packets, lying still as if they hoped their owners would one day retrieve them.

On the other side, Beatha Road was a copy of Bass Avenue, though a bit more decrepit. Several of the cars looked like they hadn't been driven for years, and two of the houses were abandoned, slowly choked by weeds and graffiti. There was a stench of rotting food.

Number 13. The Kellys. Seven, eight children? Parents used to row on the street a lot. Fifteen, the O'Connors. All girls, fat. Scared of a few of them. Seventeen, the Smiths, tough kids as well. Ran past their house. Seven, Mrs Brady. Mrs Brady oldlady. Nine, the Conways. Tom and James and Mary and Sean. Look at me arse, here, look. Two, the Barrets, four, the Galvins, then us. Galvins played marbles. Threw one at me? Scraped knee, tore trousers. Didn't want to go home because I'd get killed. Your ma is a madwoman. That smell, sickening. No, no.

Quiet here too. Distant city noise – the deep breath of traffic, birds singing, doors banging, scrapes, shouts, sirens, the hopeful clack of early evening high heels.

Tomas hurried back to Bass Avenue, suddenly sensitised to the raggedness of where he lived – the splintered pavement; cigarettes and exploded tea bags discarded on the concrete, like bodies in a war; stained curtains slung across windows in the middle of the day. Some of the houses were plastered, some exposing their desiccated grey brick; some were painted, some so neglected they seemed rinsed of all colour. They were drab and puny against a sky filled with sinister clouds.

*

CONOR HANLEY swayed his head from side to side and spoke softly, a method of presenting himself to the regular, non-movie world which he hoped might offset assumptions about his arrogance, assumptions which most people seemed to have arrived at long before actually meeting him. Because of his (and no false modesty here) success – several leading roles in some British films, along with good supporting parts in a couple of low-budget Hollywood flicks – most people who met Conor for the first time already knew something about him. They would have seen pictures in Hello magazine or on the back pages of the Sundays, usually unshaven, with some starlet under his arm, wearing a torn T-shirt which showed off his tattoos. He'd be sticking out his tongue or looking a bit pissed and there would always be some headline with words like wild man in it, which was so unfair because, really, Conor Hanley was just an ordinary guy with an unusual job who was only having a laugh when he could and it really was kind of ironic that people would think they knew Conor Hanley when they hadn't even met him.

Maybe that wasn't irony, but it was something. It was annoying because now every time he met someone new – especially women – he could feel their eyes sweeping over him, scanning for something negative, hoping that his nose was bigger in real life or his eyes weren't as hazel. But his nose and eyes were fine – no point in false modesty about that – so *of course* they'd always go for the one thing, the little bitchy, You're not as tall as I would have thought, or, Bit smaller than in the films, or just the look, the *look* – a glare down their noses like along the barrel of a gun because if the woman turned out to be taller than him (and so many of those dumb bitch models are these days), then they didn't have to say anything, did they? Just look *down*. Fuck – he was five nine. Not a midget.

So Conor was quite looking forward to meeting Karin Goldman. Firstly because she worked in the business and would be aware of these sorts of hardships, and secondly because – well, let's face it – she was a bit older than him and would probably be quite grateful of the chance to act against a good-looking younger man.

Conor sat at the long brown table in the production office and listened to Clara, the 1st AD, drone on about some club she liked to go to. Actually, Conor didn't listen, he pretended to, and made a pretty good job of it, swaying his head from side to side and wondering where the hell everyone else was. Coming this early made him look like a bit of a tool.

Eventually, David Sweeny sloped in the door, which was good because he knew David from a small production they did together at the Gate years back. They were about the same age – Conor was maybe a few years older. David, he saw, still had terrible acne. But it was good to see him because David was going to play Karin's son, who naturally was suspicious of Conor's character.

'Hey, babe,' yelled David, which was what he called everyone. They hugged and slapped backs and, nose to nose, immediately set about discussing how long it had been since they had seen each other, which, it turned out, was ages, though there had been a near-miss: David had got a call back for the last film Conor had been involved in, a piece of news which Conor greeted with 'that's absolutely wild!' before telling David that the whole project was a bit of a disaster anyway. Director was sniff-sniff all day long.

Clara, her face shining, followed this conversation for a while, then began leafing through her huge pile of notes.

Jack Forde, the scriptwriter, then walked in, lugging a huge leather bag. Big tall guy, but stooped over, like his head was too heavy. Clara stood up and introduced them all. Jack shook hands, smiled and quickly grunted by way of greeting, pushing his glasses back up his nose each time. As he retreated to a seat beside Clara, he glanced around the unadorned walls and out the large window providing a sniper's view of Dame Street.

'Good location,' he muttered.

No one responded to this observation. Conor and David continued their conversation.

'Good morning, everyone!' boomed Albert Kennedy, the jowly butt of a Glaswegian cast as the policeman on the trail of Conor's con man. Albert, a jacket thrown over his shoulders, assumed a boxing position in front of David which morphed into a half-hug and much back slapping – they had worked together before. He extended a firm hand and a sincere face towards Conor.

'Albert Kennedy. Pleasure to meet you, Conor.'

'Likewise.'

Just behind him, David was kissing Marion Russell on each cheek. Albert Kennedy wheeled around like a magician.

'And let me introduce the lovely Marion Russell, who, as you know, will be playing the part of Ms Goldman's slutty friend in tonight's production.'

The actors guffawed as Marion mock-slapped Albert and traded air kisses with Conor. Conor and David resumed their seats while Albert and Marion worked their way down the long table, trading loud salutations with the writer and the 1st AD. They glanced out the window and oohed at the view.

'So she hasn't arrived yet?' asked Albert.

'No sign,' David said. 'Probably waiting outside for the rest of us to get in first.'

Conor said nothing. He thought he detected a Tone.

'She probably is, too. I'm not kidding ya,' said Albert.

'What do you mean?' asked Marion. Albert ignored her.

Jack Forde raised his eyebrows and began scribbling on a piece of paper.

Quietly, Clara asked Marion how she had been. Marion said fine and asked Clara how her baby was.

'Oh. Not a baby any more. She's three now. Walking and yapping away. She's in everything. Has the house wrecked.'

'My God!' Marion carefully placed a hand on her sternum to underline her shock. 'Is it that long?'

Albert asked Conor was he doing much work across the pond, meaning the US, not Britain, and Conor swayed his head from side to side and said yeah, there's one or two things coming up. Some Iraqi war flick. Script is so-so, but it's a good billing. Texan accent, which is pretty easy to do. Much easier than, say—

'Hello, everyone!'

Karin Goldman threw out her spindly arms as she triumphed through the door, the width of her salutation implying not only how pleased she was to see them, but also her confidence that they too would be delighted to see her.

Which of course they were. Everyone stood up – Clara beaming and blinking, Jack pushing his glasses up his nose, Marion with a hand on her sternum, Albert applauding, Conor swaying his head and David, the closest to her, already with his arms open, as if she was indeed his disappeared mother, brought back to him through the magic of the movies. Decades of pain erased. Life rendered manageable and tidy.

Mother and son, however, did not hug. Instead, Karin waved and blew kisses. She encouraged David to introduce her to each person, finishing with Conor, who she did kiss on the cheek.

'Oh, but aren't you darling!'

Which means short. That's what Yanks say when they mean short.

Then she took Conor's hand and, her face already screwed up with the pain of having to ask, wondered would Conor mind moving down the table to another seat because, obviously, Tomas would be sitting at the top here and he had expressly asked for Karin to sit beside him. For emotional support. She glanced around at everyone else, as if they already knew about this and had been wondering how to bring the subject up.

'Things have been a little rough for Tomas lately. You understand, yes?' Her face stretched into a glacial smile.

'OK.'

The others stood to let him shuffle along the table. Clara studied her papers. Jack scribbled. Once in his new seat, Conor looked intently out the window.

'All right? Everybody here?' said Eli Gadd, holding open the door for Tomas. Distracted by what had just happened, the people around the table mumbled politely, but this built into a response of some warmth when Tomas entered the room, hands dug in pockets, his mouth bent into an impish smile.

Karin sprang up from her chair.

'It's our director!'

She led a round of applause which the others followed enthusiastically, if with a certain degree of irony. Tomas felt himself blush as Karin pecked him on the cheek and lightly ran her fingernails along his back. Eli winked and added whoops to the applause. Eventually, they all sat, apart from Eli, who announced to the room that he would not be staying long as he had a busy day of stealing camera equipment and bribing local government officials. Everyone in the room laughed, apart from Tomas, who had heard this joke several times before.

'But I just want to say that we are delighted to have you all working with us and I know it's going to be great. If you need anything, anything at all, then come to me or Clara or Jane the production manager, who's next door. We're here to help you get the job done, so please use us if you need us. If not, then leave us the fuck alone.'

The actors giggled again. Tomas cleared his throat and considered how to begin, but found he was thinking about Anna's arrival tomorrow, and that he should do something to prepare for it. Think of places to bring her. Get some food in. He realised he was quite excited, as if she was the parent, not the other way around. Look what I did, I moved to a new place all by myself.

'Well, I'd like to welcome you all here as well. And I won't hold you up today too long. Today is basically to go through the schedule for the next few weeks so you can organise yourselves and begin rehearsals. As you may know, it's not my style to sit in on the line rehearsals too much. I'll let you get on with that by yourselves and then I may sit in when it's time to start blocking it out. Though if there's anything you want to discuss with me, I will of course be available.'

He noticed that Karin was looking back and forth between him and the other actors. She was nodding, as if his words were on her behalf as well.

'Er, Clara…' he said, and Clara began handing out a stapled sheaf of notes to everyone at the table. 'So I'll just go through the schedule.'

'But before you do.' Karin plonked one of her claw-like hands on top of his. It had a distinct tremor, like an idling engine. The veins were eerily blue. She stood up. 'I just want to say – on behalf of all of us.'

Karin looked to her fellow actors for confirmation of her mandate. She received back mostly puzzled stares, apart from Albert, who nodded feverishly in support. Conor continued to look out the window.

'That it's just so special to have this chance to be working with you, Tomas. We're all terribly excited. I felt it as soon as I walked into this room today.' She looked around the table again. 'Isn't that right?'

'Hear, hear,' intoned Albert.

She placed a shivering hand over her heart and locked her gaze on Tomas, giving him little opportunity to look away. Eli assumed a sincere demeanour, but clasped a hand over his mouth, just in case.

'You are a wonderful man, Tomas Dalton, and I salute you. We all salute you.' She began applauding energetically, displaying the action to everyone else. The others copied, with both Eli and Albert adding occasional whoops. Tomas felt his face burn.

When the clapping had all but died away, Karin excused herself to go to the ladies room. As soon as the door closed, Albert began laughing in joyous disbelief. Conor exhaled loudly, then shook himself. He held up two hands towards Tomas. 'Fuck's sake.'

At this, Albert laughed even harder.

Eli and Tomas swapped a puzzled look.

'What happened?' Tomas asked.

Conor pointed at the door and opened his mouth, but instead exhaled again. He slumped back in his seat, as if recent events were far too complex to explain.

Alfred's laughter was subsiding now. He wiped glassy eyes. 'Oh, that was priceless, priceless!'

'Why did you have to move seats?' asked Marion.

Clara and Jack studied their notes.

Tomas glanced back at the door, then whispered urgently, 'Look, I don't know what happened here, but let's please try and be patient with Karin. She can be hard work – believe me, I know – but she's American, you know. She can't help it.'

He smiled weakly. Conor rolled his eyes. Alfred started laughing again.

*

'**WHAT THE** fuck did you say that for?' squeaked Eli.

'Linguini,' muttered Tomas.

'Where are you?'

'Marks and Spencer.'

Tomas successfully flipped two packets into his basket without dislodging the mobile phone on his shoulder. He studied the packets for a moment, then placed them back in the display cabinet. 'Anna's coming over for a few days tomorrow, so I'm just getting some food in. But I don't want to spend a lot of time cooking. She's impossible to please no matter what you do.'

'Yeah, yeah.'

Like a grazing beast, Tomas moved over to an orange-lit fridge displaying neat bags of rösti. 'Say what, anyway? What did I say?'

'To the actors. She's American? She can't help it? You know better than that, mate. You can't be taking sides if there's argy-bargy going on.'

Tomas picked up two bags, then put them back.

'I know, I know. I'm sorry. I was thinking on my feet. It just seemed so tense in there. And do you know what she said to Conor before we came in?'

Eli had left shortly after Karin returned from the ladies room. Other than Tomas and Clara, no one had spoken for the rest of the meeting.

'Yeah, I heard. Clara told me. She's off her nut.'

'Well, I just don't know. But perhaps it's just as well I said what I said. If I hadn't, they might have assumed I have some sort of *relationship* with the woman. On the first day I would have antagonised all the main actors.'

'Nah, a lot of them know you. They know you wouldn't play favourites. And Karin is obviously barking. Well, I dunno if she's barking, but she's…weird.'

'Eldritch.'

'What?'

'That's the word for her. I was just thinking about it. It means, as you say, weird or strange, but in an elfish way. And there is something elfish about her.'

'Eldritch. Yeah, yeah. Mate, you do have a lot of useless information in your skull.'

'Yes. Sorry. Too many books.'

As a young man, Tomas had read voraciously but with little sense of direction – linguistics, biography, mathematical physics, fiction, geopolitics, engineering, philosophy, architecture, poetry, sociology, transport planning. He had succumbed to virtually every book he encountered, a habit which took some years to break. But by then, the damage had been done – Tomas's brain was crammed with tottering stacks of random information which he couldn't forget, leaving too little room for what he wanted to remember.

Tomas rarely read now.

'Well, whatever the fuck she is, we've got to be careful with her,' Eli said. 'I'll have a word with the rest of them, let them know that if they have any problems, they can come to me to have a moan and all that. I don't want them bothering you with this shit.'

'Whatever you think is best.'

Tomas moved over to a fridge stocked with Chinese food. Does Anna like Chinese? Sort of thing she might like but not eat due to some political conviction unique to her. A woman beside him was also talking into a mobile phone, her shoulders shaking with laughter.

'I think you should bring her out for dinner again, mate.'

'Oh good grief, surely not? I thought the whole idea was to *discourage* her.'

'I know, I know. And I did have a word, you know that. But she bloody hates me; that's obvious. She loves you, though. Are you sure you didn't give her one?'

'Eli.'

'Yeah, yeah. All you have to do is tell her to be a bit more considerate of the other actors, 'cos if they see what great mates you and Karin is, then they'll feel a bit left out of the loop. That kind of bullshit. That's all. Just to keep things sweet.'

Tomas sighed. 'I suppose so. Actually, I meant to ask you – has Karin ever been ill? Seriously ill?'

'Dunno. Not that I know of. Why?'

'She mentioned that she had been in hospital for a couple of months, which is an awfully long time.'

'Nervous fucking breakdown. She's not ostrich or whatever you call it. She's a nutter. Makes sense.'

'But she is *painfully* thin and I noticed this morning that she has a bit of a shake in her hands.'

'So what do you think it is?'

'Well, I don't know.'

'Then I wouldn't worry about it, mate. None of our business. Talk to you later, all right?'

Eli hung up. Tomas pocketed his mobile, smiling complicity at the cartons of Chinese food. Such mild troubles. He glanced at the woman next to him, who still held a phone to her ear. But she was crying, not laughing, her cheeks shining with tears. Promptly, Tomas moved away.

*

ANNA FLICKED through the channels, her eyes darting between the television and the various objects which filled her father's living room. Finally, she abandoned the remote control, tossing it onto the sofa. She stood up, ignoring the early evening chat show. Two men in frantic suits slouched on a pastel couch with an attentive, long-legged woman. Many people are anchoring, one of the men told her. They are redefining their social roots because of post-consumerism uncertainty. It's a return to spiritual values.

Anna considered lighting a cigarette, then thought better of it. He'd put on a Face. Should be cutting down anyway. Think I'm doing it to annoy him. Hardly inside the airport when he started with compliments. That's a lovely skirt and blouse. You can really wear clothes. Not like your mother – everything seemed to hang off her, even though she was always slim. But you. You can *wear* clothes. It's an indefinable thing.

No it wasn't. In Tomas Dalton's world, smelly old dykes aren't supposed to have nice bodies, they're supposed to wear donkey jackets and big boots. Should have said that to him. Wouldn't have been a good start, though.

People feel quite spiritual in their cars, droned one of the jazzy-suited men. They feel completely safe.

Thursday, Friday, Saturday, Sunday. Three nights, four days. You can do this. You must do this. He's your father, for Christ's sake. Anna took out a cigarette.

The first section of the shop is known as the decompression zone.

Anna lit and sucked. Ah.

Women go anti-clockwise around shops, but men look for the high ground, to get a vantage point.

Tomas backed into the room, wielding glasses of red wine.

'Dinner's on. You do like Chinese?'

Anna, now staring out the window (cigarette tucked discreetly into her cupped hand), made a neutral sound. She usually avoided Chinese food. Always left her dehydrated. Be in and out of bed all night getting water.

Tomas carefully placed her wine on the mantelpiece, then sipped from his own.

'What are you looking at?'

Anna pointed towards the street. 'You have crusties.'

'What?'

She indicated the young couple outside. They held hands as they moved up Bass Avenue, yet every few steps the girl seemed to be attempting to flee, her thick dreadlocks whipping out from her head as she spun away from her boyfriend. Grinning, he pulled her back, now wrapping his arms around her, forcing them to walk a few paces in clumsy tandem. Then they halted, briefly kissed, and began the process again. Stroll. Struggle. Kiss. Stroll. Struggle. Kiss. Behind them, an emaciated dog of indeterminate breed unenthusiastically sniffed at the pavement.

'They're scruffy. Is that what you call them? Crusties? Sounds like a disease.'

Now past Tomas's house and heading for the cul-de-sac end of Bass Avenue, they stopped again. The boy cupped the girl's breasts while she licked her lips lasciviously. They both laughed loudly, their mounds of hair shaking. Father and daughter looked away.

'Was the street this rundown when you were young?'

'Can't remember. Are you smoking?'

Anna turned and glared at her father. 'Yes, Daddy. I'm smoking. They are bad for me. I know. I'm addicted. I know. I shouldn't smoke. I know. Are you still smoking cigars?'

'Rarely.'

He glanced at the television. One of the men was describing himself as an ethnologist of consumerism. Tomas shook his head. 'What's on?'

Anna moved her shoulders in a non-committal way. One of her odd habits. The television would be on constantly, yet she never seemed to watch it. Could become quite ratty if anyone turned it off.

Nationality is a brand, said the other man. Different races have a responsibility to live up to the identity of their brand.

'Everything's a *brand*.'

Tomas found adverts unsettling, full of selfishness and bad manners. Rudeness dressed up as individuality. Everyone a rebel, with nothing to rebel against.

One hand under her cigarette, Anna moved towards the fireplace and flicked off some ash. She picked up her wine. 'Have you got a house alarm?'

'Not yet.'

'You should get one.'

'Meaning what, exactly?'

She gestured towards the window. 'Well, come on, Daddy. It is a bit, you know. A lot of my clients live in places like this.'

Tomas slowly raised an eyebrow.

'Daddy, don't be like that. You know exactly what I mean. Look at your car. Look at your house. You're different from the people around here and they'll see that. It's up to you, of course, but I think you should take a few precautions, that's all. I would have thought you'd want to protect all your precious junk.'

Tomas tried smirking. Almost like she knows. Always hated the collection. As a toddler they could barely restrain her, barrelling around the flat, shaking, smashing and tearing whatever she could get her hands on. No matter how many times he said it – no matter what tactics he adopted: threats, actual smacking once or twice, distractions, long chats, bribes – still she attacked it, with a venom quite startling for a young child. Eventually he had to put it all high up, out of her reach, and even then she would stand in the living room, her Bible-black eyes cast upwards, her podgy hands clawing, as if trying to climb an invisible set of stairs. She would point at various objects and mumble baby words, hoping to be lifted up, knowing it wasn't going to happen, yet still slave to the urge to try. Even Marta thought it was strange.

'No, you're right. I should get an alarm.'

Anna blinked and pursed her lips, somewhat placated by this concession. It made her look like a dolly – while she had inherited her father's dark complexion and a lot of his facial features, she had also taken her mother's slight frame.

Sometimes, returning to the damp flat on the Romford Road, twisted bags from the Co-op bouncing against his legs, he'll fall back a few paces and walk behind Marta just so he can look at her, at the way the material of her skirts and mannish trousers falls gratefully against the slide of her legs and buttocks. Marta doesn't strictly approve of this objectification, of course, but she allows it nonetheless, turning it into a game where they'll pretend they are strangers, where she will glance back at him, alarmed and excited at the possibility of taking this strange young man into her bed, and all control falling away.

'I'm sorry, Daddy. I know this is where you grew up. But if you had to come back to Dublin, why this area? When there are so many lovely parts?'

Because I wanted to be close to the memory of my parents, the only real family I have left.

Such a thing to think.

Tomas said nothing.

*

ANNA MADE a face when she saw the Chinese meal, then asked why he didn't cook real food any more. Was it because he didn't have anyone to cook for?

No. It was because those I cooked for never appreciated it.

Can't say that.

Instead, Tomas made a face, hoping it would be received as playful.

Anna asked to change position at the kitchen table so she wouldn't have to look at that creepy framed scapula.

Tomas nodded his assent, but said nothing more.

Eventually, in response to a more conciliatory question about how the film was going, he told Anna that he was being pursued by Karin Goldman, the famous Hollywood actress.

Anna described how fantastic Mummy was looking, and how she could never contact her because Mum was out all the time with God knows who, doing God knows what.

Tomas related – in intricate and somewhat imagined detail – the story Karin had told him about the French man whose former lover was a lesbian and how he was forced to pretend to be a woman while they were making love.

What the fuck has this story to do with anything.

Tomas smiled, then said sorry.

You're getting at her. Stop it.

Afterwards, they sat loose-limbed on the living room sofa, almost sated from their exertions. Television chatter filled the silence. Tomas sipped his coffee while Anna rooted through her bag for cigarettes. He attempted to mentally list who other than the boys could be attacking the house. One of the other neighbours? They weren't that friendly, but he didn't sense any hostility. They nodded, said good morning. If anything, their communication was considerably tentative – not wishing to be aloof, but not wishing to intrude either. Tomas liked this. Some other buyer then? Someone with a claim on the house? The estate agent hadn't mentioned anyone else, and he surely would have to bump up the price. The house itself then? No hint of it having a dark past. The previous owner had been some blameless old lady. Her children sold the place after she died. There were a few mouldy armchairs remaining when he had taken possession. Dusty picture of the Sacred Heart which Tomas had been tempted to keep. But nothing remarkable or suspicious. A life which had simply crumbled away, as they all eventually do.

You wiped out all the remaining traces of her. Painted over her walls, ripped out the stiff carpets which once absorbed the footsteps of her children. Your life gobbled hers.

The first two rocks came through the window almost simultaneously, the third a few seconds later. Tomas imagined one of the boys – one of the twins, possibly – so convulsed with laughter that he couldn't raise his arm in time, causing the others to become serious, to upbraid him for a lack of professionalism.

Rocks through the window? Rather disappointing. Uninspired, compared to before.

So much for that fat oaf Norbert Clarke. Couldn't even pause hostilities long enough for Anna to come and go. Shouldn't have listened to him.

Nearly a week, though, since the last. They were waiting? For this? For Anna to come. No. How could—

'Jesus Christ, Jesus Christ!'

She was on her feet, pressed against the far wall, as if the rocks might leap up and attack. Startled by his daughter's voice into action, Tomas was now at the front door, already sweating as he tried to yank it open, finding that it wouldn't come, that something – not the Yale lock, not the Chubb lock, not the bolt – was holding it shut.

'Fuck, fuck, fuck!' she screamed, and Tomas would have replied but he was breathless now, oxygen only coming in short, precious bursts, his heart hammering behind his ribs. He ran trembling fingers along the frame of the door and – oh, damnandblast – leapt back when the screw sank into his index finger and vivid blood wriggled out.

'Yeah,' he said against Anna's continuing roars, putting the finger in his mouth to staunch the flow, then pulling it out to examine the damage. Bleeding not too bad, but the screw (rusty?) had gone deep into his flesh. He moved towards the kitchen to collect his toolbox, then realised the pointlessness of this until the bleeding stopped. He re-entered the lounge, where Anna was still pinned against the far wall, panting, her black hair glistening with sweat.

'What, what?' she yelled, newly alarmed by the sight of her father with a finger in his mouth. Tomas hushed and made calming gestures, which, to his surprise, had some effect. Anna stepped away from the wall, her eyes moist. She swept a hand rapidly through her hair. 'What was that? What was that? Jesus, Daddy. Rocks through the window? Has this happened before?'

The hands stopped moving and went to her hips, like a miniature gun slinger ready to draw. Tomas studied his injured finger. A neat red hole just below the nail.

'What's that?' asked Anna. There was a shake in her voice. Funny. From her job, you would have thought, always seems so much tougher. Tomas had an urge to smile.

'Cut it. I think they screwed the door shut.'

'They? They? Who are *they*? This has happened before?'

He nodded slowly, but stopped once his gaze drifted down to the rug. Almost smiled again. *So* clever. Not just rocks, but rocks covered with wet, black paint (gloss, difficult to remove), dipped then immediately thrown, leaving thick black smudges on the wooden floor and all over the Persian. Two of the rocks had struck the rug, then rolled, scoring wide tracks across it, curling out in opposite directions like the branches of a crudely painted tree.

'My God,' he breathed before sitting down. It was as if they were aiming for the rug, as if they knew it was Persian and irreplaceable, and – creatures of pure spite that they are – knew it wasn't even his.

Poor Sophie.

'My God,' repeated Tomas. He felt Anna's hand rest on his arm.

'What, Daddy?'

He stood up and headed for the kitchen. Bleeding had stopped now, so at least he could get the door open. Might have to pull the pins out of the hinges. Easy enough to get them out, but tough to get them back in. Anna would have to hold the door steady. With her tiny frame? No. Still like a little girl.

Anna's scream froze his progress. He turned back towards the lounge, realising that what he heard was anger, not fear.

'You little fucking bastards! When I get out there, I'm gonna do you! You're fucking gonna pay for this, you *cunts*.'

The words delivered with a deliberate, chant-like hatred – she was nose to the window, and from the angle Tomas watched, it seemed like she was shouting at her own reflection, rehearsing what she might say if she ever came face to face with the rock-throwers. He walked into the room, and as he did so noticed that the twins – on the other side of the glass and somewhat bemused by Anna's screaming – brightened when they saw Tomas, as if he was a favourite uncle. The tall one just stared, his mouth slightly open. He looked from Anna to Tomas, and then to the twins.

Then he grinned. A thin bead of snot dribbled from his left nostril. Opening his mouth even wider, he allowed a reptilian tongue to emerge. It swept upwards, cleaning off the snot as a windscreen wiper clears off rain. The three boys strolled away into the thin evening light.

5

FIRST HE had to speak about the owner of the rug. Sophie Ward was an Irish journalist he and Marta had befriended in London, who adored talking to Tomas about Dublin and how it had changed. She was tall and funny and slightly bawdy and Tomas was attracted to her, but of course never did anything. She had been away from Ireland as long as he, dividing her years between the Middle East and London. When the second Gulf War broke out, she was in between flats (contracts not exchanged), but of course had to go. Typical Sophie. She put her furniture in storage, but the Persian rug she gave to Tomas and Marta for safekeeping – she knew they liked it and would keep it clean. A fortnight later, Sophie was killed by the blast from an off-target bunker buster. Her body wasn't discovered until two days after the explosion, having been thrown into the basement of a building previously cracked open by mortar fire. She may have lain there for some hours before she died, with nothing to see but explosions scalding the black sky.

Tomas and Marta read about her death in *The Guardian*, and afterwards felt compelled to study the rug, as if this was the sole remaining evidence that Sophie Ward used to exist. She had no family that they knew of, no particularly close friends or lovers to claim inheritance. So they kept the rug – while making sure to tell anyone who asked how they had come to own it.

After the divorce, it came to Dublin. No discussion. Just assumed.

Tomas was sure Anna had heard this story before; heard it many times. Wasn't that long ago, after all. Must have even met Sophie a few times. But it felt proper that he should tell it again, like a benediction, and he was grateful to his daughter for listening.

Then she listened while he spoke about everything else: the boys, the cigars, the front door, the calls, Garda Norbert Clarke. He spoke for almost an hour, during which time Anna remained largely silent, her face a puzzle of frowns and tics.

When he finished, they sat in a silence made unbearable by this sudden crash of revelation. It rendered all their old talk meaningless.

They didn't know what to say.

Tomas muttered indistinguishably, got up and headed for the kitchen. He located a plaster and applied it to his finger, then got his toolbox and set about working on the front door. He shined a torch around the edges of the doorjamb and discovered a series of long, skinny screws, two inserted along the top, three down the sides. Fairly easy to dislodge with a chisel and a crowbar. How did they get them in without anyone hearing?

Behind him, Anna tidied up, jangling cups and glasses as she walked back and forth.

Probably outside the whole time, eavesdropping on everything said – all the bickering during dinner, all about not having a house alarm. Damn.

He slammed the chisel into the side of the door and wrenched it back, then again, lower down. He dropped the chisel and used the crowbar now, working it sideways until a cracking sound shrieked through the house. The door sprang open, part of the frame still clinging to it. Anna emerged from the kitchen. She watched as he cautiously moved into the front yard, shining the torch on the path, the gate and the pavement beyond. He came back inside.

'What were you looking for?'

'Well, you don't know what the little bastards will think of next. I have to check everything, just in case there's some other trap out there.'

'Is the door badly damaged?'

'Not that bad. Probably wouldn't even notice it from the outside.' He took on a sheepish look. 'I suppose I should ring the guards. Again.'

Anna snorted. 'What for? It isn't going to work. They were obviously just waiting for a chance.' She hugged herself. 'Christ, Daddy, it's creepy.'

They both looked out at the darkening street. A metallic smell drifted into the house. Gently, Anna spoke. 'Why don't you just move back to London? This is insane.'

Tomas ignored her. He got down on his hunkers and used a pliers to pull the screws out of the door frame. Anna held up her hands, as if surrendering.

'OK, OK, I'm sorry. But doesn't all this tell you something? This isn't your home any more. You're an outsider. Will you at least *consider* moving back? Please, Daddy. Please?'

He stood up, panting slightly. 'I appreciate what you're saying. Really, I do. But I'm not about to be put out of my home by a bunch of children, for God's sake. It is time to involve the police – the real police, I mean. Not Norbert whateverhisnameis. These boys came to the window afterwards to see what damage they had caused. That must be grounds to arrest them or whatever.'

Anna made a pained face. 'Not necessarily. Just because they looked in the window afterwards doesn't mean they threw the rocks. They could say they heard the smash and came to have a look. In fact, I'd bet that's exactly what they want you to do, just to make a fool of you.'

'You're joking, surely!'

'Really, Daddy. I work with people like this all the time. Some of them know the law inside out. Or at least they know enough of it never to get caught.' She tapped her father gently on the chest. 'There's only one thing they understand.'

This was the kind of phrase which, not too long ago, would have infuriated Anna if spoken by one of her elders.

'If they do something to you, you'll do ten times worse to them. Really. Scare them. It's the only way.'

She whipped up her bag, and for a moment Tomas feared that Anna was about to show him something he would rather not see. Instead she extracted a packet of cigarettes. She lit one, and sucked hard. He wished she wouldn't smoke. It looked vulgar.

'Look – do you have any idea where they live? Let me go around and have a word. I've done this before, once or twice. I can scare them, believe me.'

Little Anna playing with her dollhouse, fringe sweeping over her eyes. Daddy that's you and this is Mummy, and that's a doggy and that's me and that's a baby. Can we have a doggy?

'What? Don't be ridiculous, Anna. I'm not going to dispatch my daughter into the night to threaten people.'

She shook her head. 'Daddy, I just have to do it once and they'll leave you alone. Promise.'

'No, no. Out of the question.'

'And what are you going to do? Come on. Be realistic.'

He frowned. 'What? You think I *can't* do it?'

'No, Daddy. I don't think you can do it.'

'You better check all the windows at the back, and bolt the door after me.'
He picked up the torch and strode out of the house.

*

ARMS FOLDED, Anna watched her father march up the road – up the wrong way as far as she could tell – so obviously he's doing it for show. Juvenile. And not like him. Maybe Mummy.

No.

She slumped onto the couch. Wouldn't be here at all; well, not here so soon, when she had tons on at work, when it really wasn't convenient, if Mummy hadn't put on the guilts. You should check up on your father, really. I'm worried, and he won't listen to me at the moment, you know that. It would be terrible if, you know, something happened.

Something? What kind of something?

But this is something.

Not a very big something, though, bit of vandalism, what he gets for moving back to this dump. Could never see the obvious. Mister Magoo. Mummy, naturally, liked to pretend it was something darker. But without making a fuss, of course. Passive-aggressive drama queen.

Anna pulled over her bag and dug around until she found her mobile phone. Could ring Mummy now. No, too irritated.

*

'WHAT IS it?' Tomas whispered. 'What is it?'

He walked purposefully towards the closed end of Bass Avenue, knowing there was nothing there. He had an urge to sit on the pavement, but she was probably watching. He wished he had a cigar, to help himself think.

What are you going to do? The cheek. Really.

Calm, calm. Nothing new in this.

Even as a teenager she had treated him like a crumbling grandparent, unable to deal with the complex world spinning around. For a time, Tomas had found this endearing, a teenage affectation. But later, he worried that disapproval, even jealousy was at its root – she resented his apparently easy life, jetting to various countries, eating nice lunches, meeting gorgeous actors while she slogged for her social science degree, doggedly counting out just how much wickedness and misery can exist within the world.

Reaching the end of Bass Avenue, Tomas stopped and looked around. All curtains drawn, except for one house in which he could see a framed picture of the Sacred Heart of Jesus, the Saviour staring wistfully, hands outstretched. Shrugging. Nothing I can do. There are, what? Twenty-five, thirty houses? Never see anyone at night. He shivered. Bit nippy now.

Tomas walked back to the alleyway, switched on the torch and shined it before him, revealing circles of damp concrete, indistinguishable graffiti. Nothing. At the other end of Bass Avenue, on Clontarf Road, feral cars swooshed by. A group of seven or eight people, silhouetted by the streetlamps, moved in single file, each with an arm on the shoulder of the one in front. They produced a guttural chant, which was sometimes rhythmic, but sometimes splintered into shouts, sobs, recriminations; the din of despair. This human chain reminded Tomas of something, though he couldn't think what.

Cold now, yet his skin was brushed with sweat. Skin. Just material, really, covering the bone and muscle. A flimsy protection against the exterior world. A poor decoration.

He looked back towards the black alleyway. The wire guts of a decapitated streetlamp swung gently. Their lair. The wounded old man, prowling the perimeter, trying to look fierce. The sound of stereoscopic sirens swooped through the night sky like attacking eagles, then away again.

This city. It's seething.

Perhaps other people putting them up to it? Older kids, adults with some black grudge?

No, not here long enough.

But how can all this be just boys? Bored little boys? Their world is so *stuffed* – discs and Nike runners and streaming MPEGS and frozen shots, MTVX and cut tops and T-shirts, eBay and PSIVs and Manchester United and textting and message minding and downloaded MPZs and fan webzines and Klunk search engines and chat zones and baggies and game-boxes, digi-teen magazines and sampled Credence Clearwater Revival songs, jewellery and body piercing and drugs and a million other things which were the centre of the universe until they flopped out of fashion a week later. Not millions, either – billions of bits of information, floating like algae in the Pacific. Scrubbed of context, no moral action and reaction, no what happened next? The infinite hum of the present, defined only by what sensations it produced.

Tomas shook himself, coughed loudly enough for anyone hiding close by to hear, then moved into the darkness, swishing the torch as he progressed. He listened for sounds, but could only make out his own footsteps, a dog barking, a plane trundling far overhead.

He reached the small expanse of waste ground halfway along the alley and methodically swept the light around. Marta will hear all about it, every pathetic detail. Probably on the phone now.

A sudden scraping made Tomas jolt. He shined the torch towards the noise, backing away a few steps. Could have been a cat. Or perhaps rats. Sort of place would have rats. Tomas backed away some more.

Just what she'll want to hear. Not enough to just get away, but cripple me in doing so – illuminate my dependency.

Tomas looked at his watch. Nearly ten. They'll be at home now. Pointless looking any more. Have to find out where they live.

He turned and quickly re-emerged onto the shiny tarmac of Bass Avenue. Nothing, no one.

Been out for long enough. You're not scared. You will take action.

Tomas again noticed the metallic smell in the air. He heard the rain before he saw it, an implacable sheet of wet galloping towards him, the noise of it hammering into his ears, the huge drops saturating the street and making everything sound as if it were made of tin. And Tomas had an urge to run away, to stay ahead of the downpour, even though he knew this was foolish, that he was in a cul-de-sac and had nowhere to run to.

*

'OH, THIS is lovely. This is so…oh, exceptionally lovely.'

Karin seemed to blush slightly, as if the location had an unspoken significance.

Hiding from Anna. Pathetic man.

'You like it then?' he said.

'Yes, yes. This an old haunt of yours?'

'Alas, no. When I lived in Dublin I was far too young and too poor to come to places like this. But I've always wanted to eat here, it has a fantastic reputation.'

Through a tight grin, Clara the AD had suggested the restaurant. Sort of place Karin might enjoy. It had a French name which Tomas kept forgetting, while the walls inside were a traffic jam of paintings by some well-known Irish artist Tomas had never heard of, cartoon-like depictions of baleful people, their faces in profile, their eyes seeming to follow Karin and Tomas as they walked to their table. Still, the dining area was impressively large and not over-lit and had a certain *belle époque* feel. It would do.

'So you've brought me to the fanciest restaurant in Dublin?' Karin attempted to wiggle her gaunt backside as she walked. Her dark dress was tight and cosmically shiny and seemed to rattle as she moved. 'Ain't you nice?'

Mother in a dress — navy blue, with a fussy lace collar which makes her look curiously masculine. She hates it, hates all clothes except her long tweed skirts and waisted jackets. Her rebel outfits, Daddy calls them. But once a year, to please him, she dresses up and goes with him to the printers' Christmas dinner dance in Wynn's Hotel.

The sweating assistant manager stopped beside their table, bowed and blushed.

'Would you like to order drinks?'

'Brandy. Large one.'

'The same.'

The lie to Anna had been shameful — over lunch in the blindingly sunny atrium of the National Gallery. All morning — first in the house, then later, strolling around the city — they had affected an exhausting cheeriness. But it was discordant and slightly ugly, and she must have known that he was only pretending to ring the guards; that when he went out to search for the boys again he did no more than walk up to the shop to buy cigars; that he was relieved to escape into the front room to board up the damaged parts of the window. Without any premeditation he was aware of, Tomas announced a just-remembered dinner date for that night. She squinted at him.

What, with your actress?

Tomas held up a hand to shade his eyes.

No, no. Tom Dooley. Old, old friend from school. Just ran into him by accident. Wouldn't take no for an answer. You know what it's like here. The hospitality can be oppressive. Made the appointment ages ago, long before I knew you were coming. I'd bring you along, but Tom's had some hard times and I think he wants to talk about it. Gambling problem. Extremely tragic. And for Tom, who was so honest. You understand. I'm sorry.

For her father, Anna proffered a smile.

No, it's fine. There's loads of things I want to do that you'd find boring anyway. No, that's fine. You enjoy yourself.

Maybe we can meet for a drink afterwards? I'm meeting Tom early.

Great. Whatever. Fine.

Tom Dooley? Ever known a Tom Dooley?

She was probably relieved too.

The waiter quickly returned with the drinks. As it was only six-thirty in the evening (Karin continuing her insistence on eating early), there were, once again, few other diners – a man with a proto-handlebar moustache who sat alone and was possibly drunk; half a dozen men in white shirts, their jackets over the backs of their chairs, hung like flags to signal that work was over; a sour-faced yet pretty off-duty waitress, sipping a cappuccino. Everyone ignored everyone else.

Karin peeked at Tomas from over the large menu. One of her eyes, he noticed, was slightly bloodshot.

'Two days,' she said, giddily.

Filming on *The Marrying Kind* was due to begin in two days. Despite Tomas's trepidation, rehearsals had been going well. Conor Hanley had had a major breakthrough, realising that, as his character was marrying Karin's character for her money, he didn't actually have to fancy Karin, which was, er, you know. There'd been a little tension with David Sweeney when David suggested Conor wear lifts in his shoes, but they'd worked that out. Marion had burst into tears several times, for which she then spent several hours apologising, but Albert seemed to have developed the knack of cheering her up. She seemed to enjoy his Sean Connery impersonations almost as much as Albert did. Jack Forde, the scriptwriter, had yet to speak.

Even Karin's accent had dramatically improved, relocating from Cardiff to somewhere just north of Dublin; close enough. She was even getting on better with the others.

Tomas didn't know any of this first hand, as he had yet to attend any read-throughs. Instead he had rung each actor and received detailed reports from Clara. His absence, it seemed, relieved Karin of the need to be bossy.

'Two days,' Tomas replied. 'So how are you getting on with everyone?'

'Oh fine, fine. One big family.'

In truth, Tomas found rehearsals and actors rather boring. The former were far too repetitive, while the latter invariably over-talked their roles, stretching to apply cod-psychology to every scene, expecting Tomas to act as some brand of consultant shrink. It secretly astounded him that actors really believed they could become another person. All he saw them doing was act as themselves in different situations.

Karin wrapped a napkin around her fingers.

'Well, OK. There are a few problems, you know, small things. I could do without the Sean Connery shtick from Albert. And David…I dunno about David. There's something about him, I dunno. But hey, ain't there always little problems on a set? And it's no biggee, it's fine.'

Tomas preferred his actors at the other end of a camera lens, where he had some control over what they were doing, where they couldn't impinge. Have to look in on rehearsals though. At some stage? Tomorrow? No option. Maybe Anna will housesit.

Karin said, 'So what did you do today?'

This seemed to be her favourite conversational gambit. Tomas wondered was it like this for her two husbands, both of them silently screaming, glancing slyly at their watches until they could get out to the bar or the racetrack.

'Oh, I went around a few places with Anna, my daughter.'

'Your *daughter*? Does she live in Dublin too?' She said the words as if he had never mentioned having one.

Yes I did.

'No, no. She lives in London. Just visiting for a few days.'

'Oh! How wonderful!'

The exclamation echoed through the empty restaurant, startling the man with the moustache. He glared at them disapprovingly.

'Yes, well. She wanted to see my new house and everything. You know.'

'And where is she tonight?'

'Visiting friends. She has friends here.'

'Pity she couldn't come along. I'd love to meet her. Maybe lunch?'

'Oh, I don't know. She'll only be here until…'

'Oh Gawd!' Karin slammed fingers to her forehead, then extended the palm of her hand towards Tomas, silencing him. The men in the white shirts made faces at each other.

'Sorry, sorry, sorry. I just, you know, don't *think* sometimes. Don't think at all. *Of course* it would be *so* insensitive to be making lunch dates now with your daughter. She probably doesn't even *know* about me yet. I mean, she probably knows who I am…you know what I mean!'

She waved at him and dissolved into giggles, as if Tomas had said something tremendously witty. He swallowed hard.

'And Karin. About *that*. I think…'

'I know, I know, I know.'

She jammed her eyes shut, as if trying to remember a speech learned by rote. 'It's far too soon to be putting pressure on anyone, especially after your divorce and your move and this film.' She laid a long-nailed hand on his. 'Sorry. I keep saying sorry! Friends. Just friends until we are both ready.' Slowly, she winked her bloodshot eye. 'Any kind of friends you want to be.'

'Are you ready to order?' The waiter was hunched and breathily reverential.

'Where's the ladies room?' said Karin, still staring at Tomas.

'Just…' The waiter pointed to the far end of the restaurant. Karin left the table, attempting a wiggle as she went, bones struggling inside Lycra. Yet the composition of the scene made Tomas feel he could light and shoot it, a couple of redheads, just to bring up the green tint he now saw in the dress. Move the camera too, so that the table of now-gawping businessmen moves in relation to her. Not pulling focus, no: *physically* move the table; put it on wheels so it moves around Karin as she walks to the toilet. Light the doorway with blondes, saturate it so that the stock over-exposes when she opens the door, dissolving her into light.

What would it be? More like a musical. A musical about middle-aged lovers? Who'd buy that?

'Do you want a few more minutes?' asked the waiter.

Tomas nodded yes.

The waiter gave a sympathetic smile.

Why is she putting on this catwalk for me when she must know that I'm not—

Karin glimpsed back, reprising her bloodshot wink. She moved out of sight.

Good God.

Tomas continued glaring at the toilet entrance, the back of his neck suddenly damp.

Surely she doesn't want?

Good God.

She in there now, waiting? The toilets? Has the woman no dignity, no sense of *hygiene*? Wouldn't have done such a thing years ago, don't mind now, and especially not with a woman who.

The *toilets*?

The men in the white shirts were sitting up straight now. Some of them peeked at Tomas, to see would he confirm that the woman in the ladies was who they thought she was. Tomas locked his eyes on the menu. Definitely can't go in there now. They're watching. Oh no, so fuddy-duddy, sounds like a made-up excuse.

It is a made-up excuse.

She'll come back humiliated, and furious. *Good God*, can't have sex in a grubby toilet just to spare her feelings, just to get a film made. Good God.

He threw the menu on the table and swooped up his brandy. He took a large slug, then stood.

If I'm making my way down there, just as she's coming out.

Actually *thinking* this?

Still standing, pretending to search his pockets, he noticed that she'd left her bag behind. Couldn't have followed you in – you left your bag by the table.

No, just as pathetic. Worse.

The bag didn't really fit with the way Karin was dressed tonight, a satchel of grazed brown leather, the flap left back to expose its contents. A curling script, jar of skin cream, lipstick, perfume, keys, wallet, pens, tissues, a half-eaten Crunchie. Yet mostly, the bag contained pill boxes of various shapes, mixed in together like wrestling children – brown and white and red, emblazoned with pharmacy stickers. A dozen or more, it looked like.

Tomas whipped out his glasses, glanced towards the toilet and peered in closer. The labels were crammed with long unpronouncables. Methotrexate. Cytarabine. Vincristine. Prednisone. L-asparaginase. Daunorubicin. Doxorubicin. Thioguanine. Cyclophosphamide. Amsacrine.

Cyclophosphamide? Know that. That was? Who was taking that?

An enthusiastic *Yeah!* made Tomas look up. Karin, a hand parked on one hip, stood close to the businessmen's table, smiling and nodding while one of them took her picture. She waved and moved off. Tomas quickly pocketed his glasses and sat.

'Canadians,' she whispered, flopping down in her chair. 'I love Canadians. They are so polite!' She parked a hand up beside her face, in case one of the polite Canadians could lip read. 'But *so* boring.'

She took a sizable sip from her bandy, shook her hair, then pointed at Tomas.

'You were standing up. Were you going someplace?'

'No, I was just looking for my mobile phone.'

He reached into his jacket pocket and placed the mobile on the table. Karin ignored this evidence.

'You weren't thinking of following me into the restroom, were you?'

'No, of course not.'

'You *were!*' She took another sip of her brandy while considering her response. 'Tomas, that's…kinda disgusting. I'm surprised. But good surprised.'

Tomas looked at his hands.

Cyclophosphamide.

'Stop teasing me.' His voice was so small it had almost retreated back within him. 'Please.'

Cyclophosphamide. Marta's father can never pronounce it properly. Calls it Cyclops-amide. The one-eyed drug.

Karin examined him, her eyebrows knit together.

'Ms Goldman?' The two Canadians apologised for the intrusion. And if you want us to go away that is perfectly fine. It's just that we both have teenage daughters and they would get a real kick if you signed a couple of autographs. They really loved that film you did, you know the one where you're the principal of the high school? Boy, you were evil in that! I mean, you were great!

Their drunkenness was childlike. Karin smiled her assent, then made a face at Tomas to indicate that they would continue with the subject at hand when she returned. She scrawled some signatures, then asked the waiter – back again in the hope of receiving their order – to take the snap. Karin grinned like the pro she was, half-turned from the lens, one arm up as if engaged in conversation, as if she was having the time of her life with these fellas – eating, drinking and talking until the small hours, new friends made. Who knew? Maybe, if she was in Ontario some time, Karin might actually call in on them, because that's the kind of person she was, you know. Ordinary, just like you and me. This is the story the picture would tell.

The men thanked Karin by telling her that they couldn't tell her how thankful they were. The waiter made an enquiring face at Tomas. Tomas shrugged, then waved him over.

'I can order wine at least.'

The waiter gave his thin smile.

'OK, er, we'll have…'

The mobile rang. The waiter smiled again. Karin sat down just as Tomas answered.

'Hello?'

'I think,' Karin said, 'I feel like steak tonight. Bloody steak.'

'Hello?'

There was rustling, some breaths, the sound of an engine; a siren. Tomas closed his eyes, for a moment feeling burned by his own stupidity. Not this; not now. He heard a female voice say *No*. But it couldn't be the boys. This was an English mobile, there was no way they could get the number. *A minute, a second*, he heard the female voice say.

'Hello?'

The waiter and Karin stopped talking. They stared at him, as did the two Canadians, yet to retreat to their table.

'Daddy.' Anna sounded out of breath, or as if she was whispering. She seemed to be in a car. Or a lorry. 'I'm going to…where am I going?'

Beaumont, a distant voice replied.

65

'Daddy, did you hear that?'

'Beaumont? Beaumont Hospital? Anna, what happened?'

'I know. Shouldn't talk. Makes it bleed. They stabbed me, Daddy.'

He could hear her panting.

'Come and get me. Please.'

She hung up. Blankly, Tomas looked at Karin.

'Would you like to order *now*?' said the waiter.

6

THE MAN sitting beside Tomas had grey teeth and carried an odour of turf. His head jerked as he watched the girls at the end of their row.

'Oh no,' muttered the grey-toothed man. 'Oh no. Terrible.'

Tomas nodded slightly, careful not to make eye contact. Stale breath burned Tomas's nose as the man leaned in.

'What age would you say they are? Hard to tell, isn't it? These days, what? They look twenty but I bet they're only fifteen. Terrible.'

One of the girls had large stains on her tiny white top. She spoke to her friend, slumped immobile on one of the yellow plastic chairs.

'Natalie? Natalie?' Natt-lee.

The girl in the white top hitched up her jeans, yet still her pale midriff and most of her red underwear remained visible.

'Fucking,' she muttered.

Tomas pulled in his body as she walked past, as did most others. Some – either due to unconsciousness or a disinclination to change position – left their legs outstretched, blocking the girl's path. These she stepped over, spreading a shiver of relief through the stuffed waiting room.

Tomas sat up straight and looked like a man minding his own business. The chairs were cruelly uncomfortable, forcing him and everyone else to regularly change position.

Probably deliberate, discourage the place being used as a hostel. Doesn't seem to work, though. Half of them asleep or drunk or drooling or bleeding or fighting invisible monsters. Baby nihilists on burger-bar chairs.

It reminded Tomas of *Apocalypse Now*, though he couldn't think which particular scene. He tried to keep his breathing shallow, to avoid the mingled odours of bodies, beer and bleach. He tried thinking about *Apocalypse Now*.

A shaven-headed triage nurse with a chipped-away face emerged from behind a locked door. He glanced at a clipboard and drawled, 'Er, Dalton?'

'Here.'

The nurse waved him through the door, then pointed. 'Third cubicle on the left. They've just finished stitching her up.'

'Thank you.'

The nurse ignored him.

Slowly, Tomas made his way to the cubicle, and considered his talent for, well, making people feel better. Call it what it is. He could radiate beams of calm and comfort. He could, in his awkward, quietish way, become enthusiastic over an appalling performance or credibly fail to notice a bad wig; he could convince the vilest people they were loved by all.

Not today, though.

Tomas inhaled more antiseptic.

Don't scream. Or say anything. Just shutup, shutup, shutup.

She didn't give him a chance, urgently beckoning him to sit on the bed so she could explain that it looked much worse than it was, the left side of her face red and giantly swollen, like it had been over-inflated to the point where the skin had begun to split. The split was sewn up tightly with evil black thread and smeared with a light brown substance. Anna pointed.

'Three stitches.' She spoke out of the side of her mouth, as if impersonating Groucho Marx. 'The rest is swelling. Be gone in a day or two. I was lucky.' She pushed herself up, grimacing. 'Do you know what they do? They actually bring in a mirror to show you, just so you don't freak out.'

Tomas nodded. He put a hand over his mouth.

'I think they'll be keeping me in overnight.'

Tomas nodded again. Anna, arms folded, regarded her father.

'Not going to say anything?'

He coughed and nodded some more. 'I'm sorry. It's just, this is.'

'Yeah, Daddy. *I* got knifed. Not you. If there's anyone here entitled to put on a little performance, it's me.'

Tomas stared at his hands. 'Of course.'

He gestured towards the stitches. 'So, what will that be like?'

'Small scar. About half an inch long. It'll be white, but quite thin, they think, 'cos it was a Stanley knife. It went all the way through, you know. I can't show you now, but I've got stitches on the inside of my mouth as well.'

'Oh, Jesus.'

'Little fuckers.' Anna's eyes became moist.

'You poor, poor,' Tomas said.

Anna attempted a shrug. 'It's only a scar. I'm still me. I have people who will love me no matter what I look like.'

She glimpsed towards the mobile phone on the bedside cabinet, as if she had been speaking to them already.

What people?

He put the hand back over his mouth, whispered through his fingers. 'And how?'

'How do you think? Going after those little bastards on your street. I spotted them, right? Across the road, watching the house. Obviously planning something. Must have thought it was empty. So I go out the front door after them but they leg it down that alleyway. I chase them, screaming at the top of my lungs that if I ever catch them around the house I'll slit their throats, all that.'

She stopped speaking and attempted a smile.

'It was getting dark, so I never really saw where they went. But next thing I know I've run all the way through and onto the next street, and there's no sign of them. So like a bloody fool, I walked back to the house up the dark alleyway.'

She stopped speaking again, swallowed, reached for the glass of water by her bed. She sipped through a straw.

'Anyway, they must have let me go past and waited. I was about halfway through – and it's *so* dark in there – when a lighter, a cigarette lighter comes on, right in front of my eyes. I'm stunned, I feel a pain in my face, then the sound of footsteps running away. Over in a second. I ran back to the house and didn't realise what they'd done until I was inside.' She gestured towards the stiff surgical gown she was wearing. 'Everything ruined. And do you know what?' It was as if the question wasn't addressed to Tomas. 'It was so dark, I didn't see them. I can't accuse anybody.' She extracted a tissue from beneath her pillow and gently blew her nose.

Other fathers would be hugging their daughters now.

'Anna, why did you go after these boys, when I expressly asked?'

'Don't you start.'

'I'm not starting anything. I'm just asking.'

'That's not a question. I got stabbed because you did nothing.'

They both fell silent. Nearby, a man was laughing.

'Anna, I said that I would handle it.'

'But you didn't, did you? You curled into a ball and hoped it would go away.'

'That's not true. I just. It is *my* house they have been attacking, Anna. My home. And I think you should have respected.'

'That's it, isn't it? That's all there is for you. Your house and all that crap you've hoarded.'

The smooth and bulbous sides of Anna's face were now brilliantly red. The stiff lips gilded her accent with a Cockney twang it didn't usually possess.

'Daddy, nobody forced you to do anything by yourself. You volunteered for that. You volunteered years ago.'

Daddy, Daddy, big hugs for my little girl.

'What happened between your mother and I.'

'Oh, shut up! Did you really think I believed it this morning when you *pretended* to ring the police and *pretended* to go out looking for those kids? I deal with liars every day of the week, Daddy, and you're fucking pathetic at it. It's about the only saving grace you have right now. You were going to do nothing, like you always do – just let things rot.'

'What does that mean?'

She jabbed a shaking finger towards her stitches. 'This, Daddy, this is what happens when you do nothing.'

'Excuse me.'

'If they did this to me, what are they going—'

'Excuse me!' The triage nurse leaned steeply against the end of Anna's bed, as if the very act of speaking exhausted him. 'There are other patients here,' he said to Tomas. 'Why don't you wait outside for a little while. Have a cup of tea.'

Monstrously unfair. Anna was shouting, not me. Don't shout, confrontation not my style; family trait. Father never shouted, never even raised his voice, a real gentleman.

Among the trundling printing presses in the bowels of the *Irish Independent*, all night long he has to yell while he works, so at home he prefers to speak softly. Can make himself heard, though – if Father fancies to make it so, his whisper is thunderous.

Tomas nodded his assent and retreated to the A&E waiting room, suddenly astounded by his thoughts, at how he could quarrel with his daughter when he meant to comfort her, at the distinct pleasure curling hotly within his stomach.

*

CONFRONTATION NOT Marta's bag either. Never shouted, not even once, in how many years? Could press her view, though. That taut little voice, that way of speaking without barely opening her mouth. But never any shouting; always cold war.

Would yelling and histrionics have been any better? She'd be incapable.

Not the way we did things – the bullet shells from 1916 or the chunk of Nelson's Pillar quietly replaced by a photo of her Great Uncle Egbert or some crumbling relation in the colonies.

And he would ask, of course, and she would look momentarily puzzled, her face somehow shrunken, and say, What? Those rusty bullets? That dirty old piece of stone? Was that *something*? Her voice dry and light. You should have marked it, dear. Put some sort of label on so I would know.

And very slowly he would explain to her that men died from those bullets, men who had changed the course of Irish history. He would tell her that the dirty stone was part of Nelson's Pillar, a monument blown up by the IRA in 1966, an act of pure political theatricality. He is fifteen, giddy that explosions can take place in dank Dublin. Mother, of course, thoroughly approves. Father expresses no opinion. Days later, when Mother is finished walking around the house, a Players between her teeth, muttering, So much for Nelson, ha! Father slips into Tomas's bedroom and hands him the floury piece of Portland stone, wrapped in dry sacking. That's from the statue, now, not the base. A bit of his leg, I think. The lads at work were falling over each other to get at it. Might be worth money in a few years, son. Keep it safe.

And after telling Marta this, she would tip her head slightly, allow her eyebrows to move upwards. I see. So would you like me to put it back? I put it in the closet, along with all those old newspapers. If the lump of mud is a keepsake, then perhaps you should get it mounted on something. Or attach a small plaque. So I'll know in future. I don't always know. Would you like me to get it?

And occasionally he would say yes. But usually No, it's fine.

Are you sure?

I'm sure. I should get it mounted.

Perhaps she had wanted Yes – opposition, some grit to the marriage.

Tomas pressed the buttons on his mobile phone, shivering in the night breeze. He took a few steps to avoid a parade of tiny clouds from a smoking teenager nearby. Marta in her Holland Park flat, already dressed for bed, a baggy nightgown with big buttons. Sitting at a small kitchen table, doing nothing else, just sitting, hands folded in her lap, a book on the table not yet

71

opened. Shot from above, in low light (she wouldn't be extravagant with electricity), the static picture revealing the details of the table, the sink, the countertop, all surgically clean.

The head jerks up as the phone rings, causing a strand of hair to fall out from behind her ear. This she scoops back in place before rising from her seat.

'Hello?'

She spoke in a vaguely quizzical tone, as if it was quite amusing for someone to be ringing at this hour.

'Marta, it's me.'

'Oh, hello, Tomas. How is she?' She sounded weary.

'You know already?'

'Yes. Of course. She rang me. I was hoping you would call. You know, you never gave me your number in Dublin.'

'I still have the same mobile number.'

'Well, I didn't know that, Tomas. You never told me that either. So I've been sitting here, helpless. Anna couldn't speak to me for very long because she was having stitches put in, but she sounded terribly upset. I don't even know how this happened. How can people do such things? It's just, unthinkable. It's horrific.'

Her voice was even, almost placid. Mammoth words delivered in a tiny voice.

'Yes, yes.'

'I mean. It's just. How could you. Oh, I don't know.'

She stopped speaking. Tomas didn't reply.

Marta sucked in breath. 'How is she?'

'She's bearing up very well, I must say. She was more calm than I was. They've given her three stitches in her left cheek.'

'My God. That's terrible.'

'And there will be a small scar.'

'The poor darling. Are they keeping her in?'

'I think so, yes.'

'And is she in a private room?'

'She's still in casualty.'

'Tomas, you must insist she gets a private room. She's been through enough already and she needs to rest.'

'I'll do that, yes.'

He heard her sigh, and was struck by their physical distance – he overlooking a darkened car park, she in a dim-lit flat, hundreds of miles away.

'I assume you're going to spend the night there. In the hospital.'

'Yes, of course.'

'It's just terrible.' She paused. 'Tell her to ring me in the morning if she's up to it. Perhaps I should come over?'

'No, there's no need. She's fine now.'

Another pause.

'I would like to know the circumstances, how this happened. Is crime particularly bad in Dublin?'

'I don't know. Same as everywhere else, I suppose.'

She made a noise; this was an unsatisfactory answer.

'All right then. Well, good night, Tomas. Oh, I'm sorry, how rude of me. How are you?'

'I'm fine, thanks.'

*

THEY HAD moved her to a private room when he got back, relieving Tomas of the need to insist upon anything. He was directed up flights of stairs, past murky corridors thick with snores and beeping sounds, past plastic sheets covering construction work and into a brilliantly lit foyer where the nurses were neat and vivid, like newly made beds.

One smiled and pointed, directing Tomas into Anna's room, all smooth woods and creamy, loveless walls. Anna lay on her back, eyes closed, mouth slightly open, a sleep of relish, of the Glad to Be Alive.

Tomas told the nurses that he would be back early in the morning, his house being but ten minutes away. He jogged down the stairs and over to the Saab.

No point staying. Ghastly place. Can't. No need.

On the short drive home, he was surprised to see so many people on the streets, queuing, kissing, shouting. Not even midnight. Entering Bass Avenue – despite what had happened to Anna – Tomas felt a gush of relief as he saw that even here there was human activity: the man with the swept-over hair standing in the doorway of his wagon-wheel house, the hot light from his hall lamp glowing around him. The man considered Tomas's car, then became involved in a guttural coughing fit.

Forgetting to check the gate, the doorbell, the front door or the yard, Tomas let himself in, shot bolts behind, made a cup of tea and traipsed upstairs. He got into his pyjamas, then knelt beside a dollhouse parked at the end of his bed.

It was in a book. What was it called? No matter. What I always knew anyway. Memories are earned, not bestowed. They require care. For an impression to be successfully stored in long-term memory, the nerve pathways have to be strengthened and reinforced by regular visits, or by stimulation from sensations or objects. Consolidation, the book called it, a process whereby past events become engrained into a specific set of synapses; where memory takes on a physical shape.

Tomas eased back the hinged roof. The house had suffered severe structural damage on both gable walls – holes bashed through, extensive scrawling in various colours – yet inside its condition was close to pristine. Tomas had rescued it just before Anna's hostility towards the toy completely erupted. Inside, the tiny double bed was neatly made, the table in the kitchen all set for dinner. Mummy did some hoovering. Daddy sat in the lounge, smoking a pipe, a small dog curled at his feet. Baby slept in her cot.

Yet even with care, all the brain can really retain are ghost-images. Memories of memories, deepened through revisiting, yet possibly distorted a little each time. Shadows in the cave.

Who said that?

She had adored the dollhouse. How old? Four or five. Father Christmas brought it. The favourite toy for eighteen months, until something crashed over in her mind, making her hate it. And after so many intimate, chattering hours.

Plato, Plato – that's who. Shadows in the cave. Didn't like writing. Said it would destroy people's memory. Make them appear to know everything but actually know nothing.

Why become a lesbian?

Never spoke to Tomas about it, not once – simply started talking a certain way, dressing a certain way, saying *girlfriend* and making it sound sexual, and eventually, when he'd been screwing up his courage for God knows how long to mention this suspicion to his wife, all Marta had to say was, Well of course she's a lesbian.

Didn't you know?

No, he didn't. And it made him sad for the big-eyed little girl who had played in careful wonder with her dollhouse.

Anna wanted to kill that little girl. Only Tomas remained to keep her safe.

*

'**YOU KNOW** Jack Forde?' Karin said.

'Yes. Obviously.'

'You know why he doesn't say much?'

'Because he's a writer. They are like that.'

'No, silly! It's because his name isn't Forde at all. It's Russell. Do you see? Russell. *Jack Russell.*'

She looked back at him and grinned filthily. Tomas shook his head in mock disapproval.

'That outfit is, well, common. You utter, utter slut.'

'You picked it,' she said.

'I know. But you've such a bony ass.'

She gave a dirty laugh, cupping a hand over her mouth.

'A sick, bony ass.'

'Ha! You're the sick one!' She fingered the lacy material covering her thigh. 'Do you think I wear things like this all the time?'

'I hope so.'

She grinned. 'Sweet.' She stood up, turned to face him. 'Anyway. You like?'

'I heartily approve.'

She came forward, kneeling on the bed now. 'And these?'

She poked a curled fingernail – scarlet red – into the clump of sheets wrapped around each of his feet. 'Can you move? Can you move at all?'

'Oh no,' said Tomas, mock-alarmed. 'I can't move. I'm trapped. Help. Help.'

Crawling forward now, Karin purred. 'Don't worry, baby. I think I can help you out.'

Tomas yelled and sat up, damp pyjamas stuck to his back and arms. He switched on his bedside lamp. The bedroom was exactly as it was when he'd fallen asleep, the roof of the dollhouse still open, a half-drunk cup of tea on the floor beside it.

'Good God,' he said.

*

'**SEARGENT GRÉAGÓIR** O'Duinnshleibhe,' announced Sergeant Gréagóir O'Duinnshleibhe in a voice which dared Tomas to mispronounce the name.

'Hello.' Tomas spoke to his reflection in the sergeant's bat-like sunglasses.

Still, a speedy response.

After waking up early, Tomas had gone to Beaumont Hospital with Anna's bag, found she was still asleep, returned to Bass Avenue, then rung Clara and told her to take notes for him at the rehearsals.

Should have sat in today. Only a day left before shooting. Out of the question though; not after.

Finally, he rang one of the numbers he had been given by Norbert Clarke. The man who answered said that Norbert was on a course today, but they'd send someone else around. Was there a report made at the hospital? Tomas didn't know.

This conversation took place barely twenty-five minutes before Sergeant O'Duinnshleibhe turned up at Tomas's front door.

Tomas gestured at the sergeant to come in, an invitation which the policeman did not immediately take up. Instead he quickly glanced around, as if concerned about being followed.

Tomas also looked out. Nothing to see but an old woman tottering along the pavement. Not the woman with the arthritic scowl who lived opposite – this one was coming from a house further up the street and was, if anything, even older. She was stylishly dressed in a black and white check suit, the skirt ending just below the knee. Her thinning hair was carefully piled into a bun which glowed purple against skin so white the bones beneath could be seen moving, like animals in a bag.

With each step, the woman's body shook, the impact visibly travelling from foot up to head, her internal shock absorbers shattered. She mouthed words to herself, head weaving from side to side.

Sergeant O'Duinnshleibhe sighed. He removed his sunglasses, carefully inserted them into the inside pocket of his pristine suede jacket and indicated that he now wished to enter. He studied the house as he followed Tomas to the kitchen, taking particular note of the window in the lounge waiting to be repaired. He sat at the kitchen table without being asked, then produced a small silver pen and a brand-new black notebook.

'Tea?'

'Thank you, no. A glass of water, if it's no trouble.'

Sergeant O'Duinnshleibhe carefully opened his notebook. The first page was already filled with lines of neat handwriting. He began reading, his thick lips gently stirring as he did so. He was in his forties, solidly built, but with skin so red it may have been recently sandpapered. What little hair remained on his head had been cruelly shaved off. The bottom half of his face seemed fixed in an expression of mild revulsion.

'We already had a report. A colleague spoke to your daughter last night.'

The words were shouted, as if the sergeant was slightly deaf.

'Oh,' Tomas said. 'She never mentioned.'

The sergeant wrote in his book. 'Now, can I confirm your name?'

'Tomas Dalton.'

'T–H?'

'No, T–O.'

'D–A–L–T–O–N?'

'Correct.'

'Your relationship to the victim, Anna Dalton?'

Tomas paused. 'She's my daughter. You know that.'

Sergeant O'Duinnshleibhe looked up as Tomas sat at the table and presented the policeman with his water.

'I needed you to confirm it. For the records.'

He picked up the glass and took a long drink. Tomas said nothing. The kitchen filled up with the sound of water sloshing around the sergeant's throat, then trickling deep into his guts. He stopped drinking, loudly exclaimed *Aah*, then consumed the rest of the water. He placed the glass on the table and picked up his pen.

'Have you lived here long?'

'Just a couple of weeks.'

Sergeant O'Duinnshleibhe's look of distaste intensified, as if he didn't much approve of people living in houses for such short periods.

'I see. And where did you reside previously?'

'England. London. Hampstead.'

'Hampstead,' repeated the sergeant, as if didn't much approve of Hampstead either. 'And where is your wife this morning?'

Tomas blinked.

'She's in London. That's where she lives. We're divorced, you see.'

Sergeant O'Duinnshleibhe said nothing. 'So you think you may know who attacked your daughter?'

'Oh, I definitely know. They are boys, just little boys. About ten or eleven. A set of twins with red hair and a taller one with buck teeth.'

The garda curled up one side of his mouth and nodded his head repeatedly. 'Ah yeah, the twins – they're Mulvihills. The taller one, he's one of the Doyles. They live next door to each other, sure. On Beatha Road. All the same family anyway. They're cousins. The mammys are sisters. Not a bad lot, mind. Not the Mulvihills, anyway. Young Doyle has his troubles all right. Single parent family, you know? There's a father around the place, but they don't see much of him. What's his name? The young fella has the mother's name. That's Doyle, obviously. But the father now, the father…' He made a loud *tsk*. 'It's gone! Straight out of me head.'

Mulvihill and Doyle. Mulvihill and Doyle. Mulvihill and Doyle.

The garda stared at his notebook. 'So you think these boys assaulted your daughter?'

'I know they did.'

Tomas related the whole story to Sergeant O'Duinnshleibhe, from the day he moved in to the attack on Anna. He made sure to mention twice that the boys had gloated through the front window after throwing the rocks. Sergeant O'Duinnshleibhe hmmed, nodded and wrote. This process took the best part of an hour, mainly because the sergeant kept asking Tomas to repeat key facts, or would beckon him to hush altogether while he finished writing a sentence.

Finally, he placed the pen on the table, parallel to the notebook. His hands were large and somewhat meaty, but there was a feminine grace to the way he treated his writing materials.

'All right, Mister Dalton. I'll get this typed up so you can sign it.'

Tomas shifted in his seat. 'So what happens now?'

'We'll proceed with our enquiries. There may be some people we will want to interview in due course. And we'll let you know.'

'But you are going to go after these boys? I mean, I know they're kids, but they're dangerous. You should see my daughter.'

Sergeant O'Duinnshleibhe put away his notebook and pen. 'I understand your concern, Mister Dalton, and you have my sympathy. But we have to carry out our investigations in a certain way, in accordance with the rule of law. Anything else, I can't say. We'll make our enquiries, and hopefully a pros-ecution will result.'

'Well, you have myself and Anna as witnesses. I could contact the removal men for you if you like.'

Sergeant O'Duinnshleibhe stood up. 'You can rest assured, Mister Dalton, that a full investigation will now proceed, and hopefully a satisfactory result will come out of it.'

Tomas felt a hotness around his neck and chest. His right leg jigged. 'Sergeant, could someone be putting them up to it?'

The sergeant rubbed the back of his domed head, apparently amused by this idea, by the adorable naïvety of civilians.

'Oh, I wouldn't be suggesting that, Mister Dalton. The same buckos are perfectly capable. Yes, yes, perfectly capable.'

'Really? You're sure?'

The sergeant sat again. He gestured with his hand to indicate that this new perch was delicate and temporary.

'The Mulvihills and the Doyles are not the worst. But it's not always about the families, do you see? You can't control who these young fellas are knocking about with outside, on the street, what example they are taking. They are still young, but a lot of them, Mister Dalton, a lot of them are ruined by the time they are thirteen. And I take no pleasure in saying that. But you can see the pattern, and it's all around here – there's one parent or both on drink or drugs. There might be violence in the home, and then the child is out on the streets meeting other young gangsters and then they get into drinking and smoking hash and all the other stuff. And by then they don't care. Not scared of the guards. We arrest them and they attack us. Pull knives sometimes. These are fourteen-year-olds I'm telling you about now. Children. They have fifty, sixty convictions before they are put inside, not that it does them any good. Lot of the time it makes them worse. A lot of them have behavioural problems and the like, but the Health Board is overstretched and can do nothing. And I've seen it all happen. Nice young fella at ten or eleven. Bit of mischief maybe. But two years later and they are career criminals. Again and again I've seen that. Nothing for them at home, God save us, no help from the government. No one cares, so why should they?' The sergeant held up his hands, like a priest at the consecration. 'They have nothing, so they've nothing to lose.'

He stopped talking, then dropped the hands into his lap. Quickly, he stood up again, straightened his jacket. His body stiffened beneath his clothes. Neither man looked at the other.

'Well, yes,' Tomas said. 'I see. It's terrible. Nonetheless, I hope you'll be able to keep an eye on them. Stop anything else happening.'

Sergeant O'Duinnshleibhe put his arms behind his back. 'If there are any more incidents, please do not hesitate to contact us at the station, or dial 999.'

'But you are going to watch them? I mean, I know they are deprived and they have problems, but I have rights too. My daughter, lying in hospital with a swollen face, she has rights.'

'We will be launching an extensive investigation. It is a serious crime, Mister Dalton, what has happened both to you and your daughter. And we will be taking it very seriously. *Slán!*'

He rotated on his heel and marched out of the house.

Tomas remained by the table, aware of his burning shoulders. He decided it might be best to sit there for a while longer, to let the small domestic noises retake the house, to let Sergeant O'Duinnshleibhe get around the corner.

Eventually, he stood. On his face he wore a rather a pained expression, as if it required tremendous effort to carry out the basic tasks of existence – breathing, locomotion, speech. He located his phone in the darkened front room, then rang a glazier and a home alarm company, both of which said they would call out the following day. He rang Clara to ask how rehearsals were going, and she said fine fine fine. There was a bit of skirmish about the script. Albert wanted to change some of his lines – add in more lines, actually – but Jack wasn't keen. Albert boomed for a while, Jack went crimson. You know, the usual. But I calmed them down. It's fine now.

How's your daughter?

I'll type up the notes and bike them over to you.

Bless her. Tomas hung up, then considered ringing Albert.

Nah, fuck it.

Tomas threw on a cardigan – a threadbare old thing he liked to wear if he was story-boarding – and walked out of the house. Without looking left or right, without bothering to greet the Nigerian woman from next door, out pounding her dusty doormat, Tomas headed for the alleyway leading to Beatha Road.

They were laughably easy to find. Sat on their hunkers like Bedouin tribes-men, lined up against the stained concrete wall which edged the tiny spread of wasted ground in the middle of the alley. One of the twins sucked viciously on a cigarette while the others waited their turn, arms stretched over their knees, filthy fingernails exposed to the world.

This hour of the morning. Smoking already.

The twin with the cigarette attempted to blow smoke rings while his com-rades ridiculed these efforts, the other twin gabbling nonsense words, the tall one – Doyle – muttering 'S'crap' through a lolling fringe. They traded grins and playful shoves and didn't notice Tomas until it was far, far too late.

They didn't attempt to stand. They couldn't – he was bent over them, arms only inches from their heads. Standing would only invite it. Their mouths re-mained slightly open, their eyes spread back. The cigarette lay burning on the dry mud beneath.

Tomas glared at the first twin. 'Do you want me to put *you* in hospital?'

The twin didn't move.

'Do you?' Tomas roared, the sound blasting the boy's freckled face.

He nodded no.

He asked the tall one, then the other twin. Each gave the same reply.

He screamed at the tall one, tiny balls of spittle crashing into the boys' mucky skin. 'Then what did you attack my daughter for? Why did you throw rocks through my window? Huh? Why? Did someone tell you to do it?'

The tall one didn't move, his face, beneath the dirt, an almost perfect white. Tomas rounded on the other twin.

'Can *you* tell me? Why is everyone so keen to think that you poor disadvantaged waifs dreamed up this whole scheme by yourselves? Huh? Why is that?'

This boy shrank back, causing Tomas to bend down, almost lunge. All three of them reacted then, making tiny squeaks of fear, bringing up arms and legs against the expected tumble of blows. But Tomas stopped short. He stood up straight.

Oh yes, now the little shits are paying attention; this is what happens if I make you the subject of *my* enquiry. Overdue, this – deserved, long deserved. Oh, I'm so rude. How are you? Fuck you, you dried up old bat. That's how I am.

He took three steps back towards a patch of loose gravel, probably left there by indolent builders.

'It doesn't matter. It doesn't matter if it was you three or someone who thought this up. Put your arms down.'

They stared, puzzled.

'Put your arms down!'

Good, the shouting *drips* with violence – Eli can shout, but this is better, this would give *him* a fright.

Tomas pointed.

'My daughter is scarred for life. You ruined a priceless rug. Someone died for that rug, did you know that? Someone died.' He dropped his voice, chewing through the words. 'So if you *ever* come near me, my house or my family again.'

He kicked the gravel. A cloud of tiny stones showered the boys, squeezing grit into their eyes, stabbing redly at their skin. They squealed under the attack, bony arms and legs flailing.

'Put your arms down.'

They attempted to ignore this instruction, attempted to pretend that it hadn't been issued.

'Put your arms down.'

He didn't even have to shout, they were so cowed – they obeyed, slowly, tear-stained and scratched, shaking with the effort, managing only to bring the arms down to a point where they extended awkwardly from their skinny chests.

Oh, *yes*.

'All the way down.'

The first two complied. The third gave in to an eruption of sobs, one so overwhelming that he tumbled over, all control lost. Snot and tears glued to his magenta face, he attempted to sit back up, but each time failed, his gropes for breath growing so short that it sounded like he was laughing, or perhaps attempting to sing. His twin brother and the tall one watched this, frozen, wishing they could look somewhere else.

'I will *kill* you,' Tomas said, kicking another shower of gravel over the prone boys. 'Not whoever put you up to it. Kill *you*.'

Tomas remained still for a moment, watching them. Then he strolled back to his house.

Energy pumping. Decades since. Can take on the world, oh yes. Yesyesyes. Oh *yes*.

7

SO MUCH colour today. Like, what? After a day-time screening, in one of those grotty little places in the West End. World breaks open like a wave, super-real – sounds with tinkling clarity, colours crushed, like a 1950s pic. A period film? Would you? Could you? There's time.

An abundance of time, vast, temporal mountain ranges. Tomas steered the Saab through them and towards Beaumont Hospital, wind gusting through his open window, reflected sunlight scattering like cluster bombs between the buildings.

A scientist once – a biochemist? Where? At a dinner party? No, something like a christening. Once there is no light, there is no colour. Not that the colour isn't apparent; at night it actually disappears, that's what he said – when I was a child, my father would growl that there was nothing to be scared of, that night was exactly the same as day. But it isn't true. Night *is* different. Parents betray you, you know.

Odd feeling, this, though pleasant. Must be tiredness. After last night.

Just a dream, random electrical impulses shooting about the synapses. Doesn't mean anything.

Tomas strode across the car park of Beaumont Hospital and wondered if he appeared different. The people he would meet today wouldn't be able to provide an opinion, not having seen enough of him previously to make a comparison. Even Anna, God love her, wouldn't know.

Anna. My God. First visit, and what happens? My God.

He halted and blinked rapidly.

She won't come back. Of course not – might hate you.

No, no, how could she blame? It was them, them, their evil.

A new rule – visit London every three months. No harm in that. Maybe have dinner with Marta, keep everything civilised.

Tomas entered the vaulted foyer of Beaumont Hospital and for some seconds studied the sign high up on the wall which informed him as to the whereabouts of Anna's ward. Colder in here. And darker. People move at a slower rate, more carefully, knowing from experience what can happen. The strict hospital smells made him think of Karin's bag from, when? Only last night?

Cyclophosphamide. Marta's father had been thin too. You might never have known how ill he was until.

Tomas shivered.

Nothing but problems.

Problems that can be solved – are being solved, yes. He perched a smile on his face and kept it there as he sailed through the reception to Anna's ward. They remembered his name from last night. Impressive.

She stood on the far side of the bed, dressed in frayed jeans and a tight yellow T-shirt which featured a picture of a glittering strawberry. Some of the swelling had already gone down, though the redness remained. Anna's face and the T-shirt strawberry resembled each other. Poor choice. Probably has nothing else.

She appeared to be grimacing as he entered, as if he had caught her solving some difficult puzzle. She flicked her eyes towards him, nodded, then looked back at her half-packed bag. She seemed tiny behind the mechanical-looking hospital bed. Not old enough yet to be doing such things.

Tomas waved, then felt stupid for doing so.

'How are you?'

'Fine.'

'Swelling's gone down.'

She put up a hand, but stopped just short of touching. Grimaced again. 'Yes, I think so. A little bit.'

'Does it hurt?'

She shrugged, as if not sure.

Tomas slapped his hands together and walked around the room. He uttered approving sounds as he inspected the bathroom, the television, the phone, the view from the window. His good feeling was completely dispelled now, though he still hoped for its return.

Anna obviously being monosyllabic. Understandable.

He watched her pack and was reminded of something; he couldn't think what.

'Beaumont, Beaumont,' he muttered. 'Fletcher and Beaumont. Playwrights. A few years after Shakespeare. Big in their day.'

Anna said nothing.

'And there's a Beaumont Hospital in the States, you know. Quite a few of them. Michigan, I think it is. It's a chain, like McDonald's.'

'Thanks for sending in my bag.'

'Oh, I brought it in. Early this morning. You were still dead to the world. So I just left the bag and did a few errands.'

'Thanks.'

The day she moved out – that's it. He had watched her filling her bags, and was flabbergasted.

'I see you're packing.'

Not long after she'd finished the degree. No job, at least not a proper one. She had something in a bar, and she was going to share a place in Camden Town with a girl called Shirley or Sonya and Tomas wasn't sure what that meant, what with being a lesbian now. He didn't want to ask. Couldn't. It's *my* life – the phrase had repelled all his attempts at prying. Yet he always wanted to point out that it wasn't her life. Couldn't be. As soon as you bump into someone on the street or stop in the car for some unleaded or lift up the phone or sign a prenuptial agreement, there's always an effect, something you can't control. Your life is chipped away, sold off piecemeal to others. At best, you have a part-share. That's the problem.

'Are they going to discharge you?'

She zipped the bag shut and sat on the bed, arms folded. 'Doctor will be here in about fifteen minutes, they said.'

She stood up again, unzipped the bag and dug around until she found a box of Silk Cut Blue. She lit a cigarette, carefully blowing the smoke out the open window. 'Thanks for packing my fags.'

Tomas smiled, but not too much.

'I spoke to Mummy last night. She said give her a call, if you're up to it.'

'Did already.'

The burr of hospital life. Distant announcements, the squeak of trolleys, the swish of stiff uniforms.

Sweating. Don't stay long.

'Well, I had a busy morning. Had a garda down. I heard you made a statement last night?'

Anna shrugged.

'I told him all about it,' Tomas continued, 'but I don't know if he was all that interested. Spouted press releases. "We'll be pursuing our enquiries", that kind of thing, then ranted on about their deprived backgrounds, as if, in some twisted way, this was all my fault. I mean, I'm sympathetic. I am. But for God's sake. Very frustrating, I must say. It just felt as if nothing was going to happen. Bizarre.'

Anna hmmed and took a last drag on her cigarette.

'So after he left I said to myself, Right, that's it. I went out there and then, and it took me five minutes to find them, the boys. In that alley. Smoking, if you don't mind. And by God, I gave it to them. Haven't shouted so much in years. Didn't touch them, didn't lay a finger. But I let them know what had happened. They were plenty scared by the time I was finished. You were right, you know. I should have confronted them sooner.'

'That's great,' she said, then gazed at the floor. 'Look, Daddy, I know I was supposed to stay another night, but I've changed my ticket. My flight is in a couple of hours, so as soon as the doctor's seen me, I'm going straight to the airport. I know you're very busy with your film, so you don't have to stay.'

Tomas nodded several times. 'Well. I understand, of course. I probably wouldn't be keen to stay here either if the same thing, well, you know. No, it's fine, of course. Understand totally. I'll drive you.'

'No, Daddy. They can get me a taxi here. You're too busy.'

'That's silly. I'll drive you.'

'There's really no need. I'm fine.'

'Please. I want to. Please.'

She said nothing else, her silence taken as acquiescence.

For the rest of the time, they said little, a situation which had a surprising ease to it. Tomas stepped out of the room when the doctor came. He went down to the ground floor and bought chocolates for the nurses. They drove to the airport, making occasional comments about the traffic, the building work, what they would both be doing over the next few days. There was a tiredness to their exchanges which wasn't without generosity.

Tomas insisted on parking in short term and walking her to departures, which again reminded him of the day she had moved out of the flat in Hampstead, of the sense of unspecified regret it had summoned. They found the departure gate, she bought some magazines in Hughes & Hughes bookshop, hugged him lightly — careful to keep her swollen face from pressing against his — and then off Anna went, like she had before, tiny among the frantic crowds. Tomas watched her go for as long as he could stand it.

*

'MAAATE.'

Eli breathed the word in the voice he employed to indicate sympathy. 'How are you?'

Tomas had pulled over onto the hard shoulder. He found himself speaking in a slow, almost slurred manner which he barely recognised as his own. 'Not great, I must say.'

'And how's your little girl?'

'Not great either.'

'Yeah, yeah.'

The traffic out of the airport was a seething crawl. Anna would be in Heathrow by the time he got home. Stares on the Tube. Look at her face.

'And what happened, was she mugged or something?'

Tomas coughed, breathed through his nose.

'Yes. Or they tried to mug her. But Anna is very confrontational. So when these, these thugs demanded her purse, she didn't do what any sensible person would and hand it over. She put up a fight. So they slashed her with a Stanley knife.'

'Fuck, man. Fuck.'

'Yes. Fuck. Fuck. Fuck.' The word tasted strange in his mouth, like speaking a foreign language.

'She in hospital?'

'No, no, she's out. She's with me. In my house. Rattled, of course. Funny; no matter how grown up they get, they still want their daddy when things go wrong.'

'Yeah, mate. Of course.'

'She was lucky, really. I mean, she looks horrendous – her face is swollen up – but she only had to get three stitches. So at least the scar will be fairly small.'

'Well, that's a relief. It's a few years since I saw Anna, but she was a pretty girl.'

Tomas couldn't remember Eli ever having seen Anna, couldn't think of a situation where the two of them could have met.

'So we won't be seeing you today?'

'Well, no. Obviously not, after this. I can't leave her.'

'Well, no, mate, no. Course. I was just ringing to see how you are, and don't worry about the rehearsals, all that is fine. Karin told everyone about Anna. And that you were having dinner together. She mentioned that a few times.'

'Well, what the actors think about Karin and I isn't much of a concern at the moment.'

'No, no. Course not.'

'I'll ring them all later.'

'Sure, great.' Eli was being unusually solicitous. Tomas had a vision of monkeys cowering. 'Anyway, Clara's going to send you out some notes, so you could look at them tonight maybe and be ready for the morning. Running out of time now, mate. Fucking stress, what? You holding up?'

'I'm fine. Nothing a few glasses of wine won't fix.'

'Yeah, mate. Look, when is Anna flying back? Tomorrow?'

'Ah. Not sure. Maybe. If she's up to it.'

''Cos obviously you'll be pretty busy tomorrow, your last day with the actors. So I could drive her out if you like.'

Tomas looked at the thunderous traffic edging past. He drew back his lips, baring teeth.

'That's very kind of you, Eli. But I'd rather do it.'

'Tomorrow is the last day before filming, mate. You know.'

'We'll cross that bridge when we come to it. I'd rather leave my daughter to the airport. She would prefer that I left her to the airport.'

Both left a pause long enough to examine the tone and rhythm of each other's breathing.

'Yeah, well,' said Eli. 'We'll cope, I suppose. Look, go home, have a few drinks and take it easy. Say hello to Anna for all of us, and we'll see you in the morning. Cheers.'

He hung up.

Tomas kept the phone pressed to his ear for some seconds after this, as if he didn't want the passing cars to think he was insane and sitting there for no reason. He even kept the phone to his ear as he opened the window to the passenger seat, and then, with a pleasing athleticism, flung it out the window. The phone smashed into the guard rail, battery, SIM card and circuitry spilling out like the guts of some electronic animal. He screamed.

'Fuck you! Fuck you! Fuck you!'

*

HE DIDN'T go home. Instead, he drove into town, parked the car on Stephen's Green and wandered onto Baggot Street.

What are you doing here?

Tomas stood outside the Allied Irish Bank, hands shoved in the pockets of his baggy corduroy trousers, and watched the productive bi-peds scuttling along. Traffic slowed and sped up again, causing small bursts of tepid wind to break against his legs. This was late April, Easter already finished, Jesus resurrected without anyone noticing. Not too warm, but already the optimistic Irish were wearing short sleeves and skirts. Tomas chewed his bottom lip, uncertain of what to do next. He looked around, as if some plan might suggest itself.

Used to go for maths grinds somewhere along here. For the matriculation. Mr McMahon. Smelled of onions and whiskey.

Where exactly? Hard to tell. So much of the ancient granite plastered over with chrome and primary colours. Details flattened out. Now the street seemed only superficially familiar, as if was a reproduction.

And everyone so *young*, whizzing up and down with their neat black bags, waving at each other with the zeal of an occupying army, here to wipe away the dumb oppression of history, neatly stepping around the old crazies slumped on the pavement like toppled stacks of rubbish.

He began to walk. Looks a bit strange to stand. Merrion Square up ahead. Years since, years.

Inside the park, the shriek of the city fell away. Tomas stopped at a bench close to the bust of Nelson Mandela. At the unveiling, years before. With Marta. Doing what? Seamus Heaney read poetry. There were photos, somewhere. Tomas tried to recall how he had felt that day, but couldn't.

'Fuck.'

He sat on the damp bench and for a few minutes watched bushes rattle gently in the wind. Nice little park. Neat. Unvandalised.

No anger here, no seething.

What was that story about Merrion Square? About W.B. Yeats?

Perhaps Anna's right – should move back to London.

Yeats and George Russell. Both lived on Merrion Square but never met because they were both too preoccupied. Russell spent most of his time glaring at the pavement while Yeats would be gawping at the sky.

Don't feel lonely or out of place here. Just those boys. They'll retaliate. Maybe it is class, money, haves and have-nots. Bring five-grand sofas into the house while the neighbours struggle to buy curtains. Stupid homecoming fantasy. Could have gone to Blackrock or Dalkey or Howth, someplace by the sea.

Tomas began walking back to his car. Teenagers on skateboards zipped past. A young couple by the railings coiled around each other. He and Marta had rarely done that, even at the start, touching in public never part of their repertoire.

Can't go back to London.

He picked up the pace of his walk, marching onto the noisy clatter of Stephen's Green. Sell the house, move to a different part of Dublin – get a hotel room for the time being – after the shoot look for a place to rent, don't be so hasty this time. Simple.

Almost immediately Tomas felt his mood lighten, enjoyed a melt of relief in his stomach. As he drove home, he even found himself singing. 'The Boys of Mullabawn'. Something Mother does occasionally, late at night. Eyes closed, legs spread under her long skirt. Nip of whiskey clutched in one of her big paws. Hasn't much of a voice really, but she has conviction.

Upon the Monday morning early,
As me wandering starts to take me,
Down by a farmer's station,
His meadows and green lawn.
I heard great lamentations,
The wee birds they were making.
Said we'll have no more engagements
With the boys of Mullabawn.
My pardon to you ladies…

He couldn't remember any more, but safely sealed inside his sound-proof car, Tomas Dalton sang on, humming any words he didn't know, half-grinning with embarrassment, yet not wishing to leave this song incomplete.

From the words he could recall, 'The Boys of Mullabawn' seemed to be about a group of girls missing their boyfriends, a subject so trivial his mother would normally have treated it with yelps of scorn. Perhaps they all perished after some skirmish with the English. Usually the way. Back then it was the recent past. Now it seems as if the past never happened at all.

They were waiting for him outside the house, and making it quite plain to anyone who chose to look that this was exactly what they were doing, lined up at the gate, the three sets of eyes cast expectantly in his direction. And when Tomas saw them he didn't stop smiling or become alarmed, because it reminded him of the day he had moved into Bass Avenue, and how much he had welcomed the sight of these children. There was something about them, too, the way they leaned against the railings, so tiny in their floppy clothes, having their big serious talks about really important things. Anyway, he was too tired to become agitated again. Acted like a madman. Understandable. Yet still. Shouting and lying. A lot of lies lately. Like a teenager. Too much upset. Far too much.

The History of Things

He considered where he might get a hotel room. Not the Shelbourne. Wouldn't want Karin knocking on the door in the middle of the night; maybe something a bit further out of town, even a nice guesthouse, bit more homely.

They didn't move as he got out of the car. They stared, each wearing a fixed, U-shaped smile.

Go with it, see what happens.

Across the street, the man in the wagon-wheels house was out again on the pavement. He was, from the look of things, in the middle of washing his car, but had paused to chat to the old woman who lived directly across from Tomas, again strapped into her plastic coat and hat. Both scowled as they spoke, as if sharing an intense mutual disgust.

Tomas tried to keep his face neutral. Immediately, the twins set up a staccato gabble, some of it apparently addressed to him, more of it to each other. Tomas closed one eye and tried to follow, but could only make out the odd word, or what sounded like words. Home. Crutch. Poodle. Snag.

The tall boy smiled now, glancing back and forth between each twin, but gradually shifting more of his gaze towards Tomas. He nudged the twin on his left side.

'Shurrup!'

This process was repeated with the other boy. They slapped hands to mouths and made small *eek* sounds.

The tall boy – Doyle, wasn't that his name? – took a step towards Tomas, hands hooked into his jeans pockets. He nodded backwards.

'They go on like that for hours. Bleeding pain in the hole.'

Tomas shifted on his legs, not sure how to respond. This seemed like *conversation*. The boy gestured towards the Saab.

'You've a nice motor.'

'Thank you.'

'Did ya get it with your job?'

'Er, no.'

Tomas found himself staunching a smile. The boy contemplated the car. 'You bought it,' he said with a certain wonder. 'Are you, like, a manager or something?'

'Sort of. I suppose.'

It seemed dangerous to be talking to them in this way, yet irresistible also, like meeting a long-admired celebrity and discovering that they are as nice and interesting and beautiful as you'd hoped.

'The twins there,' Tomas asked. 'You understand them?'

'Course not. But, like, you get used to it. They go on that way all the time so you don't pass any remarks about it. Used to piss me off but if I get thick they only start laughing. Do ya know what I mean?' He shrugged – a little boy with a little boy problem.

Tomas shivered. 'So do they ever speak normally? Can they understand you?'

'Oh, yeah. When they're at school and that they talk proper all the time – though when they were nippers their old dear – my Auntie Sharon – had to bring them to the doctor to learn them how to speak. She says when they were babbies they spent too much time alone together, so they made up their own way of talking, like.'

'Really?'

No, no, no, no, this can't be right.

Tomas glanced at the outside of his house. Seems OK.

'But if they get, like, excited or anything they go off into their own talking and all that, do ya know what I mean? You should see a lot of the kids at school, they get *really* freaked out.'

'Yes,' said Tomas, not looking at the boy, now carefully examining the exterior of his house, leaning over the rail to study the front yard.

'We didn't do anything,' said the boy. 'I swear.'

Not right, not right.

The twins were whispering in each other's ears, giggling in turns.

Tomas said nothing.

'Look, Mister…Dalton, is it? When you moved in we pulled a few stunts and that, but it did get a bit outta hand, do ya know what I mean? And like, you know, me and the lads feel a bit sorry about it all. Do ya know what I mean? So if you want us to do any messages or any jobs for ya, like, to make up. Ya know, you can ask us. 'Cos the cops called up to the house and me ma said she'd skin me if I get in any more trouble.'

NoNoNoNoNo.

The twins behind him nodded furiously, then fell silent. The tall one, speech finished, crossed and uncrossed his arms. His bottom lip, stained with some blue substance, hung outwards and shook slightly, like a rattling goalpost. He had the face of someone used to rejection, ready to pretend he didn't care.

Tomas walked into the house.

The front window was boarded up – an obvious way in. But no sign of tampering, the glass still intact, save the three fist-sized holes. The back door was fine too and nothing in the garden.

'Fuck.'

Tomas kicked a cupboard door in the kitchen. It made a light crunching sound. *Of course* they're lying, sneaky little rat-boys. Let's pretend to be sorry. Not a sliver of remorse. Or fear. Animals.

Tomas sat at the table and waited for his breathing to slow down. Then he briefly examined the kicked door (seemed to be fine) and went into the living room. Outside, they were still by the railings, one of the twins dancing while the others nodded their approval. Tomas picked up the phone and checked his messages. One from Eli, from that morning. Clara. Everything is fine. I'll send out notes. Bless her. Karin. Hi babee. How are you? Her voice rolling around like a drunk on a ship. Tomas grimaced. I couldn't sleep last night thinking about you and your daughter. I hear you won't be in today. But maybe later.

He hung up. Placed the phone on the sofa.

Think, think.

But instead, Tomas yawned. Looked at his watch. Twenty past five. Still early. Up at the crack of dawn, though. Strange dream, tied up with sheets, good God.

Take a bath.

He trudged up the stairs with such difficulty that by the time he reached the top he was dizzy and out of breath. He had to lie on his bed for a minute before getting up to turn on the taps, get a fresh towel and find the toenail clippers.

Then, reluctantly – as if being nagged into it by some other presence – Tomas checked the back rooms for signs of intrusion. Nothing. Windows closed. Everything where he had left it. He checked the walls. Photos of Anna where he had hung them, photos of various film sets in the other room. Couple of small paintings in the hallway, the four framed letters, all fine. Back in his own bedroom, a series of postcard-sized film posters on one wall, a watercolour of Clew Bay on the other. The dollhouse, intact. No. Everything's fine.

Calm down.

What are they up to?

A glance out the window. Still there, waiting. For something. Across the street, the old woman in the plastic coat had tottered off to the shops, leaving the man outside the wagon-wheels house to get on with cleaning his car. He seemed to do it half-heartedly, looking around to find some other distraction.

Tomas flopped back on his bed and listened to the digestive sounds of the bath filling up. He rubbed his hair a few times, then stood again, tried to smile, peeked out the window. Still there. He began unbuttoning his shirt, looking in the direction of the hallway now, at the four framed letters, lined up on the wall like staring faces at a zoo. And when finally he did see, Tomas found it difficult at first to believe the testimony of his eyes – why trust the electrical impulses from his optic nerve when they had failed him so miserably just moments before? He had looked – *specifically* looked – and seen nothing. Unless some other part of his brain was failing him now. Perhaps he had already seen it, seen it seven or eight times, and marvelled at the purity of the vandalistic ethos behind such an act, at the evident craft which had gone into its execution. Then sat, devastated, face buried in his hands, forgot what had so affected him, stood up again and saw, as if for the first time, the nail. A large nail – perhaps five inches, the sort used on a building site – had been driven through the centre of the third frame, puncturing the glass, the letter, and the wall behind: driven in so firmly that the letter would be damaged even further by any attempt to take it out. It had been inserted with such care that the glass had remained within the frame, splintered like lightening, distorting the scrawls beneath. *Dearest Kitty, As I write these words...*

The other letters remained as they were; untouched.

He had looked.

It hadn't been there.

This is madness now.

Tomas didn't shout, didn't open his mouth, but did emit a series of pained growls, the sort of sounds Marta had made when giving birth to Anna. She'd heard other women in the ward yelling their heads off, and found it terribly embarrassing.

Water spilled from the bathroom taps.

Tomas ran from the room and thundered down the stairs, his shirt flapping behind him like an army pennant. He flung open the front door to find – as he knew he would – that the boys were gone, that any further searching would be pointless. Wouldn't be in the alleyway or hanging around on Beatha Road. Wouldn't do anything he could think of.

Upstairs, the bathwater waved towards overflow.

He walked to the gate, looked around. A scraggy dog eyed him from across the street. Inside one of the cottages, he could see a woman in a tracksuit hoovering and smoking a cigarette. Somewhere in the distance, a car alarm wailed. Everyone had their dustbin out. Rubbish day. No one told me.

He felt calm now, but knew this must be bogus. Some sort of shock, a stalled reaction which would smack him like a typhoon later on. Noticing now that his shirt was unbuttoned, Tomas pulled it across himself, and saw he was being watched intently by the staring woman in number 16, her frizzy hair giving the appearance of someone recently electrocuted.

Tomas nodded. She continued to stare.

'The boys,' he ventured, pointing at a spot in the stained, uneven pavement. 'The boys that were there? Did you see where they went?'

The woman didn't look where he pointed. She remained frozen, not uttering a word.

8

THERE WAS rain the next morning. Not torrential, but the misty, insidious sort which leaves the air cold and a film of dampness on everything it touches.

Hopeful, though – if the weather gets worse, cancel the shoot tomorrow. Stay here.

Now ring Eli. Tell the truth. Oh, God.

'What?' the producer said. 'What?'

Eli, still in his hotel room, only half-dressed, didn't know what to say, didn't know where to start. Boys breaking into his house – not the sort of thing you easily keep to yourself. And the law refusing to do anything? Sounds potty. Mad. And Tomas already told a *completely different* story about how Anna got stabbed: muggers in the city centre. Now it's kids – *kids* – who live down the road.

Bloody strange.

Eli Gadd liked to keep a positive outlook – you had to in this game – but he'd always feared that one day a project would run past his control, like the gunslinger who knows that eventually he'll meet someone faster. And always from the last place you expect. Christ, Tomas was so dependable he was boring. Dream director, none of your artsy shit. No ego. Believed in the product. But since he'd come to Dublin. Something going on. A reluctance, like he's looking to get out.

But Tomas? Not Tomas. He's a proper pro. He knows you have to work on shit every now and again and pretend it's top-notch. You smile. You say yeah it's great and get on with the job. Be a professional. Done that before and made his money, thanks very much.

Maybe the divorce. Or Karin. Maybe he's a secret gambler or queer or a nonce or a junkie or into rubber – doesn't bloody matter. Problems at home stay at home. That's being professional.

But after all these years? Nah. Wouldda known.

Tomas was never too keen on the read-throughs, course, but this time he hasn't looked in on one minute of rehearsal. Not one minute. Actors throwing wobblies. Bills piling up. Money too tight, too tight. The whole fucking thing has disaster carved into its arse. Fucking disaster.

And who gets all the shit and all the blame? The poor fucking producer, that's who. The only sane bastard.

'Fucking hell,' Eli said. 'This is a right mess.'

'Yes. That's one way of describing it. Understating it. It's, it's…there are no words. Obviously I can't come in today. You see, I had it all decided – I was going to move out, get a hotel room or a nice B&B. Someplace not too far but far away enough from Karin, if you know what I mean. Ha! I was going to sell, yes. I had accepted that it wasn't working out. It was silly of me to go back to where I was born. Maybe buy a place in Howth or Dalkey. Near the sea. But visit London a lot. Yes. Anna made an effort, so I should too. But they got into the house, do you see? Inside. And I have no idea – no idea at all, Eli – of how they did it. They want me to know they can come into my home any time they want. That's the message. So I can't leave today, you understand that. All my things are here, Eli. *Everything* is here. One of the Boland letters has been destroyed. Do you know how much they are worth? No, no, no. Can't leave the house. Impossible. And, and it's as if they *know*; they know exactly what to go for. They are eating me, bit by bit. They got in, you see? Got inside *me*. How did they do that?'

'I don't know,' Eli said. It seemed as if Tomas was asking a real question and wanted a real answer. Too late for a replacement director now. Clara too inexperienced; the actors would never wear it anyway. Had to be Tomas. Not impossible – plenty of directors are totally barking and still work. Drugs. Little boys. All that. Just a matter of getting him out of that house.

'Tomas, listen to me. We've worked together a long time, yeah?'

'Yes, Eli.'

'So I'm going to say some things now and I want you to really listen to what I'm saying. I don't want you to get mad. You know I respect you, think the world of you.'

'Eli, I know I'm letting you down.'

'No, no. Wait. Look, of course I want you to show up for work today. This whole film is looking a bit dodgy and I'm worried about that. I'm bloody frantic. But I understand what's happening to you, Tomas. I do. And I know what these little gits are doing to you. They're getting into your house but really they're getting into your head. Do ya know what I mean? *They don't want you to leave the house.* They want you to be too scared to ever go out again – that's what this is about, mate. It's about showing fear, about having the most bottle. You stay at home, all terrified, and they've won. You got to keep going, mate. Keep living your life, keep directing this picture. 'Cos we need you. I need you.'

There was a pause. Eli was slightly breathless. He scanned the room to locate his cigarettes. From Tomas's end, there was the sound of chewing.

'Yes, yes, I appreciate that, Eli. I do. And you are right – I can't let them win. I won't. I am going to move out, I am. Soon as I can. But it's all my possessions, do you see? I assure you, it's just for today. It's too late to organise someone to mind the house now. But I will be there tomorrow. I will. I'll have a look at the schedule tonight to see if we can rejig it a bit. We'll do read-throughs before we shoot any important scenes. I'll get on top of it, Eli. I will.'

This sounded like Tomas. This sounded like a sane person.

'Hey, mate. That's all I wanted to hear.'

'Just give me today. OK?'

'Well, yeah. If you really need it. But I could organise someone to housesit for you, you know? I could get a security firm.'

'Please, Eli.'

'You wouldn't feel safe with a security firm guarding your house?'

'Eli, there's a knock at the door. Better go. I'll see you tomorrow. I promise. And thank you.'

Tomas hung up, and for a moment remained still.

You sounded like a lunatic. Fuck.

What about tomorrow?

He got up and moved towards the door, pausing to punch the code into the new house alarm. *1441.* Best keep it on at all times, the man who installed it said. The man had also changed the locks, but hadn't a clue how the boys got in. Did you not call the guards? Really? It reminded him of a joke. A vegetarian in an Irish restaurant. The waiter asks, Will you have chicken, so?

Tomas wrenched open the door with one hand, the other resting on a golf club he had parked in the hallway. He prepared a strict face and a sarky speech for the glazier who was already an hour late.

'Hello, Mister Dalton.'

Garda Norbert Clarke removed his hat. His head shone whitely. 'Are you busy? Could I have a word?'

Tomas stepped back, swept a hand towards the living room. Unsmiling and professional, Norbert Clarke went as directed. He marched stiffly, a stance that distracted from the blubbery quality of his body.

Outside, the young dreadlocked couple strolled past, arms wrapped around each other's shoulders like attacking octopi. The closeness of their embrace made them stagger slightly. The girl looked briefly in Tomas's direction, smiled, then looked away.

In the living room, Garda Clarke studied the boarded-up front window. 'This?'

'Another gift from my little friends.'

'Hmm. Rocks?'

Tomas pointed at the rug. 'Covered with wet paint to do the maximum damage. This rug was quite valuable, given to us by a close friend who has since passed away. And now.'

The black smears resembled scorch marks in a forest. They had begun to flake, scattering tiny flecks of black on the wooden floor. It looked like people, viewed from a satellite. Garda Clarke thumbed his chin.

'So it was after this that your daughter…?'

'She went to have a word with them and they stabbed her.'

Garda Clarke put out a hand. 'Well, we don't know that.'

Tomas glared. 'I beg your pardon?'

'Mister Dalton. I know who you *think* attacked your daughter. You made that plain in your statement. To be honest, I think so as well. But there's no evidence linking them to the crime, other than a few circumstantial facts. I'm sorry. I really am. We haven't given up, though.'

Tomas, his face red, pointed at the ceiling. He felt the hotness return to his neck and shoulders.

'They did it again, you know. Last night they *broke into the house*. No idea how. I haven't slept a wink.'

Norbert Clarke looked down at his feet. 'I'm so sorry to hear that. Was there much damage?'

'I have, or I had, a collection of four letters written by Harry Boland. They are very, very valuable. Six-figure valuable. Now I have only three.'

'My God. How did they get in?'

'Haven't a clue. Nothing was disturbed.'

'You did call the guards, didn't you?'

'Well, aren't you here now?'

'Yes, yes.' He tipped his head, as if he couldn't quite frame in words the complex point he wished to make. 'But you should have reported it, Mister Dalton. You have to make an official report. It looks funny if you've waited for a day. For the insurance, I mean.'

'Insurance? Is that what you are? Claims adjusters?'

'Mister Dalton.'

'Have you no interest in actually catching criminals any more?'

'Mister Dalton.'

'Because you have failed to make any effort to catch these boys. That's why I didn't ring you. What's the point? You know who they are, you know where they live. But you do nothing.'

'Actually, I spoke to them.'

'And then my daughter got stabbed! So that was a big help, wasn't it?'

Garda Clarke closed his eyes and looked at the ground.

'Yesterday they were standing outside the house. Calm as you like. Engaging in conversation with me. Practically admitted to everything.'

Norbert Clark looked up.

'No, Norbert. Don't get excited. I'm getting the hang of this now. All they said was that there had been a few pranks, that's all. Far short of the signed confession and photograph you need before you act. It was just to taunt me anyway, because they had already broken in here – in *here* – and destroyed something that is part of our heritage, that was passed down through my family. Of course, I don't expect you to appreciate that, but at least you can recognise the seriousness of the situation when something worth hundreds of thousands is destroyed just for fun.'

'Well if it's that valuable, why do you keep it in your house?'

'What, I have to *expect* people to break into my home? Well, don't worry, Garda – not that you are – the remaining three letters are in a safe place.'

They were still on the wall of the upstairs landing, all four of them: the second from the right stabbed through the chest. *Dearest Kitty.*

'But what am I to do with everything else? Would it be easier if I just moved out altogether? Saved you the bother of doing your job? These little...bastards can break in here at will and do whatever they like and oh, it's nothing to do with you. Not your job to catch criminals. Actually, it's my own fault for having furniture in my house!'

'Oh, for fuck's sake!'

The exclamation surprised them both. Coming out of Norbert Clarke's mouth, the words contained a muscular vulgarity quite unlike anything he seemed capable of. Tomas had a brief urge to smile, but Norbert was talking now, his face growing pinker with each word.

'The world is full of people, Mister Dalton, other people. You can't avoid them. Some will be bad, some of them will be good, and there's nothing you or I or anyone else can do about it. You have to live in the world as it is, and some of that involves taking precautions. Not looking for trouble, but not being stupid either, and Mister Dalton, you...'

He stopped, panting now. A grin began to crack Tomas's face in half.

'And I'm stupid?' Laughter spluttered out of Tomas Dalton. He held his chest and shook, then bent double like a vomiting man. Incapable of speech, he sat back onto the sofa and waved at Norbert Clarke to do the same. The garda perched on its edge.

'Sorry, sorry,' Tomas eventually breathed. 'Didn't get much sleep last night. Just stress, I expect.'

'That's all right, that's fine,' said Norbert Clarke in a quiet voice.

Tomas scratched at some paint flakes clinging to the rug. 'So why are you here? Not just to tell me I'm stupid?'

Norbert Clarke smiled, though unconvincingly. He waved his head. 'Well, er, there is something, yes. Are you sure this is a good time?'

Tomas held up his hands. 'I'll be good, Norbert. Honest. The bestest boy.'

Norbert Clarke shifted on the sofa, causing the leather to squeak. 'Well, it's about the boys, of course.'

'Yes.'

The policeman leaned forward. He dropped his voice to a deep hum. 'After your daughter was, er, attacked. Did you speak to them? The boys?'

'Yes I did. Put on quite a show. Not that it made any difference.'

'What did you say exactly?'

Tomas frowned, jutting out his lower lip. 'Oh, what you might expect – Anna was still in the hospital, after all – don't come near my family or else; that kind of thing.'

'Or else?'

'Or else I'll do the same to you, I suppose. I can't remember exactly. It was just to frighten them.'

'But you did threaten them?'

Tomas frowned again. 'I *suppose*. But as I say, it was just to frighten them.

They're children. Have you never threatened your kids with something you didn't mean?'

'I don't have children.'

Tomas held up a hand. 'Yes. You told me that before. Sorry.'

Both men fell silent, like timid soldiers waiting for the enemy to pass by.

'Look,' sighed Norbert. 'The problem is. The parents have complained to us that you threatened the boys. Threatened to kill them.'

'*They* are complaining about *me*?'

Somewhere nearby, a drill stuttered.

'Yes, Mister Dalton, they did. Now we don't have to take the matter any further, and on this occasion we won't.' He closed one eye, as if aiming. 'But I must warn you to be a bit more careful.'

'For Christ's sake. I, I just can't fathom…'

'All right, all right,' said Norbert Clarke, on his feet now. 'I just came to say that. I don't want to antagonise you any more, Mister Dalton. I really don't. It's ridiculous, I know, but there you are. The law can be an ass.'

Tomas was suddenly smiling again. Something teddy bearish about Norbert Clarke, hilarious the way he uses words – *fuck* and *ass* – obscene and innocent at the same time, like a toddler aping a grown-up. Tomas followed him to the front door. Outside, the glazier's truck had just arrived, the driver decoding the contents of his clipboard.

'Funny,' said Norbert, speaking quickly as if he didn't want to give himself time to think. 'There's something *familiar* about this. Just then, with the painted rocks. Just a flash, but I can't…probably nothing.'

He jammed on his cap and strode away. Tomas watched him go while waiting for the glazier to amble up to the front door.

'Daltry, is it?' The glazier had big ears and a disappointed face.

'Dalton,' Tomas corrected. 'And while we are on the subject of getting things wrong, I see you are, what? An hour and a half late? I can't just wait in my house all day for you. I do have a life to lead.'

*

HE SAT, eavesdropping on the creaks and settling sounds the house secreted, a language of whispers which might reveal why it had acquiesced to these boys.

Nothing; guards haven't a clue. Some time after Norbert Clarke left, a small young woman weighed down with a huge box of forensic tools had poked around the back of the house, but seemingly found no evidence. She didn't admit it, of course. Obvious though.

Been so bloody reasonable with Norbert, too reasonable. Now they complain? Little fucks, parents no better, obviously, mongrels breed mongrels.

They must have weaknesses, something they want to protect, at least until the move; enough to distract them, wound them into considering what to do next.

After the glazier left, Tomas had spent an hour phoning removal companies. Only one of them did storage. We'll get back to you. No room at the moment. Maybe a week or so.

A week. A week. Survive a week of war with little boys.

Are they all like this?

Tomas scoured mental images of his own childhood. Not much came. Stone throwing. Shouting 'Bastard!' at a passing drunk. A fat boy he punched in the stomach. Trying one of his mother's untipped cigarettes, and feeling sick almost immediately. Lying when she confronted him about it. But she knew; she always did.

Did she?

Stupid, stupid, how can you remember? When decades of adult disillusion have elapsed?

Tomas sat and listened.

*

'HELLO,' MARTA said.

Jesus, the gall. The bloody cheek.

Lost the right to ring up and expect her voice to be recognised – she should announce herself like everyone else.

Calm, calm.

Can't pretend not to know who she is – juvenile, give her the advantage.

She already had surprise, and in their unspoken rules of combat, to ask Marta why she was ringing was considered a concession. Tomas's job was to guess what she wanted and refuse before she asked, thus depicting her as selfish and, worse still, predictable.

'Hello,' Tomas replied, as neutrally as he could.

'How are you?'

Marta's voice was twangy and rather girlish, yet suffused with a pre-emptive scepticism, prepared not to believe anything she was told.

Take the lead.

'More importantly, how is Anna?'

Dangerous. Vulnerable to accusations of blame. Unlikely, though, an obvious assault. Insinuate it, rather. Hint at guilt.

'Oh, she's OK.'

Not wishing to sound negative, Marta had, over time, developed a method of describing the universe using just three adjectives – *fantastic*, which was reserved for special occasions; *good*, which described an arc ranging from adequate to poor; and *OK*, which usually meant very bad indeed.

'Poor thing. Putting on a brave face, I suppose?'

'Yes. But I must say I was very concerned when I heard the circumstances of her attack.'

Concerned meant furious.

'Well, so was I. In fact, I had specifically asked her *not* to approach those boys.'

'Yes, she mentioned that.'

Tomas took the phone away from his ear. Anna rarely defended her father to Marta. This put him beyond the immediate reach of Marta's blame.

Must be something else.

'It's astounding. The whole thing.'

'Yes, it is.'

'I didn't know Dublin was so violent.'

'As far as I know, it's not. Least it's no different to most places. I just appear to have been very unlucky.'

'Yes.'

There it is: the *tone*.

'I mean,' Tomas said, trying to keep his voice flat, 'have you ever heard of such a thing happening to anyone, anywhere?'

'Indeed not.'

Stupid, played straight into her.

'These boys don't know me, nor I them. Everything else is fine. It's a lovely place.'

'That's not what Anna says. She says it's badly deprived.'

'Now Anna was only here for a few days. It's a bit rundown, yes…'

'Well *she* is the social worker, Tomas.'

'You don't need to be a social worker to tell what condition an area is in. Common sense will tell you.'

Marta made a noise, a faint squeak escaping from the back of her throat. What would you know about common sense?

He shifted on his seat. His stomach gurgled. Virtually nothing in the house. A few slices of bread and some pasta. Can't risk going to the shops, though, even around the corner.

'And the condition of the area has nothing to do with it,' he continued. 'It's just these boys, they're disturbed somehow. It's a freak occurrence.'

'Well, yes, Tomas. Obviously. But it all sounds so…pre-meditated, so *thought out*. Cigars full of urine. One would hardly need to be Doctor Freud to work out the symbolism. There must be some reason why they have initiated this feud with you.'

'It's not a feud. I've done nothing to them. I've told you – I don't even know them.'

'Well, that's very strange.'

'What do you mean, *strange*? Do you think I'm lying? Why would I do that?' His voice grew high and tetchy and he knew the hotness in his limbs would soon erupt again. She'll be thrilled now. What's wrong, Tomas? What are you not saying, Tomas? Are you depressed, Tomas, ga-ga, Tomas? Smug bitch.

'Of course I don't think you're lying. I rang because frankly, I'm rather worried. If these boys can stab Anna, they can just as easily stab you.'

'They won't stab me.'

'How can you be sure?'

'Because I'd kick their fucking arses.'

'I beg your pardon?'

'You heard me. And what has this got to do with you? We are not married any more, so where and how I live is none of your business.'

She paused. 'Well, I suppose you could look at it that way. But just because I'm not married to you doesn't mean that I'm not concerned about your welfare. We were together for nearly thirty years, Tomas. That can't just be erased.'

Good answer. She was admirably, annoyingly calm. Completely ignored the swearing – something he'd never done much of before. She was usually squeamish about bad language, like it was all aimed at her.

'Really. I thought when you left you were trying to erase thirty years of marriage.'

'Oh, Tomas. Don't be immature, please.'

'Immature meaning I don't say what *you* wish to hear.'

'Tomas, you really don't sound like yourself. Perhaps you should come over to London for a few days. Just get away from things. See a doctor.'

You're ga-ga, Tomas.

'Ha! They'd burn the place to the ground if I did that. Marta, *I'm* fine. *I* have a problem which *I* will solve. *I* also have a film to make. And *I* have a new life which has nothing to do with you. So why don't you go and fucking interfere with somebody else.'

'Tomas, please.'

'Somebody who fucking might want to hear your bullshit.'

'I'm going to hang up now, Tomas.'

'Because, Marta, I'm not—'

The phone clicked off.

Fuckbitch, fuckbitch, Thomas muttered as he threw down the receiver, seeing himself on crutches. Torn ligaments in his ankle. Eight, ten years ago? Stupid, really. Walking up Rosslyn Hill. Slipped as he stepped off the pavement. Collapsed in front of her, gripping his foot, barely able to speak under the giant clamp of pain. And she'd been calm, calling a taxi, getting him to the Royal Free to get strapped up, then back home. But later, just as dusk was slowly diluting the colour of the day, she came into the bedroom, eyes averted. Sat on the bed, half-turned from him. She reached back and gripped his hand so hard it left a mark.

You gave me a terrible fright today.

Her voice croaked.

When you fell down, I…I didn't know what it was. Imagined all sorts of terrible, terrible things.

She sniffed.

I was scared, Tomas.

In silence, they waited for the evening darkness to swarm around them.

*

HE SAT on the stairs, nibbling a piece of dry bread.

What's on the list?

Put the Boland letters in a bank. Do that tomorrow.

Talk to neighbours. Done. The Africans, anyway. Saw nothing.

Ring Norbert. Done. Mustn't have that much to do if he can spend all day keeping an eye on the boys.

Screw all the windows shut. Done.

Buy food. Can't do that. No.

The sharp knock on the front door prompted Tomas to look at his watch, as if he was actually expecting a visitor. Wearily, he turned off the alarm and gripped the golf club as he opened up. This process made him hunch slightly, so that Karin Goldman – dressed in a light brown calf-length suede coat and black winkle-picker boots with a two-inch heel – was almost the same height as him. She pushed sunglasses back onto the top of her head.

'Hi there.' The words failed to sound calm and friendly. Not much of an actress today.

Still, she could make an entrance.

Karin held up plastic bags.

'Brought dinner. Pasta. Nothing fancy.'

Tomas gestured a welcome. Karin took careful steps inside.

'Oh, your house is charming.'

'Thank you.'

'The street, though…it's a little funky.'

'By funky, I assume you don't mean cool and hip.'

She cocked her head to one side, like a puzzled dog. 'That would be correct, Tomas.' She pointed. 'Kitchen this way?'

He nodded and followed her, Karin tottering slightly on her high heels.

'I just thought you could do with a good meal, what with everything you've been through. And how is your daughter? No, you can tell me when we sit down. Anyway, when you didn't turn up for rehearsals today, I was worried about you. Last rehearsal day and no sign of the director? Well, I knew that wasn't like you. Eli made a little speech about how you were in shock after what happened – they all know about it, of course – and that you'd be in tomorrow. But I was worried anyway and spoke to him afterwards. And do you know what? I think he's worried about you too. I mean, I think the little guy does care about you, so I've kinda changed my opinion of him. I thought he was pretty creepy before, but now I think he's not so bad.'

Tomas sat at the kitchen table and listened. It was surprisingly pleasant to have another voice in the house, filling it up, making it warm. And food. His stomach juices bubbled.

'So I said to him that I'd like to call over and cook a meal. To be honest, I like to keep busy the night before shooting starts – you know, just to keep my nerves in control – and Eli said he thought it was a great idea. He said to be sure to tell you that it was him who gave me your address.'

She stopped unpacking the bags and regarded the ceiling, as if remembering some long and complex piece of dialogue. 'And if you don't like it, you can eff off. Though he didn't use that exact word. He also said he'd see you in the morning.'

Karin turned back to the shopping bags.

'Eli prides himself on his subtlety,' said Tomas.

There was a pause while Karin looked around. 'So, how are you?'

The question was addressed to some cupboards in the kitchen, her back half-turned to Tomas. But now she spun around, her long pink nails extended from her hands like a pantomime cat.

'No. Hold that. First I want you to be honest. Is it OK for me to be here? I mean, barging in uninvited like this when your poor daughter has just been attacked and everything? I can be insensitive sometimes, you know?'

Karin pointed to the sky and dropped her voice to a whisper. 'Your daughter, she upstairs?'

Tomas stared blankly at Karin. 'No,' he said eventually. 'She's gone home. To London.'

'Oh. Eli said she was still here. Still, my point is, if you'd rather be alone, Tomas, that's fine. Really.'

Karin's eyes carried a bit too much mascara, and were wide and watery, hinting at tears. Tomas grinned, his even teeth a white shock.

'I'm glad you're here, Karin. Really I am.'

*

AFTER DINNER he showed off some of his collection: cameras, bullets, bits of stone. The scapula, and finally, the four letters at the top of the stairs. Objects have a sort of immortality, he told her. What my mother always said. They are frozen moments, like the first footprints on the moon. Things are memories, material embodiments of what the brain tries to store. That bullet from 1916 charts a man's death; the framed set of braces belonged to my father, who wore them every day for twenty years, as much a part of his life as his fingerprints, his speech and the air he sucked into his lungs.

Karin did lots of nodding, and seemed to understand.

It's a silly Western attitude, he said, to feel uncomfortable about liking objects. Christian guilt that, say, the Japanese don't have. They treasure their possessions like friends. They feel they have expanded their universe by bringing things into it. And this is not the crass collection of *possessions*, acquisition for its own sake – this is much different. More like archaeology.

All things have an entire life behind them, Karin said.

Yes. Yes.

American Beauty. It's a line from that film.

Tomas smiled.

She looked down, almost whispering now, her voice shushing through the darkening hallway.

It's funny. About the past, you know? The older I get, it's more like the past won't go away. Like, it's still here? Like you and me are here right now, but in our minds we're in all sorts of places at the same time. When we were kids or when we got married or when we got our first job, that's all still going on. The past hasn't passed at all, do you know what I mean? Time is supposed to go in a straight line, a beginning, middle and end, but it doesn't feel that way. It's all jumbled up and sometimes it seems to connect up in ways that don't make any sense at all. Does that sound crazy?

No. Not at all.

They looked at the letters again, watching a tiny rhomboid of reflected evening light slowly close over. Dusk slowly enfolded them.

I know what I'm like. I mean, I know how I come across.

Her words were soft. The twilight had altered the terrain of her face to black and white.

I'm loud. I lack class, I know all that. My father, you know? He was a drunk. Not that I remember. I was only a little kid when he died. But my mom, she...I dunno. For years she acted like it was her fault, like she coulda stopped him drinking. Or he was drinking because of her. Still don't know what really went on. But we were poor, you know? Crappy jobs, food stamps. So many things we couldn't have, couldn't do. Everything was grey. Our house was grey, our street was never sunny, our clothes were always washed out 'cos we had to make 'em last. That's the way I remember it, anyway. Jesus. Kansas in *The Wizard of Oz*.

She lit a cigarette, the lighter flame throwing a brief orange shadow across her long, smooth nose, closed eyes with stately, Egyptian eyelashes. A queen on her deathbed.

And when I was twenty-one I moved to New York and suddenly there was all this *colour*, you know? And that was the first time I realised I was alive. Can you imagine? The first time I realised my childhood was over, that it wouldn't last forever, that there was more than one way to *exist*.

She sucked on the cigarette, exhaled extravagantly.

So, man, I leaped all over colour. You should see what I used to wear back then. I dunno, just, loud and garish says alive to me. I've tried to change over the years, wear black, all that, but it never worked. I always felt a fraud. That's me, I guess. I...

She tsked.

Listen to me, rambling. It was all a long time ago. And I've been lucky. I've nothing to complain about.

Tomas nodded slowly, looked at the framed letters, then back at Karin.

I saw all the drugs in your bag.

She stared, her eyes wide, a slight shudder in her chin.

I recognised one of the names. Cyclophosphamide. Marta's father was prescribed it. For leukaemia.

She continued staring at him.

Is that what…?

She looked towards the ground, biting her bottom lip.

Sorry, said Tomas. I'm so sorry.

*

SHE STOOD with her arms folded while Tomas explained.

'These letters were written in 1922 to Kitty Kiernan, who was Michael Collins's girlfriend. Popular legend has it that Collins was introduced to Kitty in 1918 by his friend Harry Boland. This is true, but what a lot of people don't realise is that at this time, Harry was the one seeing Kitty. Michael was seeing Kitty's sister, Helen. But when Helen married someone else, Collins also became interested in Kitty.'

'OK.'

'So between, say, 1919 and 1921, during the, er, War of Independence, both Boland and Collins were wooing Kitty Kiernan. Difficult for both men, as Collins was in hiding a lot of the time, or in London, while Boland was in New York. Collins sent him there as an envoy.'

'Convenient.'

'Yes,' said Tomas. 'Exactly. By all accounts, Kitty appears to have chosen Collins over Boland by the end of 1921, which was when the Civil War started. Boland and Collins took opposing sides.'

She scrunched her eyebrows, interested now. 'Opposing sides? Because of the girl?'

Leukaemia. My God.

Tomas scratched his head.

'Well, most people think not. But most people haven't seen these letters. They were written in 1922, *during* the Civil War and shortly before Boland's death. He is very angry towards Collins.'

'Wow. Yes. But would that affect what side he joined in a war?'

Tomas held up a finger. 'Never underestimate the power of jealousy. Or bitterness.'

He pointed at the fourth letter. Karin's eyes had strayed several times to the frame beside it, still torpedoed by the nail, but had said nothing.

Eli must have told her about the boys. She is not without generosity.

'See this section here? It refers to a period Kitty and Harry spent together the previous summer. Boland did come back from the States for a spell during 1921. And see this – "*that piece of news you presented as disaster, yet I would have welcomed as a blessing. Was it an accident Kitty? You have little to lose now by resorting to the truth.*"'

'Sounds like he was angry with her.'

Tomas smiled, a conjurer about to reveal. 'Yes. I imagine so. It's impossible to know for sure what this is a reference to. But see the word he uses – "blessing".'

Karin slapped a hand to her mouth. 'You mean she was pregnant? With his kid?'

'Maybe.'

'And the bit about was it an accident. She got rid of it, right?'

'Maybe.'

'My God.'

They stood for a moment, contemplating the four letters. Eventually, Karin pointed. 'So nobody knows about these?'

Tomas shrugged. 'As far as I'm aware.'

'But shouldn't you tell somebody? I mean, aren't they of historical importance if this guy switched sides in a war because of a girl?'

Tomas gave an awkward smile. 'Well, that's true. But I did inherit these letters from my mother, and I know she wouldn't approve.'

Karin blinked. She cocked her head to one side.

'My mother was a Republican. Big admirer of Boland. She wouldn't want it getting out that he chose his side in the Civil War because of something so, well, trivial.'

'Love ain't trivial, mister,' Karen said. She looked back at the letters again. 'Well, if she didn't want it getting out, why didn't she destroy them?'

'That was her problem. She knew the value of objects like this. She couldn't do them harm any more than she could have to Boland himself.' He pointed at the black nail. 'She would have been horrified with *this*.'

There was a pause.

'But are you comfortable?'

'How do you mean?'

'You know. If the facts don't suit, then keep them quiet? You're comfortable with that?'

Tomas folded his arms. 'Well, I don't think it's that important. To be truthful, I haven't given it much thought.'

Karin shook her head, grinning also. 'You Irish are weird. I thought Jews were bad. Not that I'm Jewish, really.'

'You're not?'

'My dad was Jewish but my mom's side were Welsh-Americans. Not that she told me. I had to go look it up.'

'Welsh-Americans? I didn't know there were any.'

'Yeah. It's funny. We were kinda forgotten about.'

She pointed towards Tomas's room, at the structure nestling by the foothills of his bed.

'What's that?'

'Oh, it's just…it's a dollhouse.'

*

THEY BOTH knelt, their legs almost touching. Tomas heard her draw in a long, deep breath. She extended pink-topped fingers towards it.

'My God. It's lovely. But what happened at the sides?'

'At some point Anna decided she didn't like dollhouses. So I rescued it.'

She put a hand on his shoulder. 'That's sweet.'

They are right beside the bed.

Heart thumping. Don't stay here too long. I'm dying for a coffee. Get up and let her follow. Right. OK.

'It's perfect inside,' he said.

He eased back the lid and felt a flutter of concern.

Karin oohed and edged a little closer. But Tomas was now scanning the tiny neat rooms, feeling the high-pitched whine of blood through his temples, a sensation which increased in intensity until he saw that the mammy, the daddy and the little baby have had their heads carefully removed. There was a light thump in his oesophagus and Tomas emitted an *Oh*, which sounded more like surprise than horror. Yet it was enough to catch Karin's attention, enough for her to notice that his facial muscles were frozen, that his eyes were swimming with tears he couldn't possibly control. And she crooned

Baby, baby, baby in that squeaky, startled voice of hers, sliding her skinny hands across his back and shoulders, and Tomas didn't want to think about what they had done to the dollhouse – a firewall went up in his brain. Instead, it was like praying: Oh my God she's touching me and I'm crying and we're in the bedroom. Oh my God. Not here. Not now.

9

'ALL RIGHT?'

The grin loitered unconvincingly around Eli's face.

No.No.No.No.No.No.No.No.No. I'm not all right, matey-boy, what a stupid fucking question, how could I be all right? What miraculous change in circumstances do you imagine has taken place that now I could be suddenly all right? What? What?

Stop.

Stop.

Unfair. Eli's been patient. Beyond all right to expect. Acted like a friend, even though. Fondness, yes, but not.

'I'm fine,' Tomas said. 'Great. Feeling much better.'

Tomas's skin was red and itchy, his throat dry, and he didn't like being here, out in the open, where he could be seen, where he could feel the light wind and shots of sea spray coming over the Bull Wall, where the seagulls cawed interrogatively.

Whatchadoinhere? Whatchadoinhere?

Sweating again.

Should have stayed at home. Don't be foolish. Couldn't. First day of shooting. No show and that would be it. Film cancelled. Rumours scampering around. Tomas had heard many of the nasty stories, had been at the birth of one or two. Someone raises their voice and it's a tantrum. Or a fistfight. Or they are out of control on some awful drug.

Tomas waved to the skulking Jack Forde and talked to Joe the cameraman and looked through lenses and viewed filters and reflector boards. Only just staying; could go home right now.

Home. Home. It is home. *My* home, my, my, my.

114

Something familiar about this. What did Norbert mean? Fool. Perhaps not a fool. Perhaps not saying.

No, no. Calm down.

Panic stalked Tomas, circling him, digging its paws into the dirt, leering through fangs. Yet no one else noticed. The crew, mostly men and women in their late twenties, mostly dressed with a careful sloppiness, moved around or stood in expectant clumps talking about what time they left home, the woeful traffic up the coast road. Any news on that bus strike? Is it going ahead? Jesus. I got clamped there last week. Out of the car for two minutes. Stupid. Forgot my wallet. Had to leave it there and take a taxi home.

Norbert Clarke had promised to keep an eye on the boys today. Some comfort in that, though not an extravagant amount. Curiously, to employ someone from the film to baby-sit his house was, for Tomas, an unthinkable option, a form of defeat, though he had no idea why.

Anyway, luck is changing. Has to. Just the previous night he had managed to evade too much embarrassment with Karin Goldman. She had let him blub for a while, then followed him down the stairs. Didn't even ask what he had been crying about. She left shortly afterwards, having deposited a faithful peck on his cheek.

This was a positive development. And – deploying the logic that positive developments travel in packs – an indicator that this was the best time to risk leaving the house. For a few hours anyway. He'd already rung Norbert Clarke to remind him of what had been agreed. Norbert, just awake, gave a bleary Don't worry.

Amazing you can be here. After what they did. Little Anna.

Tomas stood near his TV monitor calling out directions as the Jimmy Jib operator moved the camera this way and that. Tomas sipped from a polystyrene bath of tea and toked on a thick cigar, a convention he always observed at the start of shooting. The sight of a cigar-smoking director, he believed, calmed and cheered people, made them think of Hitchcock, of debonair, powerful men who never panicked, who were never victims. The cigar, however, made Tomas dizzy, made him wish all these young people would stop whizzing around, carrying their clipboards, rolls of thick wire, tripods, slabs of coloured plastic, chunks of silver scaffold. A city's worth of activity, crammed onto the skinny bridge out to Bull Island. At least the scene was easy, little more than Karin strolling thoughtfully by the sea. Four lines of dialogue, and what with the racket from the wind and the screaming seagulls, it would probably be dubbed in later anyway.

The camera moves decided, Tomas looked across the scuttling mesh of people. Eli already on his mobile phone, his face pale, one hand sliding through his thinning hair. What time? 7:45? Eli was not usually up this early.

They'll be eating breakfast now. Guzzling some muck laced with chocolate. School starts at 8:50 (Tomas had rung and asked). If they knew the house was empty, try something on the way? Ring Norbert and warn him.

When did they vandalise the dollhouse? When they attacked the Harry Boland letter? On another occasion?

While I was there?

Tomas shook himself, then noticed Clara wearing the sort of expression which usually preceded apology.

'Everything OK?'

Sound calm. Good.

'Yes, yes. It's just Karin is in make-up and would like a word.'

They exchanged grins. Good kid, Clara.

Moving towards the lopsided Winnebago which served as the make-up department, Tomas passed within greeting range of Eli. Tomas winked, and in return Eli proffered a thumbs-up. Boyishly optimistic.

This will end badly. I'll be Judas.

Karin could be heard from some feet away.

'Patches, patches, you know? Not for cigarettes. For HRT. Oh, why am I telling you this? You're a child. Have you hit puberty yet? *You* have a child. I don't believe that. How old? No, I mean how old are you? My God, that's insane, you look about fourteen. That skin. How did you get that skin? You don't smoke, right? That's always it. But even you, my beauty, even you: one day your ass will be hanging down to your calf muscles, believe me. And suddenly you won't be able to talk in sentences any more. Then you'll know you need HRT. Haven't had it myself. But my mom, she's sixty-four years of age, I swear to God, she only started last year with a patch after my sister Janie begged and begged and begged. Now I'm from Trenton, New Jersey, you know where that is? Two months after my mom starts with the patch, she's dating again. My old man died years back and believe me, no one missed him. But not only that, she goes on one date and afterwards she's bragging to my sister – *bragging* – that after dinner she and this old geezer went into Cadwallader Park and had sex against a tree. Can you believe that? Sixty-four years of age? I don't know whether to cheer or throw up.'

Tomas paused at the door. She had moved on to some new story now. Karin's father, the drunk. *He died and no one missed him.* The worst of punishments, to be forgotten. The absence of memory. When there is no light, there is no colour.

Tomas couldn't imagine how one parent could be retained in the mind, the other crinkled into a ball and discarded. His mother and father blur into one person, a familial double act, almost meaningless if regarded individually. She is tall, long limbed, something equine about the way she carries herself. The same height as Father, but nowhere near as thick and weathered. Tommy Dalton looks as if he has been left out in the back garden for a few years, but hasn't even noticed, such is his engine-like presence. He has an awkward muscularity, his limbs as solid as anvils, each movement a studied effort at not destroying the frail world around. His sleeves almost always rolled up – because of the printing, of the constant assault from oil and ink, he scrubs his hands ten times a day. Rises slowly from the chair, and as if in a funeral procession, moves towards the little toilet off the kitchen. The heavy clank of his belt buckle being opened. The thunderous torrent of his piss into the shining bowl. The explosive flush. The squeak of the taps being opened. The fervent shush and slap of his hand washing. Mother smiles at these sounds.

She does most of the yabbering, yes – and there are some who may think him the hen-pecked husband – but scarcely a word comes from her mouth without his consent. Isn't that right, Tommy? What do you think, Tommy? Usually he nods his assent, but sometimes he shakes his head.

No.

Tomas and his mother sit up then, almost surprised by the sound of his voice, which is deep and curls all the vowels to breaking point. And he explains why, often referring to books and thinkers – Plato. Karl Marx. Saint Thomas Aquinas. Padraig Pearse. Bakunin. And this is always a wonder because they never see him with a book in his hand, ever, and have no idea how he knows such things.

She rarely disagrees. And when she does, there is no argument, as far as Tomas can detect. His father listens, his expression blank, then extends a flat hand, as if serving an invisible drink. He goes back to reading his paper, allowing a thick silence to fill up the house. Her face reddens, and she becomes frantically busy, baking bread or putting black on shoes. And for this short period Tomas experiences an excruciating anxiety, a worry that everything in the world he knows is in danger of crumbling to powder.

Eventually, his father stops reading. He carefully folds up the paper, places it on the table beside.

Are you right there, Peg?

And she glances at him and smirks. Not because of the words so much as the way his eyes twinkle, sitting on his cheeks like they don't belong to his face at all, but some babyish creature thousands of years old, someone impossible to resist. Then she goes back to the stove and he returns to his paper. He smokes a pipe, fingers straying through his thick moustache. Makes you look like Mister Connolly, Peg says. And they exchange a look Tomas doesn't understand, yet still makes him happy.

He knocked on the door, then pulled it open.

Was it really like that? How do you know?

'Everyone decent in here?'

He stomped up the stairs. The make-up woman grinned back at him. Karin also smiled, her face made ghostly by the harsh mirror lights.

'Hi,' Karin said, lengthening the syllables as if her words were a secret code. 'How are you today?'

The make-up woman glanced interrogatively between them.

'Fine, fine. You wanted to see me?'

'Oh, just to talk about this morning. Block out my moves.'

'Of course. There's no rush. Get your make-up on first.'

Karin jammed a thumb backwards.

'Actually, we should be finished by now but I kept yakking with young Peg here. Girl talk, you know.'

'Peg,' Tomas said, his eyes creasing with pleasure. 'That was my mother's name.'

*

JUST AFTER eleven he called the break.

Eleven already? My God.

He had spent the first hour of the day glancing compulsively at his watch, so much so that it annoyed Joe the cameraman, who never liked to show his irritation. Is there something wrong there?

Tomas apologised, a conversation which had brought Eli sweeping over. Everything all right? Good, good. Sweet.

And this was the odd thing – for the rest of the morning, he didn't think about *it*, about *them*. He relaxed, concentrated on the images of Karin in her cheap plaid overcoat, walking along the Bull Wall, staring across at the twin towers of Ringsend Power Station, two striped fingers presented to all who approached the city by sea. He told her, Don't *try* to look lonely. Just walk. She looked lonely anyway.

So when Tomas called the break, he did so with a flowering sense of accomplishment – he had come here today to construct the appearance of work, not actually do any.

The life you used to have. There it is.

He turned on his phone and rang Norbert Clarke.

There was a background mash of drilling, footsteps and Latin-sounding music. The policeman had to shout slightly to make himself heard.

'Hello, Mister Dalton.'

The words seemed slightly slurred, as if Norbert was tipsy or tired.

'So how's it going?'

'Fine, fine. They haven't gone near your house.'

'They're at school?'

'No. They went on the mitch today. Into the city centre. They've already been to Burger King and now they're in an amusement arcade. Must have come into some cash. I don't know if I can do this all day. I could have kept an eye on them coming and going to school, but this is much more than I anticipated. I do have work to do, you know? This is outside my area. I'm not even supposed to be in this part of Dublin. So, you know, I don't think…'

'They're playing truant?' Tomas almost sang the words. 'Isn't that something? Can't you report them for that?'

There was a pause, during which Norbert Clarke may have been changing position.

'I *could* report them. But, you know, it might be better if we keep that one in reserve. Now we have something to threaten them with, do you see?'

Tomas hmmed. 'Yes. OK. One other thing. Yesterday you said there was something familiar about this. Have you had any other thoughts?'

Norbert made an uneasy noise. 'You know, I wish I hadn't said that, I shouldn't have. It was just a feeling, you know, whatdoyacallit, déjà vu. It was nothing, I'm sorry.'

'Oh.'

They exchanged stiff pleasantries and hung up, the inconvenience to Norbert successfully dodged. Tomas drummed his fingers on his phone, one eye closed. Useless. Keeping something back?

No, no. Don't get paranoid.

'All right?'

Eli held up a steaming cup of tea. Tomas accepted it with a nod.

There was more colour in Eli's face now. He had combed his hair.

'That went well, didn't it?' Eli breathed the words cautiously, as if saying them out loud might make the facts cease to exist.

'Yes. Yes it did.'

Eli winked, wiggled his shoulders. 'Knew it would. Knew you'd get things sorted, mate.' He lightly nudged Tomas. 'Oh look, here comes your bird.'

Eli moved off as Karin swaggered towards him, swigging from a small bottle of Ballygowan. The shoulders of the plaid overcoat were covered with a protective plastic bib. It gave her a nunish air.

Tomas found himself tempted to smile, but before he could speak with his leading actress, Jack Forde had weaved into his field of vision. There was a light coat of sweat on his forehead and his eyes were hypnotically bulbous through bottle-top glasses.

'Er, sorry,' muttered the eyes.

'Jack, how's everything going?'

Jack quickly glanced to each side, as if there was a possibility they were being watched.

'Er, er. I heard. What they did.'

'Yes.'

'To your daughter.'

'Yes.'

'Fuckers. Cunts. Fuckers.' Jack coughed up the words. Tomas made his neutral face. Jack rubbed his nose vigorously, glanced around again, then leaned in closer. He kept moving his hands, apparently undecided as to what to do with them. He spoke to Tomas's feet.

'The thing is, the thing is that they are let away with it, all the time. Do what they like. Running fucking riot all over the place. You know, we go to school and college and work hard. You know, we don't deserve this. If these fuckers don't want to contribute, they should fuck off. Eastern Europe or something. My brother-in-law, now, has a juice bar in town. Worked his arse off, but then these little…bastards, young fellas, start coming in, ruining his business.'

He paused, slightly breathless now. A tiny glob of moisture dangled perilously from the tip of his nose.

'But he got a few blokes, do you know what I mean? And he sorted them out, do you know what I mean? Problem solved.' Jack Forde grabbed Tomas's forearm and urgently crushed it. 'If you have any more hassle and you want to do something, you know? Just ask, you know?'

The scriptwriter looked directly at Tomas now, their faces only inches apart. Jack's breath carried a hint of chocolate.

'The good people have to fight back, you know?'

Delivering one last numbing squeeze, Jack scrambled away.

Karin, having paused, now approached. She jerked her thumb towards the retreating Jack. 'He looks agitated.'

Tomas swayed his head. 'He's a writer. They can be earnest.'

Karin now moved her still-outstretched thumb in the direction of where the scene had just been shot. 'So how was that?' The question sounded rhetorical.

'Couldn't have asked for more.' He glanced at his watch. 'Listen Karin, sorry. I just need to make a quick call. Sorry about this. Won't take a minute.'

He walked away, leaving Karin to pose where she was, a hand cocked on one hip, the other to lift the water bottle to her mouth. She shook her head occasionally to get rid of the stray hair flapping into her eyes. She had, Tomas observed, the ability to look comfortable wherever she was, to give the appearance of belonging. Acting has its uses.

Digging in his baggy trouser pocket, he extracted the slip of paper on which he had scrawled a number and the words *Holy Family School*. He dialled the number, then said, Yes. I thought you might like to know that some boys from your school are playing truant today.

*

CHRIST, EVEN the school isn't interested. But why be surprised?

He had to repeat the names several times and reassure the phlegmy-sounding woman on the other end that yes, he was sure they weren't sick or at some family function, and yes, he would give his name, and finally, after all that, she sighed – *sighed* – long and mournfully, as if she had so many other, better things to be doing today, like writing an opera or going on that once-in-a-lifetime holiday.

He let the irritation curl in his stomach. Supposed to be at school. And a school, any school, even one in a – oh, God – *disadvantaged* area should take truancy seriously. No excuses. No wonder they are the way they are.

Tomas knew why he had done it: simple spite, an act of unpasteurised revenge which would probably antagonise them even more. Still, done now – we'll see, we'll see.

And after the annoyance melted, Tomas felt better – better than better. The commission and execution of the phone call was gloriously energising, not just for him, but for the whole cast and crew, for the gliding sky which glowed an almost metallic blue, a vast screen before which Karin performed her poignant little walks.

The good people are fighting back.

He even made jokes, standing petrified-still so as not to distract Joe the cameraman; shouting over to Jack the scriptwriter (skulking tall at the edges of the crowd, glasses still slipping down his nose) that this walking scene had the best dialogue in the film. He lit another cigar, an unheard-of development for Tomas. He pointed, he smiled, he waved.

He continued to smile even after he first saw her. For a few seconds, while he recalled the string of events which meant she shouldn't be here now, which made her, perhaps, a ghost from the future or the past, haunting his film set.

Tomas looked away, then back, a cartoon double-take; his face grave now, hers showing the tiniest smirk. She moved her lips.

'Hello, Tomas,' said Marta.

*

SOME OF this crew had worked on Tomas Dalton films before and knew her. She had already exchanged several hellos and waves before swapping air kisses with Eli. She looked slightly flushed and pleased by the time Tomas came over, his face wriggling between puzzlement and annoyance. Marta was Jackie O-smart: the skirt with matching jacket, discreetly fitted to her small, neat body; the rectangular handbag held in front; the hair bob length, but scooped behind the ears, showing off her pixie face.

'Looking great, doll,' Eli slurred.

'Thank you, Eli. How are you?' Marta liked to speak evenly, her voice rarely succumbing to any slip of emotion. Like a 1950s announcer. This is the BBC.

'Never better, film is sweet as a nut. You're old man's doing a bang-up job, as usual.' He pointed and winked at Tomas. 'And now he's here. I'll be off.'

More air kisses. Vague promises of dinner. Marta turned and appraised her ex-husband.

'Hello, Tomas.'

'Hello.'

He said nothing more. Neither did she. It was up to Tomas to guess. He sighed, looked around.

'What are you doing here?'

'I've come to see how you are, Tomas.'

The words arrived with regretful finality, as a summons server might speak; as if, despite their divorce, she had retained the right to inspect and judge his condition at any time of her choosing. A great power, but not one she took any pleasure in employing. His fault she was here.

Tomas considered how best to reply – not something to put him in a good light or even to sell the idea that he was more balanced and happy than she

– but something simple and nasty, designed to wound. He could just walk off, leave her there. No; silly to ignore a person when they are only feet away; juvenile. Best to be insulting.

I don't love you any more might work, though Tomas wasn't sure if this was actually true or not. He wasn't sure if he loved anyone or felt anything. Strange internal deadness. When did that start? *Our marriage is over, Marta.* Could do it.

Tomas glanced at his watch. Just after four. Have to ring Norbert.

'Look, our marriage…'

'Hi there!'

Karin stood with a hand on each hip, the plaid coat now unbuttoned and spread back. Underneath she wore a black dress which showed off her boniness and contained too much glitter for this time of day. Most of the thick make-up had been scraped off, but some remained in the folds of her face, making her appear older and dotty. She shot out a hand, like a tiger showing its claws.

'Karin Goldman.'

Marta took the hand loosely. 'I'm Marta Dalton.'

'You still use his name?'

'Yes, I do.' Marta half-smirked, as if the question was ridiculous.

Hands still on her hips, Karin stared back. 'Yeah, well. I just heard you arrived. The director's wife is here. That's what I heard. Amazing how quickly *everyone* knew about it.'

'Yes,' said Marta, her voice still a crystal lake. This is the BBC. 'Well, a lot of the people here would know me from previous productions Tomas has worked on, going back, oh, years and years in some cases.'

She smiled, as if Karin would enjoy learning this. She scooped a hair back into place. Karin rotated her face towards Tomas.

'You weren't going to tell me? Wifey-poo is on the way back and you weren't going to let me know? Christ, Tomas, I thought you were different. I thought you were a *man*.'

Tomas remained silent.

Karin leaned into him, as if confiding a great secret. 'But what are you? You're the same as every other pathetic guy. Oh, you hate 'em for a few months, but as soon as the apartment gets dirty or you get hungry or horny…' She whipped her head around, squinted down at Marta. 'Well, maybe not horny.'

Marta's right cheekbone shuddered.

Karin let her arms fall, her body slouched. 'Look, Tomas, I'm not gonna give you a hard time. I'm too old. And I thought you would have been too old for lies and bullshit. I'm disappointed, that's all.' She put a hand to her face, breathed deeply. 'I mean – last night I hold you in my arms while you cry like a puppy. And now?' She gestured towards Marta, as if asking her to provide an explanation. Marta remained still.

'Well, actually, Karin,' Thomas started, mildly surprised that he was speaking at all.

She swooped a flat hand in front of his face. 'Please, Tomas, please. You'll embarrass us all. I've said too much already. I wish I hadn't come over here. I wish I could have stood by and bitten my lip like some classy English-woman. But I can't. I'm white American trash. It's my fate to be trash and lie down with trash and have trash shoved down my throat.'

'Karin.'

She marched off, cutting straight through the zig-zagging crowd.

Tomas watched her for a moment, then looked back towards Marta.

'So,' she said. 'Are you finished work for the day now?'

*

IT STRUCK Tomas that he might actually hate her now, sitting beside him in the car, sweeping her head back and forth like some sort of robot assessing the terrain.

Just got in; didn't even ask.

She wasn't speaking because he wasn't, because through silence she could maintain that he was in a childish huff. Don't blame me if your girlfriend became angry. I didn't even know you had one. I came over to see how you are. Because I am worried, Tomas. This isn't like you. See how angry you are? You need help. You do.

Simply by showing up, Marta had said her piece.

Tomas wrenched a mobile phone from his pocket and poked the keyboard with his thumb. But it was new and unfamiliar (Eli had organised it after Tomas claimed the old one had gone missing), so it took a few attempts to get the number right. Marta watched.

'Isn't that illegal? Shouldn't you use a hands-free kit?'

This, he ignored.

Norbert Clarke answered on the third ring. He sounded breathless and agitated.

'Now *that* was an interesting afternoon.'

'Really?'

Norbert stuttered slightly. 'Well, actually it was quite boring, most of the time. After the arcade they went back into Burger King, then they bought cigarettes and strolled around. At about three they got the bus home. But when they got off the bus, the tall one – Doyle – got a phone call.'

'Yes, yes.'

'Whatever that call was about, it seemed to get Doyle quite excited. Did a lot of shouting, and even from the distance I was at, quite a bit of swearing.'

'So who was it?'

'No idea.' There was a smile in Norbert's voice.

Tomas imagined Norbert's pink face, animated by the zing of doing real police work for a change. The fat kid, finally allowed to play on the first team.

'Anyway,' Norbert continued, 'once the call was over the boys changed direction – they *were* going home – and headed for your house.'

'Jesus.'

He felt Marta sit forward. They were a couple of minutes away from Bass Avenue.

'So I think this call may have had something to do with you. I don't know.'

'And?'

'And I followed them. Now don't worry, they definitely didn't go in. But I think they must be getting into your house from the back. Miss Switzer, you know, your neighbour in number 16?'

'I've seen her. She doesn't say anything.'

'No, no. That's true. Anyway, Miss Switzer has a side gate which leads to the back garden. I saw them jumping over the gate.'

'So what did you do?'

'I followed, of course. That's trespass. I made a lot of noise and they legged it home. That was two hours ago and they've been there ever since.'

'Little bastards.'

Marta was staring at him now. Norbert took an apologetic tone.

'Now I know you've been hearing this a lot, but it's pointless arresting them just for trespass. At their age it's a minor offence, probation. What we want to get them for is breaking in and malicious damage. Now we have some idea how they are doing it, I think we could catch them.'

'Good. That's good.' He felt like Norbert's boss, praising him for his hard work, giving him tips on how to crack the big case.

Can't depend on this fool to protect the house; it will overwhelm him.

They agreed to talk later.

'Was that about these boys?' Marta asked.

'A garda followed them today. They tried to break in again but he chased them off.'

'My lord.'

They pulled up in front of the house, gravel crunching like breakfast cereal under the Saab's tyres. On the far side of the street, one of the old ladies headed for the shops. She held hands with what at first glance appeared to be a child, but was in fact a middle-aged woman, Downs Syndrome causing her to breathe through her mouth, to twist to the left slightly with each step, to look around Bass Avenue as if it was a wondrous place. Her hand was held greedily by the older woman, who tottered along dourly, eyes forward, mouth moving with silent mutters.

Marta squinted at number 17. She was careful not to look at any other part of the avenue. Tomas found himself appreciating this, then irritated by his gratitude.

'Nice house,' she said.

Outside, the air had turned chilly. Clouds bulged with threat. Yet Tomas and Marta didn't hurry inside. Tomas had a good look at the gate before touching it, then kicked a banana skin and a discarded packet of Tayto crisps off the pavement. In the yard he carefully examined the windows, then the front door, the handle, the letterbox, the bell. Marta said nothing, standing quietly with her small overnight bag.

Finally, Tomas gestured her inside. She smiled weakly, but still said nothing. He wished she would. She pointed at the bag.

'Where will I put this?'

'Leave it there. I'll bring it up later.'

Anna had slept in the back room upstairs, but had complained about the amount of junk cluttering up the room. Better to do a quick tidy-out. Marta gestured with her head.

'Kitchen this way? I would like a cup of tea.'

She took two steps, then peered back at him.

'You do have tea?'

He closed his eyes, tilted his head. 'If man has no tea in him, he is incapable of understanding truth and beauty.'

'Pardon?'

'Japanese proverb.'

She smirked. 'Your head is still stuffed with trivia, I see. The house too, I have no doubt. *Do* you have tea?'

'Darjeeling? Sencha? Oolong? Earl Grey?'

'Tea bags will be fine.'

The History of Things

'In the cupboard to the right of the window. Sugar is in there as well.'

'Thank you,' she whispered and walked into the kitchen. Tomas had meant to sound snide, but it came out playful. They were both voracious tea-drinkers. For years it had punctuated their at-home days, each in their own study. Breakfast, elevenses, lunch, mid-afternoon, dinner, supper, bedtime, plus one or two other cups produced as a fond surprise or in response to some minor crisis.

'Would you like one?' she called back.

'Yes. Thank you.'

He moved into the lounge and wondered would the tea taste the same now, the way cigarette smokers don't enjoy coffee as much once they have given up.

Tomas assessed the room. Seemed normal. So much of their life together had been calmly arranged. He'd be getting ready for a film or fiddling around on the internet. She'd be preparing her classes or reading some obscure book, meeting every couple of hours for tea and almost-whispered chats about Anna's new flat, or how the flowers on the balcony were doing or the ongoing medical crises of Lobelius, Marta's malevolent cat, now deceased. When did these things become insufficient for Marta? It was so sudden, and still largely unexplained, as if she wasn't entirely sure herself, as if she woke up one morning and forgot why she loved him. Just like that.

Tomas fluffed cushions on the sofa and noticed that the floor could do with a sweep. Bits of white gravel and dust, probably left behind by the glazier. He imagined how much tea he and Marta had consumed over the years – thousands of gallons, sluicing through their systems. He crouched to scoop some of the larger pieces into his hand, then noticed that it was also on the paint-splattered rug. The gravel on the rug, however, seemed to have taken on geometric order: a thin white line, crossing traversely, which might, at a glance, appear to be part of its pattern.

Everyone was surprised at the time. Tomas and Marta? But they seemed so complete, so utterly content with each other. Was it an affair? Illness? Money? That there seemed to be no reason made it baffling; that it was Marta who initiated the break-up transported the news into the realm of the totally astounding. As far as anyone knew, Marta had never made an impulsive decision – as if, because of this lack, Marta had decided to be impulsive. Just once. Just to see what it was like. But having no previous experience of rash actions, she had chosen a course with the most devastating consequences. And being Marta, didn't see any point in not playing out her decision to its natural conclusion. Even Tomas had toyed with this theory.

He sat on his haunches and exhaled. With the care of a bomb disposal expert, he leaned his face in as far as he dared, so close that his breath dislodged some of the smaller pieces. Hundreds of them, carefully ground down and set in a line, a miniature army crossing a rectangular world.

He stood, breathless suddenly, heart clanking.

Think, think, think. The side table, the Pearse book. Back wall: five frames. Two watercolours. Picture of Anna in school play. Braces. 1916 Proclamation. Bookshelves. Wireless. Bolts. Bullets. Mantelpiece. Movie poster.

'Where did you say the sugar was?' Marta called.

Mantelpiece.

'It's OK, I've found it.'

It was gone. Or more precisely, in the way of the physical universe, it had changed form – from chunk of stone, once part of Nelson's Pillar, to worthless dust. To dirt, the enemy of Western life.

There would be more than this. The spiteful logic demanded it. Revenge for the phone call to the school. Shock and awe in your living room. Tomas took two steps onto the rug, dispersing more of the dust. It felt like desecration. Too late now. *The Complete Works of P.H. Pearse*, he saw, was sitting at a slightly awkward angle and required no more than the movement of his hand to completely disintegrate, the unthreaded pages becoming a sudden snowfall which fanned across the room. He took another step, first edition paper crunching beneath his feet.

'It's ready!' Marta called.

The braces within the frame. Still there, but slashed into tatters, possibly with the same knife which had penetrated his daughter's skin. Now it had destroyed the thin echo of his father's working life, decades of sweat and purpose, reduced to scraps of cloth.

Tomas remained still, schooling himself to feel nothing; guilty for doing this. No. Not now. Not with her in the house.

He headed for the kitchen, his feet squashing pages from history, further grinding down the tiny pieces of stone his father had scrambled through O'Connell Street to retrieve more than four decades before. And beneath this, the Persian rug which took a father of nine from Al Hasakah six eye-aching weeks to produce, yet which had given little comfort to its lonely owner, dying in a bombed out hole in Baghdad, her eyes full of light and wonder.

Marta cowered in one corner, arms up as if defending herself against invisible assailants. Tomas quickly looked around, but saw nothing.

'What?'

The History of Things

She pointed. The table. Pot of tea. Two cups. Plate of biscuits. The sugar bowl, contents moving, undulating like a white sea, subject to its own lunar cycle. Tomas squinted. The sugar had clung to the bodies of the ants, their stick limbs swishing in panic, robbed of all purpose by the gigantic world.

'Please,' she hissed. 'Get rid of that.'

10

THE TICKING woke him, though when he sat up and listened, he could barely make out the sound of any of the clocks. Perhaps a dream.

Tomas got out of bed, the floorboards spreading a cold ache against his feet. He went into the bathroom, peed, slugged some water from the tap, then padded to one of the back rooms, jammed with tea chests, stacked, empty frames of various sizes and designs, busts, tripods, black plastic bags, a stack of old records, some of them 78s. The bulb was weak and threw an anaemic glow over everything. It resembled someplace hidden, a tomb or a hidden arms dump.

Carefully, Tomas picked his way through. Why not attack up here? Ran out of time, perhaps, or were disturbed by Norbert. Norbert. *They didn't get in.* Useless. Perhaps they were a decoy, the damage done by someone else. Instructed to run in, run out, confuse the bastards. Who, though, who?

No, silly, paranoid.

Is it?

The boys did exactly what was intended – one act of sacrilege each, plus the ants for good measure. Tomas went to the window and peered down at the yard. Can't be getting in at the back. Windows all screwed down, no sign of anything forced. Changed all the locks. Unless they can pick locks? No. Shit.

He rested on the corner of an overflowing tea chest and examined a long orange beanie baby spread-eagled on top. Anna had collected them for a while, but in some ironic, post-modern way which Tomas hadn't detected at first.

He sighed, a bit more loudly than intended.

Tomas had a mental flash of the boys as Peter Pan-like sprites, impervious to locks or doors, and with the nasty cartoon faces of the witch in *Sleeping Beauty*. Disney understood evil. Marta always said he was a Nazi, like evil is a sort of innocence. Hitler. Stalin. Saddam Hussein. Living out their personal fairy tales.

Has to be a reason, has to be. Even children have motives beyond mischief, even they wouldn't go to all this trouble without some greater purpose in mind.

Has to be.

A sudden gust of wind lightly shook the house, bringing with it a drum roll of rain on the roof.

Is motive relevant now? This is a siege, a test of the will to exist. A week before the removal company can collect. Said they'd come back with a date two days ago; annoying. Oh sorry, I was busy. No one is that busy. Bastards.

Marta, once they calmed down, had produced the expected argument. Let them have it, Tomas. Is it worth it now? After all that's happened? Is it?

He said nothing. She hated the collection, always had. Spent years thinking up objections – not just that it was messy and ate up space; she had *ideological* problems. Tomas was the living embodiment of what Marx identified as the personification of things and the reification of people, a fetish for products where people and things become interchangeable.

Stupid woman. Stupidly clever.

Tomas attempted a smile. Still calm. Yes, you are still in control of this. He padded back to the bedroom and watched the yellow haze from the street light fall across his bed. Marta was so small, you'd hardly know she was in there. She slept on her back, arms folded across her chest, head to the side, mouth slightly open. Even in slumber she was neat. Her breath sounded like air through a seashell.

He shook his head. He looked at the hallway. He peeked out the window, then at his feet, then at the hallway again. He felt separate from himself, like a different version of Tomas Dalton had peeled off and made different decisions, all these people operating within the same space. Finally, he climbed back into bed with his ex-wife.

*

SHE WOKE him with tea, a boiled egg and soldiers.

She sat directly in front, the tray between them, and watched in silence as he dunked a sliver of toast into the yoke. It re-emerged yellow and sloppy, small drips pattering onto the duvet. Marta grimaced at this, but did nothing to clean it up.

'You're not eating?' said Tomas.

'I will. In a while. You have to be up early for your shoot.'

Your shoot. Like this is some hobby.

They both fell silent again, slightly horrified by what was so familiar.

Your house; speak, be in charge.

'How did you sleep?'

'Well, thank you. It's a good solid bed. Where did you buy it?'

'Neals.'

'You didn't buy it here?'

'I didn't want to waste time when I got to Dublin. I had to get straight into work.'

'And what did you do with our old bed?'

'Gave it to the Salvation Army.'

'That's not like you.' Silence again. Marta looked down at her hands. 'That wasn't meant as a judgment, Tomas.'

'I know.'

She looked back up, cracked a half-smile. 'I thought you might like me to stay here today. Keep guard?'

Tomas nodded. Silently, he succumbed to a great rush of relief.

'That is, unless you've decided to get rid of all…this.'

'No, no. Not yet.'

She was like some sort of preacher, trying to coax him into accepting Jesus, armed with that self-gratifying smirk. Oh, you'll come around.

How can she believe that? Especially now, when the loss of so many pieces makes the others that more valuable?

Last night she had seemed to understand. After they had got rid of the ants and cleaned everything out and finally had a cup of tea (neither of them ate; they couldn't), he had shown her Anna's dollhouse and she sang an *ahh* when she saw it, an involuntary gust of air and emotion.

You kept this? All these years? Didn't know you had it. My word.

And he didn't have to tell her why, because she too remembered watching Anna play – she seemed to realise, at least for those few minutes, the agonising decay of everything which he was trying to resist. And when he showed her the toy family inside, and what the boys had done to them, her eyes became wet. She placed a hand on his shoulder.

Oh, Tomas.

It was so easy to go to bed together, almost impolite not to. Slow and undramatic. Everything where they had left it.

While Tomas finished breakfast, Marta cautiously peeked out the bedroom window, like a fugitive worried about snipers. She studied one of the cottages across the street, painted cake-pink. A rusting iron sign announced that the house was named Inisowen.

'Very quiet here,' she said. She was trying to sound calm.

'Yes, it is. I've barely met anyone since I moved in. I think there are lot of elderly people. Retired.'

She looked back. Some strands of mousy hair had escaped from behind her ear. 'Even older than us?'

'Even older than us.'

Tomas and Marta fell silent, united in the shock of time passing.

'You better get up,' she said, 'or you'll be late.'

Tomas nodded, but stayed where he was. 'Today,' he started.

'Yes?' She scooped the hair back into place.

'Be careful not to leave anything unlocked. And you can't afford to leave the house empty. Even for a couple of minutes.'

She placed a hand on her hip, mock-stern. 'Yes, Tomas. I'm aware of that. Now get up. You'll be late.' She went back to the window, then turned again. 'Unless you want me to leave the room?'

*

'CROWLEY INTERNATIONAL Removals?'

The woman chanted the words with a lazy despair. Tomas attempted to drive and keep the phone balanced on his shoulder. Won't hear the end of it from her if there's a crash.

What are you thinking? None of her business.

Hotness spread around his chest and shoulders. He had a sudden urge to yell.

'Is this Keelin?' Tomas said in a moderate voice. 'I spoke before to a Keelin.'

'Yes, this is Keelin.'

Indifferent, even to her own name.

'I'm Tomas Dalton. I was on to you the day before yesterday about moving out and having my house contents put into storage. You'd said—'

'Hang on.' The clicking sounds of a computer keyboard, like a scuttling spider. 'No, no. Nothing here.'

'But I spoke to—'

'Tomas. That T–H?'

'T–O.'

'Right, right. Dorton, is it?'

'Dalton. D–A–L–T–O–N.'

More clicking. 'Ah yes. Tomas Dalton, 17 Bass Avenue?'

'Correct.'

'Well, Mister Dalton, we have no storage space available at the moment. But the situation can change on a daily basis. As soon as storage space becomes available, one of our customer service representatives will contact you.'

'That's what you said to me two days ago.'

'Yes. Well, we have no storage space at the moment. But I can get one of the customer service representatives to call you.'

'But you said two days ago that you would ring me and give a date when you could take my furniture. *You* said a week or so.' He pulled up at a traffic light. The man in the next car was picking his nose and talking back to the radio.

'Well,' said Keelin, 'I don't know about that, Mister Dalton, but there is no storage available at the moment. But I'm sure one of our customer service representatives—'

'So do you have any idea when some space might become free?'

'Well, I don't directly deal with that. The customer service representatives—'

'So you have no idea when storage will become available, and when you said it would be a week you were just plucking a figure out of the air.'

'I didn't say a week, Mister Dalton.'

'So I'm making this up? I spend my time ringing up removal companies to accuse them of saying things they didn't say for some sort of perverse thrill? You specifically said a week because I pressed upon you how urgently I wanted the job done. You specifically said you would ring me back within twenty-four hours to give a definite date.'

Tomas was sweating. It grew along his back like a swelling jellyfish. Doing that a lot.

'Mister Dalton, I don't know who you were talking to, but I definitely didn't say that.'

'I was there, you know! I was involved in the conversation! My memory hasn't deteriorated to such a degree that I can't remember conversations I had two days ago. You probably have dozens of conversations like this but I only had one, so – excuse me – but I think I have a better chance of remembering what was said than you do.'

'Mister Dalton, I couldn't have said that because it's not my job. That would be the job of a customer service representative.'

'Will you stop fucking saying that!' He was screaming now. Holding the phone directly in front, not looking at the road, spittle and howls flying from his mouth.

'Will. You. Stop. Fucking. Saying. That! Will you? Will you?'

Keelin didn't answer. She had already hung up.

*

FUNNY, SHOULD be dreading this. Looking to calm everyone down, avoid her resentment.

Yet now he hoped she would come over, try to make a scene, relying for her power on the assumption that he would wish anything but that.

Give her the fright of her fucking life.

Not like you, all this.

When Tomas arrived at the shoot he didn't, as was his habit, get himself a mug of tea and amiably gossip with whoever he met. Instead he paced about like a boiling prisoner, challenging the gaze of anyone who looked his way, making sure to place himself directly in *her* line of sight. She sensed it too, cleverly effecting blindness, turning this way and that at just the right moment, even dropped a scarf and part of her script to avoid looking. She was rescued then by the arrival of Albert Kennedy, arms outstretched as if he was about to pick her up. Like a tour guide, Albert gestured to the cloudless sky, to a group of electricians, to a pigeon waddling along the pavement, his mouth constantly moving, Karin's smile carefully fixed. A few feet away, Marion also listened to Albert, her body bent forward slightly, suggesting a supplicant at prayer. Marion kept her eyes fixed on Albert. Karin followed Albert's sweeping hands. The actor glanced back and forth between the two women, and then upwards, to let imaginary theatre lights create a sparkle in his eyes.

I know what you're doing! Not looking at me!

Shout it out, that would fix her. Insane even to consider it.

The crew scampered around. They nodded at Tomas, but seemed reluctant to chat, as they normally would, as if the arrival of Marta (which of course they all knew about) was an event so cataclysmic they wouldn't be able to resist mentioning it – there was nothing else. Having an affair with Karin Goldman and then the wife turns up. Time and history slammed to a stop. Tomas shook his head, letting them see his displeasure. Not just Karin or the little thugs – Marta pissing smugness all over the house. Few humps into her scrawny pelvis and everything is all right now, is it? (How could you?) And that droning half-wit on the phone and the mongoloid police and the ugly neighbours, the chisel-eyed citizens of Dublin; a conspiracy of annoyance.

To his left he saw Conor and David, slouched against the catering truck, Conor wearing three days' worth of beard and cowboys boots with a two-inch heel. He rubbed his hair, stretched, then shook his head furiously at whatever David was saying, his spittle-covered lips only inches from Conor's ear. David's acne seemed to be more pronounced today, glowing slightly against his white skin. Conor turned to look at his friend and for a few moments they shared a look filled with flirtation and hatred. Both men smiled, then Conor grimaced. Conor said something, shaking his head again. After a speedy glance around, David reached for Conor's free hand, but this was smacked away.

Don't want to know about that. Just keep your pants on at work, chaps.

Standing alone, like a tree amidst the milling film workers, Jack Forde stared directly at Tomas, not at all embarrassed that he had been caught watching his director. Jack waved as if they shared a secret. Tomas returned the thinnest of smiles.

Nutcase. Never employ him again. Employ? Ha.

'Morning, mate.' Eli clasped and unclasped his fingers, as if embarrassed about his hands. He spoke softly, as one might at a funeral or an execution, while addressing relatives of the condemned.

'So let's hear it then.'

Taken aback by this directness, Eli glanced about. He leaned into Tomas. His skin was so pale it almost gleamed. 'Well, you can imagine it, can't you? Went bleeding mad, she did, when Marta showed up. Not that the bloody cow would admit it. After you went she had a go at Conor, for fuck's sake. Hasn't even done a scene with him yet and she's saying her leading man can't act and keeps missing his cues and he's ugly. She's saying he's ugly. Fuck's sake, I know which one I'd rather shag.' Eli shook his head and lit a cigarette.

'So it took me ages last night to calm all that down. You're at home with your fucking legs up and I'm trying to stop your female fans from going apeshit. Anyway, eventually she admits that Marta pissed her off. So I told her, I did – I said Tomas was just as shocked as you were when she showed up. But she wouldn't take that from me – all you boys stick together, you know, all that stuff. The right hump. Haven't talked to her this morning. Couldn't face it. Bloody hell, she goes on, don't she?'

Tomas nodded. 'Yes, she does.'

'Look, mate. I don't want to pry. But what's going on?'

Tomas shrugged the question away, as if it had been asked dozens of times before. He scanned around for Karin, so he could hate her as he spoke. But she'd disappeared into the make-up caravan.

'Nothing is going on. With either of them. Karin – you know – is indulging in some fantasy relationship with me. Marta turned up because of what happened to Anna, because of these boys. She's worried about me, she says.'

Eli squinted through his cigarette smoke, but said nothing.

'I know what it is. Marta thinks – hopes – I've lost it. Having some sort of breakdown.' Tomas went to sip his tea, then halted. 'Plus, she also seems to want me back. Well, that would have to involve her admitting that she made a mistake in the first place, which of course she'll *never* do. So she wants me back as long as we pretend that the divorce was somehow *my* fault.' Tomas attempted a derisive laugh, but it came out squeaky. He slugged on his tea, which was slightly too hot. 'I suppose you want me to talk to Karin.'

Eli moved his shoulders to indicate their collective powerlessness in this situation. 'Sorry, mate. I know it's not your fault and that, but you're the man. I thought she did some nice work yesterday, you know? And I think she did it because she wanted to please you. If she's pissed off with you…well, you know. The whole thing could go belly up.'

'Yes, I know,' said Tomas, his voice not indicating if he felt going belly up would be a bad thing or not.

'So mate, be fucking ruthless. Got to be now. Know what I mean? Tell her what she wants to hear. Tell her you love her and that you'll marry her when this is all over. Just get her back onside again. Keep her sweet for the next month and we'll never have to see the crazy mare again.'

'Except if we win an Oscar.'

For a moment, Eli attempted to consider this as a real possibility. He crinkled his mouth and made a *hmm* sound, but this pose lasted no more than a few seconds. One glance at Tomas's red face and he too began to smile, then cackle loudly, the two of them roaring with a loony mirth as the busy production staff carefully moved around.

*

SHE STARED rigidly at a floral arrangement of make-up brushes. Silly. Comical, what people do. Tomas wanted to laugh about it – he wanted Karin to do the same, as if they had jolted forward in time and he'd said his piece and she'd accepted it and everything was fine again.

The make-up woman looked between them.

She knows all about it.

'I'll just go for a quick fag.'

'You will not.' Karin's lips barely moved as she spoke. 'You will stay here and finish your work.'

The young woman froze. She glanced pleadingly at Tomas.

'Peg, isn't it?' he said. She nodded. 'Go and have your cigarette, Peg. We won't be long.'

'You will stay here, Peg, and finish your work or I swear to God…'

Peg took a step, then froze again, as if operated by a remote control which Karin and Tomas were squabbling over. He beckoned towards the door.

'Go, Peg.'

'She is my make-up artist.'

This was addressed to Tomas.

'But she is my employee, Karin. I pay her wages, so she is obliged to do what I say or she won't get any wages. She has no choice. She has to get out.'

'Oh, that's the way it is, is it? Suddenly we're Mister Big Muscles?'

He wanted to smile again. She'd be embarrassed about saying that. Mister Big Muscles? Is that what I said?

'It is simply a fact.'

With Karin distracted, Tomas nodded towards Peg, who gratefully slid out of the Winnebago. He shut and locked the door behind her. Almost immediately, Karin stood, the large plastic bib again covering her plaid coat. Without much make-up, her skin was creamy and surprisingly smooth, her hair scraped back into a loose bun. It revealed the healthy young girl she had grown from. Playing catch. Riding on her bicycle. Wondering what Mom had done to Daddy to make him go away.

'Please excuse me.' She reached out towards the door.

'No.'

Karin retracted the hand and blinked up at him. 'You are going to *prevent* me from leaving?'

'If I have to.' Tomas found himself ambushed by a tingle of exhilaration. Such a movie cliché. Hero forces dizzy-headed girl to face her feelings. What film? Something with Cary Grant?

She closed her eyes, sighed, opened them again. She addressed her words to Tomas's chest. 'If you don't move out of my way this instant, then I'm off the project. I'm gone. Tomas, I'm serious. No more film and you are Eli are in the hole for a few million bucks.'

He folded his arms and leaned back against the door. His fringe flopped over one eye. 'Don't care. I don't care about the film, Karin. I came here to talk to you. Not as the director. As Tomas. You know, the man you've been, whatever you want to call it.'

Karin tipped her head to one side. Tomas pointed. 'Would you please sit down? This won't take long. Then you can do what you like.'

Slowly, she retreated to her chair.

'Let me tell you something about my divorce. Marta left me, not the other way around. It was very sudden, very unexpected. I didn't drink or hit her or have women on the side. We never rowed. We got on rather well, I thought. A little boring, perhaps, but I thought we were both happy. We gave each other room to pursue our own interests and we met in the middle. But then one day she announced that was it, and she left. I'm still not entirely sure why. She said I kept things from her, that I shut her out.'

He put a hand to his forehead, as if momentarily confused.

'Anyway,' he continued, 'that's not my point. My point is I had to get over that. I had to make a new life for myself. I spent the best part of a year in the flat I used to share with Marta, and then I decided – quite rationally, I felt, and after a good deal of thought – to move back to Dublin, specifically to the area where I grew up.'

'Tomas, I know all this.' She grimaced, as if pained or embarrassed.

'No, no, no.' His face grew red. 'You don't know all this. What I'm saying to you, Karin, is that I worked hard at getting over my wife. I was over my wife – I *am* over my wife. So I don't want you thinking for *one moment* that I was in any way pleased when Marta showed up here yesterday.'

'Really?'

The hand was under the chin now in a poor attempt at ironic distance. Tomas's face grew redder.

'Yes, really! I didn't want Marta to show up here, I didn't ask her to. I brought her to my house because I was married to the woman and because she is the mother of my child, but I didn't want her here. I want her to go home as soon as possible.'

'Do you really expect me to buy this?'

'Did you ever think for a moment to ask me? You couldn't wait for it to be a disaster, could you? For me to be some sort of playboy? I'm not one of your husbands. Or any other man you've met, by the sound of things. I'm sorry to disappoint you, Karin, but I haven't told you any lies and I don't have any secret problems. I am actually the man I appear to be.'

Tomas realised he was screaming these words; even the busy clatter outside seemed to fall back obediently. Suddenly they were both aware of a silence that compacted around, that connected them like twins in amniotic fluid. Karin opened her mouth, then shut it again. Tomas put up his hands, his eyes glassy. He whispered, as if talking to himself.

'I know a lot of men go back to their wives, but I don't intend to. In fact, even as I say this I realise *how much* I don't want to go back to Marta. She arrived here, Karin, completely unbidden by me, pretending to be worried because of what happened with Anna. She's the one who wants to get back together. She had her mid-life crisis and made the only impulsive decision of her life and now she wants to have boring Tomas back again. But it's not going to happen. Do you understand, Karin?'

She stood up, but didn't reply. Tomas jerked a thumb over his left shoulder. 'She's at home now, but only because I need someone to guard the house for me.'

Karin dipped an eyebrow. 'So you're using her to house-sit? Your wife flies from London to win you back and you use her to house-sit?'

Tomas slumped into a chair. 'I had no choice. If there isn't someone there, those boys will just destroy everything. I'm under siege. You saw what they did.'

Karin made a noise, as if not entirely convinced. Yet she remained where she was. Tomas looked at the floor. He felt he was spinning and didn't want to move until the sensation stopped.

'So that's it?'

'That's it. What I wanted to say.'

'Well, Tomas, if what you say is true, then you should go home and tell Marta. I mean, it's kinda weird to be using her to guard your house.' Karin looked at her hands. 'Look, this is my fault too. I know I came on a bit strong.

I dunno why. That time we met before, the first time I mean? At the BAFTA thing? Christ, that was four years ago, and I know this sounds a bit crazy, Tomas, but…there was just something about it that stayed with me. I know we only talked for twenty minutes or so. I can't even remember what we talked about…'

'The Old Town Bar in Manhattan. We talked about that.'

She smiled.

'And Madrid. You told me about Madrid.'

She gently fingered the make-up brushes. 'Look, thank you for telling me this. For going to this trouble.'

'Which means what, exactly?'

'Which means I will think about what you said, Tomas. Just give me a little time.'

'OK.'

She straightened up, looked at her watch. 'It's getting late. I'll go get a cup of coffee and find Peg. You take a moment and then we'll get back to work. Deal?'

'Deal.'

As she opened the door of the caravan, she lightly brushed her fingers against his right cheek. Then she was gone. Yet it felt as if she had imprinted the air molecules around her, left a shape, a jumble of views of Karin from different perspectives, like a cubist painting. They crowded in on Tomas as he fought to catch his breath.

*

HE COULD imagine Marta taking tiny peeks out that bedroom window, pulling a cardigan around herself, even though it's not cold, mentally baking in the silence. The boys close by, sitting in a primitive huddle, craning to watch her, scratching, shoving each other, picking their noses and flicking it at the pavement.

Energising, this. Adrenaline, must be. Satisfaction like revenge. Someone else finally knows what it's like, trapped in that house, hearing nothing, seeing nothing, as if the place is subject to gaps in space and time, like drop-out on video tape. Moments and events which, through some galactic technical error, fail to take place. Babies not born. Wars never won.

She answered on the second ring, her voice small yet deliberately solid.

'Yes, yes. It's been very quiet for most of the morning. Very quiet. Didn't see a postman or a milkman, even.'

This was animated for her, as if she had just regained her voice and found pleasure in using it.

'And no sign of the boys?'

'Hmmm. Well, no visual sign, if you like. But just a few minutes ago there were a few phone calls. I thought you were another one.'

'What did they say?'

'Oh, nothing to be alarmed about. Schoolboyish obscenities.' She stuttered slightly. 'In fact, I think they were in school. I heard what sounded like a playground. I just hung up. Didn't say anything.'

'Good, good.'

He heard Marta inhale deeply. 'It is…rather *disturbing*, I must admit. Should I ring the police?'

'Well, you can if it would make you feel better. But to be honest…'

'Yes, yes.'

At school, safe for another few hours. End the shoot early. Be there before they get out. Tomas tried to sound jaunty. 'So that's it. Did you do anything else? Talk to anyone?'

'Read a little. That's all.'

'Didn't talk to Anna?'

'Oh yes, I did. Of course. Naturally.'

Naturally. When Anna was seventeen she became pregnant by the son of the Jewish cardiologist who lived three doors down. This, Tomas presumed, was before she became a fully fledged lesbian. Or perhaps not. Tomas didn't know because he had never spoken to Anna about it. Marta had strictly forbidden him to, and he – wishing to be told how to react – had complied. According to Marta, Anna had cried for several hours, which wasn't like her. Marta made a few phone calls, and the next day they went to a clinic in Shepherd's Bush for the termination. Tomas had been on a shoot in Vienna when all this took place, so by the time he arrived home everything was back to normal, the whole unfortunate episode apparently forgotten and unspoken about. Marta told him about it as if the abortion had happened months, even years before. Tomas asked was there anything he could do? Buy her flowers? Give her money for a shopping spree?

No, nothing, said Marta. Anything like that would only upset her again, so what's the point? It's a mother–daughter issue, Tomas. I'm afraid you can't be involved in this one. And would you want to? Really?

Tomas had said nothing. He would have dreaded talking to Anna about her abortion. Yet still.

'Right, better go,' Tomas said. He wanted to scream into the phone. *You stole my daughter, you bitch.*

*

TOMAS FELT a delicate boom of power as he put the car into fourth gear. He was surprised by the words which had charged out of his mouth. Liked himself. Liked Karin's face, too: that's how to film it – risky, but she could do it, you know, she could actually act. (Unlike a lot of dumb fuckers over the years. Think posing is the same as acting; think pretty means talent.) Anyway, anyway, the whole thing with the camera parked on Tomas's shoulder so all we see is her face, her hurt, her attempts at sarcasm, her surprise when he explodes, the tenderness which eventually emerges. (My God, when she stroked your cheek there was something, you know, down there.) Only her face, yet really it's about you, you changing, morphing into a different beast. A man, for a change.

Changing too fast to keep up; giddy – like a first motorbike ride, when was that? Had it happened? Ever?

Said things to Karin, perhaps too many. Yet, yet – now come on, own up – still enjoyed it; *playing* at having an affair. You acted too. Could have acted, professionally – older roles, executives, presidents; people have said; lots of people. All your own hair and teeth, not much of a belly.

Stop. Now – first things.

Get rid of Marta. Tomorrow, though, no one else to mind the house – another night? No, can't do that, too much. Decision, good.

On the car radio, a woman with a squeaky voice was using words. Acceptance. Self-development. Self-esteem. I'm a very spiritual person.

Nice, making decisions, good, firm decisions – ring Eli, get someone to mind the place, or ring Norbert again? Should do it, bit excited, playing at cops and robbers.

But what use? Boys fooled him.

Validating. Nurturing. Life experience. You have nothing to fear but fear itself.

'For fuck's sake.' Like that phrase. Never used it before.

But then the fear can become a fear of fear, said the woman. A bored-sounding man gave out a phone number.

Tomas thumped the dashboard. Oh, Marta, I will separate the smug look from your face. He pulled into Bass Avenue and imagined it from high above.

Camera on a jib – the Saab sparkling in the blustery sunlight as he pulled in behind the police car parked in front of his house. The rooftops gleaming, newly painted, arcing off to infinity and bedecked with rows of cherubim and seraphim blowing loud and true on their long golden trumpets to welcome the conquering Cary Grant back to his castle where no one can defeat him.

Should shout at her. Be abusive.

From the high crane shot, Tomas saw himself laughing, slapping the dashboard of the Saab.

You're acting very strangely. Very, very strangely.

11

'**WHAT? WHAT** is it?'

Marta and Sergeant Gréagóir O'Duinnshleibhe had sat up guiltily when he arrived. Thought I didn't notice; think they're clever.

Marta smiled. 'Nothing, really.'

Tomas began examining the walls of the living room.

Marta opened up her voice, as if speaking to a deaf person. 'This is Sergeant O…I'm terribly sorry, Sergeant, but I can't pronounce your name.'

The sergeant's pale head creased into a grin of satisfaction. His tongue peeked out from between purple lips.

'No worries. O'Duinnshleibhe. 'Tis a hard one to get the tongue around if you don't have any Irish.' He grinned again.

Tomas, peering at the far wall, muttered, 'The Irish are a fair people. They never speak well of one another.'

Gréagóir O'Duinnshleibhe nodded slightly, as if he had heard this before, then turned back to Marta. 'But as I told you, Mrs Dalton, I already met your husband.' He held up his black notebook. 'I took a lot of details at the time.'

The policeman swivelled his head to find Tomas, now studying the front window. 'Your wife tells me you've been getting more abusive phone calls. I'm afraid I made her blush by getting her to repeat some offensive terms.'

He grinned again, perhaps mildly titillated. Tomas turned to face them now. The sergeant seemed to be wearing the same clothes as last time, the same black notebook perched on his knee, a half-drunk glass of water. Yet today he seemed decidedly jolly, what with getting Mrs Dalton to blush and, better yet, getting to *meet* Mrs Dalton and use words like *husband* and *wife* in what was previously a broken home. Tomas's lounge bathed in the newly won approval of Sergeant Gréagóir O'Duinnshleibhe. Tomas glared at Marta.

'My *wife*? Really?'

Sergeant Gréagóir O'Duinnshleibhe produced a large brown envelope. 'So it's as well I called in, though from what your wife says, she was thinking of giving us a ring anyway.' He turned to Marta. 'Which I would recommend you do in future. And right away.' Now to Tomas: 'I have here the statement I took from you the other day. You could give it a look over and sign if you agree with its contents.'

Tomas stared at Marta long enough to make her shift uncomfortably on the couch. Hands in his pockets, he shrugged. The sergeant cocked his head.

'Is there something wrong?' He seemed to shout everything. Perhaps a bit deaf. 'Do you have something to add?'

Tomas shrugged again. 'No. Not at all. I simply think it's pointless. They are going to get away with it anyway. That's my statement.'

Marta produced a dark frown. Sergeant Gréagóir O'Duinnshleibhe's face grew slightly flushed. He shook his head, as if he was worried by flying insects.

'Indeed, and it is not pointless.' With a surprising grace, the sergeant got up from the couch. He contracted his brow and pointed at the brown paper envelope. Despite his bulk, he was distinctly unthreatening.

'Documents like this, Sir, are the way the law operates. Now I know you've been resident in the United Kingdom for some time and you may have forgotten the way things work in this jurisdiction.' He turned to Marta. 'No offence, now, Ma'am.'

She waved this away.

Tomas smirked. *Ma'am?* Curiously old-fashioned. Victorian. Would he call an Irish woman *Ma'am*? Pathetic. The twenty-first century and still kow-towing to the Brits. Maria Edgeworth. What was the name of that book? Mother loved it, of course. Paddy takes over the Big House, in the end.

'But I imagine the law in Britain is not too different to the way it is here, so I must say I'm surprised by your attitude, Mister Dalton. And I would suggest to you that if you took a bit more mind of the law and a bit more mind of officers of the law like myself and my colleague Garda Clarke, then we might not have had so much of the bother. Do you see?'

Tomas grinned drunkenly.

Castle Rackrent.

He looked at the sergeant. 'What are you prattling on about?'

'Tomas!' Marta hissed.

Sergeant Gréagóir O'Duinnshleibhe pursed his lips and shook his head. His face grew even redder. 'Very well, so, I will be more specific.'

Tomas smirked again. Lots of smirking today. Feel like smirking. Funny anyway, lapsing into this quasi-parliamentary language. *Sir* and *I would suggest to you*. And with that culchie accent. Culchie – haven't said it for years.

The sergeant flicked open his notebook and scanned the neat lines of text. 'According to my colleague Garda Clarke, he informed you that the boys in question were playing truant from school. He said he would take no action on this matter, as it might antagonise the situation further. Yet you, knowing this, took it upon yourself to report them.'

'What's this about, Tomas?' Marta said. Both men ignored her.

'Of course I did. They were mitching from school. They shouldn't be. Your attitude seems to be to let them off with whatever they want.'

'Well that certainly is not our attitude. What you don't seem to realise is that Garda Clarke was doing you a favour. He didn't want to annoy the boys' families any more than they were already. Because legally they have the right to demand that we come here and arrest you, Mister Dalton.'

'What?' Marta said.

'As you have admitted, you threatened those boys. You threatened them physically.'

'You *threatened* them?' Marta said.

'Now, while I may understand your frustration, Mister Dalton – and I certainly don't condone what you did – you know the way it looks whenever an adult is arrested in connection with anything to do with children. People jump to the wrong conclusions. And that certainly wouldn't help you, Mister Dalton.'

'Excuse me,' Marta said, now also on her feet. 'But I *am* here and I asked a question.' Neither man spoke, as if admitting to Marta's presence was a concession. 'Tomas, you threatened these children? Is that what started this?'

All in a moderate, civilised tone; even the exchange between himself and the sergeant. Do this hand-held, like one of those American cop shows, darting back and forth between himself and the sergeant, Marta's alarmed little face caught in between. Eli would have a fit. Too bloody avant garde, mate.

'I'll explain it to you later.'

'No, Tomas. Before you make things worse, I think you should explain now.' The words came gently, but in a slightly too-loud tone, the voice for the bewildered old man.

'Will you ever shut up, woman, for fuck's sake, and mind your own business?'

He didn't shout either, delivering the sentence with just the right amount of force, enough to strike Marta silent, for Sergeant Gréagóir O'Duinnshleibhe to quickly decide that he should interfere no further. A perfect volley. Tomas looked back at the garda.

'Well, thank you for your advice. But all you've done is prove what I said at the outset. These boys are systematically destroying my home yet it is I who seems to be getting into trouble. No, I won't be signing that statement. Now I think you should leave what remains of my house.'

Sergeant O'Duinnshleibhe had already placed his notebook back in the inside pocket of his jacket. He nodded solemnly. 'That's your decision, Mister Dalton. I'll say no more other than we will be keeping an eye on things. If the law is broken, we will intervene.'

'The law has already been broken, and you've done exactly nothing.'

The sergeant ignored this. Instead, he pointed at the envelope left on the coffee table.

'It's there if you change your mind. Good day to you, Mister Dalton.' He looked at Marta. 'Mrs Dalton.'

Sergeant O'Duinnshleibhe headed out the front door while Tomas bounced upstairs.

*

HE MOVED slowly from room to room.

System in place now, good – something of comfort. Method in my madness.

Check the edges of the windows.

The door frames.

The match fragments secreted among the black plastic bags and dusty vases. Method, method. A – B – C. Who wrote that book? Silly thing. First chapter contained only words beginning with A. *Africa* something? Stupid idea. Hard enough to write a decent sentence without that. Hard enough to get anyone to read it.

Nothing, nothing. Haven't been. Why? When they can ghost in and out so easily?

He listened. Still. Quiet. Dead as a do-do. Stupid bird. Not a peep from her downstairs. Probably sitting with the lights off. How many Irish mothers does it take to change a light bulb? Don't worry, I'll just sit here in the dark.

He shifted some of the bags around, the plastic crackling like fire, then squatted cross-legged on the floor. The bags stood around him like ancient monoliths erected by some extinct race. Tomas was regularly haunted by the idea that something in his collection was missing, either lost or not yet found. Marta would complain that the apartment was stuffed with rubbish, yet to him their home never felt full enough.

He rustled one of the sacks. Obsession, hmm, mad Tomas, crazy-booby Tomas. Fuck her; better than what she has, and she knows it – here to get me back because me was all she had, really; once she left, well.

Thought me mad for years. Gave her power, or the illusion of – thought she could mediate, filter out anything from the world I wasn't able for – leave him with his toys – that was her blindness. Couldn't see anything transformative. What she didn't get, she labelled odd, simple, weak in the head. Insane. Talk about film, about art, but never felt it, blather about Bergman in that dull voice, the symbology, the character motifs, the references to God and death – those who can do, those who can't – even if this isn't any great shakes, has to be better than her airless existence.

Ever say this?

No.

Never even thought it out loud.

While on holiday once in New York, he had brought Marta to an exhibition of the American surrealist Joseph Cornell, art out of old clay pipes, faded photographs, glass beads, maps, toys, medicine bottles, marbles, plastic ice cubes. Tomas walked behind her, pointing, saying, Look, this is junk too. But it's beautiful. He read her sections from the catalogue. He knew Dali, you know. Yoko Ono was a fan. She went to one of his exhibitions wearing a see-through blouse and bought ten pieces. Not long before his death.

Marta's mouth cranked downwards at the edges.

Probably what killed him.

Days later, on the plane home, she said, Tomas, that exhibition.

Yes? He opened his eyes. Marta liked to talk on planes, finding the uneven engine noise and the threat of terrorism unsettling. Tomas liked to sleep, to escape the boredom and the enforced bodily smells of others.

I found it more enjoyable than I thought I would.

Tomas smiled, but attempted not to look smug.

I did like the pieces made from old toys and junk. Quite affecting, if you think about who owned them previously. Even if it is materialistic and typically American.

Good. I'm glad you get it now.

That's what worries me, Tomas. I don't think you get it. That was in the context of art – they were presented in a certain way, to interface with the viewer. Your collection is just, old things.

Tomas folded his arms. I'm not claiming my collection is art. But I thought you might appreciate the idea that things can be more than just things.

She sat up, her head slightly tipped to the left. She had taken on that eager, clinical stance.

Yes, and I do appreciate that. I'm not debating that possibility at all. But what you are doing with your collection is in no way art. I think it's religious.

Tomas crinkled his brow, not sure whether to smile, not sure if he would like what was coming. Religious?

Yes, in a very primitive way.

Now he smiled. Thank you.

I think you are engaged in some sort of animism. You're investing physical things with a spirit.

Marta, for God's sake.

No, no, wait, Tomas. I'm not finished. What you are doing ties in with your background. It's transubstantiation.

It's what?

Is that not the correct term? For the Roman Catholic rite?

Don't ask me. I haven't been to mass in decades.

But of course he knew. Daddy believes, in a silent, unshowy way. Mother mocks the idea behind Tom Senior's back. Witch doctors. At mass, if Daddy can't hear, she whispers into Tomas's ear. Wait for it now, little Tom, here it comes. See that bit of bread? That's turning into God right now. Can you not see it? Can you not see the spirit of the Lord descending to take residence within the wafer? But he was tiny under the grey, vaulted church and couldn't see anything. Not wanting to lie, he said nothing. Later on, when he realised the sarcasm, he would smile, just to please her.

Transubstantiation is what takes place at the consecration of the host. Marta, still the cleverest girl in the class. Roman Catholics believe it *becomes* the body and blood of Christ.

Yes, yes.

A physical object takes on a spirit, which is a form of animism.

Tomas tried to look bored. So?

So, Tomas. She smiled, as if explaining to a child.

This is what you have been doing, practising a sort of mock-Catholicism. By adding these objects to your collection, you feel you are consecrating them in some way.

Tomas squinted. How do you come up with these theories?

You should think about it. Really.

He put his head back, closed his eyes, patted her on the hand. I will, dear. I'll give it a lot of thought.

She picked up her book.

Tomas wriggled in his seat, to make himself more comfortable before sleep arrived. But he couldn't. He was furious.

Bullshit anyway. Screwed up by atheism, not the other way around. When he was a child, people expected to suffer and die; anything else was a bonus. Now in this godless century, everyone has to ENJOY, ENJOY, ENJOY the few miserable years they have – that's what starts the worry, the gym, the skin cream, the tummy tucks, the mania to cling onto every precious second.

'Christ.' Tomas looked around at the plastic bags, which remained mute and unmoving. 'Christ,' he repeated.

She was downstairs, ears pricked.

Good.

He laughed, as mad-sounding as he could make it.

Tomas was swept with a lightness, a sense that all that was clear and bright and honest about him had separated out from the rest, that the Tomas Dalton he deserved to be now floated above the inferior version cross-legged on the floor.

Such a selfish, oblivious creature. Can't even see why he came back to Ireland – not to start a new life, but to continue the one he already had, this time safe from her interference. He had come here because he thought she wouldn't follow. Alone with his things. That was what he wanted. Not other people. Other people implied relationships, implied the distorted feedback of what they think you are, what they think you should be, an audition for a part he could never get and didn't want.

Both Tomas Daltons laughed.

Other people are vile.

*

MARTA SAT. She didn't move, as if afraid to. Like she had an appointment and the other person was unexpectedly late and she was unsure of what to do now.

Best remain. Can't follow him around the house. *His* house. When he's ready to come out of hiding, then say something.

That man up there. Barely like Tomas. Gone so far. The anger, the bad language, this pugnacious air. Something dark in him. Tenebrous.

Last night he seemed to be coming back to himself. Gentle again, child-like, considerate. Those thick, comforting arms. The old Tomas, before he began all the obsessing on his mother.

Silly girl.

Last night could have been nothing, probably was nothing, part of his mental landslide.

Get him out of this place; get some help. Counselling. Therapy. He might come back to his senses. What little he has left.

Can't stay here all by himself, going crazy. There's nothing for him except the past, and that's long gone. Inconceivable that he can want to remain when there is so much in London. His career, Anna, friends, me. People who know him.

Anything is better than being alone.

Even he must know by now.

She had noticed the photos all over the house. Pictures of just about every-one they knew, yet not one of her. Rather pointed.

Sad that you would notice. At least you didn't say.

When he was out at the shoot, she had a gentle poke around (as he used to say) and found several objects long forgotten about. A leopard-skin bra and knickers which she blushed at the thought of ever owning. A pair of old reading glasses. A flaking copy of *Ways of Seeing* in which she had inscribed *I see nothing but you.*

He remembered.

But this house – the junk seemed to have finally taken over like moss on a wall. And the ghastly street, the whole area. Never liked Dublin. Rural parts are quaint enough, but there's something edgy and mean-spirited about the city, as if it doesn't really believe it's as good as anywhere else. Behind all the glitzy new buildings, it still says, Hey, what are you looking at?

Marta stood up and walked to the kettle. Cup of tea, I suppose. That po-liceman was rather odd too. Pomposity about upholding the law, then brags about bending it. Reminded her of something she saw on the news. In Iraq, after the war – a skull-faced doctor says that medicines are being sold by gov-ernment officials on the black market. One day a child was admitted, seriously ill. The doctor administered out-of-date drugs, having none other. The child died of anaphylactic shock. I'm still guilty, says the doctor. But what choice did I have?

A thump from upstairs, a voice, then the creak of floorboards. Marta quickly studied the kitchen. Sit? Be ready for him? No – go on making tea. Get him out of this horrible, horrible place. Bring him home.

Home was gone. Tomas had given it away, or more accurately, drifted from it.

That is the problem – that will be the problem. You left. You walked out.

But by then there had been nowhere to leave; by then it was the only strategy left. He'd hardly spoken in weeks, crouched in his maroon leather desk chair, slowly leafing through photographs like something was lost in there. Even Anna couldn't get him to talk. Been like this before, of course, many times, drawn by the gentle tug of the past. On those occasions, even the implied threat of her departure had been enough to wrench him back.

But this time she had left it too late, allowed too much of him to dissolve. He became a ghost-Tomas, with sunken, puzzled eyes, trapped beyond a veil neither of them could breach.

Yet he did, eventually, leave the apartment. Sold the place, moved here. Decision, action, interaction. Sign of something, perhaps something salvageable, deep in there. Have to try, of course, even if there's a remote chance.

She warmed up the china pot and waited for the kettle's boiling climax. The floorboards had stopped creaking now, replaced by a rhythmic thump down the stairs. He panted as he entered the kitchen, like a dog looking for his dinner. The sigh, as if he was sick of everything.

Marta gestured with the teapot. 'Cuppa?'

Another sigh. 'Oh, all right.'

She turned to face him, tried smiling. His clothes could do with being ironed. His hair was greasy and dangled in lank grey streaks on each side of his head.

Looks appalling.

A few years ago she would have told him this, or a version of this, without any hesitation. He would have placidly accepted the criticism, probably flashed off those nice teeth to show he hadn't completely lost it. Marta considered the fact that they never rowed to be a buttress of their relationship, a mark of civilisation. They would spar instead, wishing to avoid any serious damage.

Not now, though.

Irritating, having to coax, cajole, charm. My own husband. How could this have happened? We're good people. We didn't do any harm.

She smiled again, as pleasantly as she could.

'Tomas, can we have a little talk?'

He nodded, but didn't say anything. Instead he emitted what seemed to be a sort of growling sound. Marta poured two cups and brought them over to the table. She sat and cleared her throat.

Tomas folded into the chair opposite. He didn't look at her. 'Did I ever tell you the story I heard the first night I moved into this house?'

She shook her head no.

In a rambling, uninterested manner, Tomas told Marta about Dave the removal man and how he had beheaded a horse. When it was over, Marta said nothing. She carefully scooped hair behind her ears.

'So? What do you think of that?'

'I don't know what to think, Tomas. Do you want an opinion on the story?'

'Yes, go on.'

'Well, it sounds very Freudian to me. Your friend obviously made it up. Tomas, I don't want to talk about that. I'm sorry. Perhaps another time. Let me ask you something. How long have you got left on this shoot?'

He stood up, stretched. She never remembered him stretching before. His arms went directly out from his body, crucifixion-like. The stance tugged up his crinkled shirt enough to reveal the black kink of hair below his belly button, the band of blue underpants peeking out over his trousers. It seemed lewd.

'Oh, weeks. Only just started. Why? Do you want me to go back to London?'

Marta found herself surprised by this guess, though now that she considered it, there was no reason she should be. Hopeful, actually. He's thinking about you.

'Well. Perhaps for a spell. Just to get a little break from, you know, all this.'

He put his hands on the table and leaned down. He smiled awfully. 'You must be *so* pleased.'

She looked up at him. 'Tomas, please don't.'

He sat down again. Leaned back in the chair, one leg cocked on top of the other. 'You're such a hypocrite.'

She stared at him for a moment to divine the tone of this assertion. 'Tomas, I came over here because I am worried about you. Anna is worried about you.' She held up hands on either side of her head, as if to keep out sound. 'Look at how you are living. You're a prisoner in this house, Tomas. You're obviously not sleeping. You're paranoid—'

'Ha!'

'You're threatening little boys, Tomas. That's not like you. You must know this is not like you. Even when you get... distant. It's not like you.'

Tomas said nothing, looked away.

Marta softened her tone. 'I know your collection is important, and I know I haven't always understood why you are so attached to it, but really, is it worth it? Having this feud? Arguing with the police? I mean, they are only *things*.'

'Yes, it is worth it. Wars happen, people die, all the time over things. Oil – that's a thing.'

'But Tomas. Threatening children.'

He pointed towards the front door. His fingernails were stained with something tea-coloured.

'This isn't Hampstead, my dear. The rules are a bit different. Should have done a damn sight more than threaten them.'

'Tomas, how can you say that?'

Smack.

He slapped a flat palm on the table. The shockwave travelled outwards from his thick hand, jolting the teacups and Marta.

'Because that's the way things work. To make yourself heard, you have to do a bit more than have a little chat about it.'

'So you threaten children? And then what? You attack them? Hurt them?'

He folded his arms and shrugged. Marta put a hand to her forehead, like she was trying to hold it in place.

'I just don't understand why you would want to live this way. If it's the norm for children to be attacked in this area, that's bad enough. But for you to come here and join in?'

Tomas slowly nodded. 'Oh, yes, here we go. The uncivilised Paddies. That's why you're here now. To gloat because you think you've been proved right. Well sorry, darling, I'm going to stay here with my own kind, the dirty muck savages.'

'For God's sake, this is nothing to do with being Irish. This is about being civilised.'

'Civilised meaning English. Meaning speaking in your toneless accent and sitting with your legs together with your hands in your lap and chewing your food slowly and always saying please and thank you and *may* I have another currant bun, Vicar.'

'What are you talking about? Tomas!'

Now Marta slapped the table. She had tried to yell, but found herself unable, perhaps because she never had before. Her voice had deepened somewhat, taken on a bit of weight, but failed to achieve any significant volume. Yet slapping the table had grabbed his attention, forced him to camouflage his shock with a pretend-laugh.

'I really don't see the relevance of any of this. Nationality, Tomas, it's…it's *redundant*. Heaven knows, it's only people our age who give it any thought. Anyway, it might have escaped your notice, but you are fifty-two years of age and for over thirty years of that *you* lived in England.'

'So I'm English? So I should be grateful and act like a Brit?'

'No, no, no. Tomas! What I'm saying is that you've been away from this place for three decades. It has changed. You have changed. Whether you like it or not, you're an outsider here.'

He laughed again and made a flicking motion with his fingers, as if brushing away crumbs.

'For God's sake, Tomas, you're a film director, not a plumber. You've this big house to yourself. You have a nice car parked outside, which I'm amazed hasn't been stolen. You are not one of these people, Tomas. You can't be. And that's obviously why these boys are attacking the house – because you're *different*. That makes you a target.'

Tomas pointed at the wall. '*I'm* an outsider? There's a load of bloody blacks living next door. Can barely speak English. They're the outsiders. Let them be attacked.'

His arm dropped down. Marta looked at the far wall, then back at her ex-husband. She put a hand to her mouth but spoke through her fingers. 'That is an appalling thing to say. I can't believe you're now a racist. Now think, Tomas. Please. Listen to yourself.'

'I didn't mean it like that.'

'That's how it came out.'

'I meant according to *your* theory. About being an outsider.'

Marta didn't reply.

They sat in silence, Tomas drumming his left foot on the ground. Abruptly, he stood, letting the chair clatter backwards onto the wooden floor. Marta folded her arms but didn't look at him.

'Why am I doing this? Why am I even indulging you? Let me make it clear, Marta. I came here to get away from you.' He screwed up his face, as if he smelled something repellent. 'From you and your tidy little life where fuck all happens. I don't want any part of it. I didn't want you to come over here, and now I want you to leave. It mightn't look so great at the moment, but I like my life. I like how I've changed.' He stopped, panting. 'People I've met…'

Marta jolted her head back slightly. 'The American? Is that what you mean? She's hardly your sort, Tomas.'

He squinted. 'The American has more courage than you'll ever know. Diagnosed with leukaemia, yet still she's over here, working away.'

Now Marta squinted. 'No, no.'

'Christ, you're such a bitch.'

She placed a hand on her sternum. 'Tomas, my father died of leukaemia, so I do know a little about it. And that woman doesn't have leukaemia.'

'You heartless cow.' He walked to the door. 'I'm going to ring a taxi. You pack your bag and get out of my house. *My* house. And don't come back, ever. Is that clear?'

Marta said nothing. The thumping in her chest was so intense it shook the fingers still spread across her sternum.

He screamed, 'Is that clear?'

Slowly, Marta nodded her agreement.

*

THE DAYLIGHT was starting to weaken as the taxi pulled away. Tomas stood in the front room where she could see him – ignoring her, finally happy in a world of his own creation, one she couldn't render sterile. Bye-bye now, off you go.

Bit late. Will she get a flight? Who cares. There'll be ramifications, yes; apologies. Eventually. I was tired. Stressed. Under a lot of pressure, you know. Making a film. Besieged in my own home. My God, you can't imagine. But not now.

Now it felt like an emergence, a slow dissolve from black and white into colour. Now he was aware of the oxygen being sucked into his lungs and efficiently dumped into his bloodstream, circulating round his fizzing brain, his back, legs, arms. Ahead there would be feelings – sorrow, regret, anger. Yet Tomas treasured this prospect.

Been in a stupor for years, extremes of feeling sucked away, an event horizon of emotion.

Now – think. Concentrate. Telling the school put a halt to their gallop. Worth the sacrifice. Phone calls to Marta was all they could do. Pathetic. Probably under the cosh to go straight home.

Tomas nodded repeatedly and cracked a small grin, as if he had just finished decorating this room and was satisfied with his work. He walked to the kitchen, then back to the living room. He clapped his hands together a few times, shook himself. Can't stay still. Don't want to stay still. So much to do, so much I *can* do. Anything, really. Be a hero. Change the world. James Blackwell – there was a man. An Irishman leading the attack on the Bastille, saved his future wife from the gallows. Didn't they ask Mao Tse Tung about the French Revolution? What did you think, Mao? (Or would it be Mao Tse?) Oh, he said, scratching his yellow chin. Too soon to say. Right too, yes. It's always too soon or too late. Timing, yes. Timing, that's the key. With will and belief, anything can be done. And I will. They don't know what I am, what I can be.

I'm waiting, you little bastards.

Wonder how the scar is healing. Poor face, poor face. Marta probably rang from the airport, Your father, he's become so…brutal, not our kind of person any more. And what will she say, what will she think of me?

She, she, she. I can't, I can't, what's her name? What's her name? I can't remember my daughter's name.

12

FISHING LINE, fishing line, long spindly fishing line. There was a phase. Phrase? Phrase that pays? There was an ould woman and she lived in the woods, Weile, weile, wáile, There was an ould woman and she lived in the woods, Down by the river Sáile. Phase, no: day, single day; Gideon Rosenberg, the actuary (from the Latin, actuaries, meaning a scribe or clerk). Actually I'm an actuary. Lived on the floor below and who, despite having never married, was not gay (silly word; why do they like that word?), suggested to Tomas that he give it a try. Fresh air, served up in newspaper, straight from the air farm. Quiet. Kind of lulls you. Tomas was keen on fresh air back then, a needy junkie, massive binges of hill-walking, piggish feeds of quiet and scenery, empty places bereft of human interference. Not that there were any left. Go up Scaffold Pike on a sunny day and it was like a shoulder-bumping supermarket – a mocking place because suddenly there were all these wiry Northern men – men a good ten years older – who were running up the bloody mountain. Fell jogging or something they called it. Anyway, the descents played murder with Tomas's Achilles tendons, which for some reason were always weak; maybe genetic, maybe he came from a long line of weak-ankled men. So he had begun to abandon some walks halfway through, fearing agony on the way down.

When he was on his own.

When no one saw.

Fell jogging bastards.

So the fishing seemed a good idea, and Gideon was always pleasant company, despite the boring job; so splendid, give it a go, try anything once, what?

Set out at about four-thirty in the morning, which didn't bother Tomas, he was used to early starts – in fact he liked them, the imminence of the sunrise, the dark exclusivity of night, when everyone else was tucked up, even freezing his arse off, waiting for dawn to completely break and for the actors to stop moaning and yawning.

But it left Gideon cranky – never saw that before, pussy-faced like a pouting girl (he *did* look gay then), his skin white like a baby's, making this half-cough, half-sigh sound as if he strongly disapproved of something but was too stubborn to say what.

Didn't travel that far. Somewhere above Reading. Either the Thames or the Kennet. A mist when they first arrived, which soon lifted. Yet in Tomas's memory the fog loitered around them all that day, a blur of bushes and green frothy water, kamikaze insects, a fold-out seat which soon numbed his bottom and a half-seen array of shiny, fiddly devices which Tomas didn't understand, no matter how many times they were explained. Ledgering. Light quiver tips. Feeder rigs. An inescapable stink of fish, though he couldn't remember Gideon catching any. Tomas certainly didn't, soon becoming passive and indifferent as Gideon boringly outlined what they were trying to land and how the delicate use of this equipment would aid their endeavour. Tomas had found he didn't want to catch anything, that he was content to watch Gideon the actuary casting and recasting, his reel clicking away. It was dreamy and pleasant, and Tomas would have gone again only on the way home Gideon made it clear that he shouldn't have bothered coming if he wasn't going to try. Tomas shrugged, tried grinning his way through Gideon's pique. It was some time before Gideon spoke to them again.

Afterwards, he discovered a roll of fishing line cuddled into his pocket. Tomas had no hesitation in keeping it. Might come in useful. And it would remind him of the day, which had a quality he wanted to covet.

Years later, Tomas examined this line. He pulled out a small section and bit it, satisfying himself that it was still intact. This *has* come in handy. Didn't usually happen with most of the rubbish.

See? You can joke about it too. Nothing but jokes from you, Mister Ha Ha. You're OK.

Not going mad. *She had a baby three months old, Weile, weile, wáile, She had a baby three months old, Down by the river Sáile.*

He opted to start upstairs. Rearrange the storage rooms. Put everything closer together and the most fragile pieces in the centre. More difficult to penetrate, no time to choose the target.

Next he began tacking up long strands of the fishing line across doorways and windows, in the middle of the upstairs and downstairs halls and in each room, attempting in each case to blend in the line with some object or piece of furniture. To all of these he attached keys or cowbells or small bottles.

Within a few hours of Marta's departure, Tomas had established a silver network of threads, each one delicate enough to betray movement. He toured the house a few times, memorising the position of each. He practised jumping over the line in the upstairs hallway, ducking under the line in the doorway to his bedroom. Jump. Duck. Duck. Jump. Outside it was dark now, the pavement shimmering from a recent spill of rain. A cat curled around some railings three doors down. A man emerged from one of the ratty houses at the cul-de-sac end. He threw a soggy carrier bag into a bin, then smoked the last inch of his cigarette. He glared around at nothing, then went back inside. Tomas could see his shadow moving through the front room, lighting another cigarette, then moving towards the back of the house. For food or bed.

Busy tonight. Good, good. *She had a penknife long and sharp, Weile, weile, wáile, She had a penknife long and sharp, Down by the river Sáile.*

It was after ten when he decided to sit down, to look in the fridge and the cupboards. (Is there a smell? All the rubbish, must be a smell.) There was a handful of penne, two slices of bread and enough milk for one cup of tea. Should have got supplies today. Fuck.

He sat at the kitchen table, munched dry bread and listened to the chugging sounds of the boiling kettle. There's a smell. Fish? Bad fruit? Cheese? After a couple of mouthfuls, he flung the bread into the overflowing bin. Right across the room, direct hit, *yes*. Alert, every creak and click, every change in the powdery light. Not hungry, though. No – *don't need* food – other nourishment, some deep psychic source. Revved up, ready to go, like a poised samurai sword. Tomas walked about the kitchen. He positioned the seats neatly under the table, carefully washed a cup and plate, scratching at some congealed stains with his thumb. He considered organising the food cupboard. No, not enough there. Fridge nearly empty. Do something with the rubbish? What, though? Can't put it outside, can't put it anywhere. No, nothing to do now. Thought of everything, finally – everything has passed through this mind, been filtered, judged, graded for quality. Every. Single. Thing. God is a being who has thought of everything. Tonight, Matthew, I shall be a deity, I shall have dominion over all the spare parts from my life, in the house and outside, the street corners.

Avoided them, when? Eight? Malachy Duignan to box your ears, the son of the rebel, look at the state of him.

Malachy Duignan. God, wonder what happened.

The rebel.

Not everyone loved her.

People are sheep, Tomas, they'll do what's easy – too scared to support the rebels in 1919, too lazy now to finish the job, get the rest of the country back – they're scared of people like us, Tommy, people who have taken a stand. It reminds them of how useless and cowardly they are.

She's dabbing something. On my split lip.

This happen a lot?

Only one child in the house. This is suspect – something wrong with her, or him, or worse. Using the rubbers – wouldn't put it past that one.

Overhear this?

To your face? A hot, steely arm wedged under your chin, bigger boys discussing her, as if you're not there, as if they pity you a little, victim to that madwoman, that atheist.

Tomas grabbed a broom and brusquely swept the kitchen floor. He inspected the cupboard doors for dust, then the top of the pictures. Nothing, too soon for dust.

She stuck the penknife in the baby's heart, Weile, weile, wáile, She stuck the penknife in the baby's heart, Down by the river Sáile.

He jumped, ducked, jumped, ducked to the front of the house, peered out the windows again. Nothing. Jump, duck, jump, duck back to the kitchen. Slap hands a few times.

Do some exercises.

Sweating slightly, but feel *so* good.

Try running.

Tomas did this, on the spot, but after five minutes or so felt foolish. Press-ups instead. Yes, better. Sweat going into eyebrows, heart hammering behind the ribs, but yes, yes, this is it now. Up, down. Slower, slower, let arms feel the strain. Not too flabby at all, at all. See those muscles popping up? Glistening in the dark, pumped, ready to slip round your scrawny necks and squeeze.

See how you like it.

*

THE PHONE was ringing, though it was an old-fashioned sound: a full metallic ring rather than a bleep. *Three loud knocks came a-knocking on the door, Weile, weile, wáile, Three loud knocks came a-knocking on the door, Down by the river Sáile.*

Keys in the door. OCD, they call it. Boots scraped on the mat. Just at school time, Daddy is home. Oily from the presses. Howya kiddo.

Tomas made a noise as he sat up, then scolded himself for doing so. Should be more cautious. He peeled back the duvet and slipped white, bare legs off the sofa. The hair on his thighs stood erect, as if caught in a gale from upstairs. Definitely.

Ding. Ding.

Like a diver about to enter water, Tomas took three deep breaths, then threw himself out of the living room, knowing he had laid the thread in such a configuration that he could bound straight up the stairs if he kept his head low, knowing that the flat *ding* sound came from a miniature tourist cow-bell he had bought in Austria, given to Marta for a joke. To infuriate her, a little bit. It carried the inscription: *The Sound of Music.* It now rested at the doorway to his bedroom. Jump. Duck.

It was still there when Tomas arrived, and plaintively dinged in his presence to demonstrate that the noise was not caused by intruders, but by some distant vibration, probably night-time drilling streets away.

'Shit.'

*

MARTA WAS crying, sitting by the side of the road at the spot where Tomas had thrown his mobile phone out the window. The phone protruded from her forehead, like a car crashed into a wall. She rubbed around the impact point, revealing white flashes of bone. *There were two policemen and a man, Weile, weile, wáile, There were two policemen and a man, Down by the river Sáile.*

Are you talking to me?

She nodded, no. But let him know that even though she couldn't get a plane, the headless horse would be along any minute. And it's called OCD.

She didn't leave. You left her.

'Shit.'

Tomas had intended to shout, but found a whisper was all he could manage. His throat felt burned and constricted, his head throbbed as if his skull had dramatically swollen, straining the skin around it to tearing point. The slightest movement could begin the ripping – around the neck, at either side of the face. The eyes, the nose, the mouth: everything could become detached and slide from his head in a bloody trail onto the sofa and floor. He would be found in pieces.

Don't be silly; stop.

Don't want to move though. Can't. His head and body felt far too heavy, as if weights were crushing his chest. The most Tomas could manage was to flick open his eyelids, force his aching pupils to search for any signs of light.

Nothing.

Hear anything? No.

Tomas lay where he was, pinned down by thoughts too heavy to bear. An odour of sweat curled up from his armpits, packing his nostrils, sliding into his bronchial tubes. Sickly bile rose up his throat. Must wash.

Eventually he managed to move his right arm, feeling around on the floor until he located the watch. 3:35. Not a sound this time, just a bad dream. Wasteful. Need sleep. Stupid. Really overdid it. Like a madman, bouncing around the house. What got into you?

Exhausted, yet still down there, a certain stiffness – a lot of them lately, like my twenties, almost constantly erect and couldn't believe that a girl would, especially a girl like Marta. And then hold and stroke. Say Love. I love you Tomas.

They won't be along tonight, not at this hour. Rest.

Tomas tried to shift position, but didn't have the energy. No gas in the tank. Yet he didn't mind. Don't mind anything, really.

Sniff. Clear the tubes.

Behind the sweat, other smells. Musty, but slightly sweet. Haven't opened the windows for days. He felt like some ancient pharaoh tucked up with his worldly goods, hoping they might be of some value in the next life. Unable to leave this place, yet unwilling to die.

Obsessive compulsive disorder. Six months before she walked out? Should have seen that coming. Now it was a *disease*. The energy she deployed, completely blind to her own obsessions. Jealous, probably. Jealous of things. Sad. Even a bit theatrical, which wasn't like her, following him for the best part of a day, reading out from studies and medical texts she had found on the internet.

Central to the disorder is an inability to resist the urge to acquire objects, even though acquiring or possessing such objects may create problems like excessive clutter. Look around you, Tomas. Clutter.

Smiled. Ignored her. Kept moving around the flat.

Listen to this, Tomas. Hoarders often cope with their behavioural deficits – and that is what it is, Tomas, a *deficit*, something is *missing* – they cope through avoidance. By saving things, they avoid the uncomfortable process of decision-making and the stress caused by having to discard a possession.

Have you *ever* thrown anything away? Have you?

Oh no, it's all true! I'm a nutcase!

Are you the woman who stabbed the child? Weile, weile, wáile, Are you the woman who stabbed the child? Down by the river Sáile.

Tomas, this is serious. She would have shouted if she could.

Now this is you. Some hoarders need to maintain control over their possessions. This results in increasing isolation and *suspiciousness* of others. That is definitely you. If you had to choose between me and all this junk, you'd take the junk, wouldn't you? Wouldn't you?

Marta. Please. Don't talk rot.

People who hoard identify their possessions as central to their identity. Be honest, please. That would be true of you, wouldn't it?

He stopped walking, tipped his head from side to side.

Yes, I suppose.

Well then, don't you see? These are from studies of people with OCD. They are describing you.

No they are not. They are nothing like me. My collection is important to me, that's all.

She rifled through the papers. Pilot interviews are consistent in finding that childhood experiences of abuse, neglect or *instability* in the family may play a role in the development of hoarding.

He stopped, turned to her, veins in his neck pulsating.

Don't bring that up.

Well Tomas, it could be—

Don't you dare bring my family into this.

Tomas, I'm trying to help you.

By attacking my family? It's...it's sick.

Eyes moist, he went to the bedroom, slamming the door behind him, astonished that she would choose to attack him in such a nasty way, baffled as to why. Sick bitch.

*

'YOU KNEW, didn't you?'

Eli took a couple of steps backwards when Tomas burst out from behind the front door. 'You knew we weren't filming today?'

'Yes. Of course. Why?'

'I dunno. You just seemed surprised. Nah. Course you knew. Sorry.'

Eli gazed around, keen to change the subject. He nodded in the direction of number 16. 'Who's the weird-looking mare next door?'

Reluctantly, Tomas padded out, glanced at her, then quickly retreated to his hallway.

'Don't know. She won't talk to me. Crazy.'

'She stands there all the time?'

'A lot of the time.'

Eli took a few more steps back, his eyes fixed on the woman as if she was an old friend and it was only a matter of time before she recognised him. Tomas remained in the hallway, glancing back over his shoulder. He shifted from one foot to another.

'Morning,' Eli called. The woman ignored him, preferring to stare at a Jack Russell jerkily sniffing the cracked pavement across the street. The dog's coat was dotted with bald patches, revealing vivid pink skin, like crop circles manufactured by tiny aliens. The woman's hair, black and almost impossibly frizzy, stood up straight from her forehead. A tsunami of fuzz.

'Morning,' Eli ventured again. Still ignored, he gestured helplessly towards Tomas and rolled his eyes. He dug his hands into his pockets and slowly came back towards the door. 'So,' he said.

'So?' Tomas didn't look at Eli as he said this, but across the street to where the girl with the dreadlocked hair was carefully guiding an old woman along the pavement. The old woman was wrapped tightly inside a plastic coat and hat. The dreadlocked girl pointed towards the end of the street, as if to encourage the old woman into believing that she could make it that far. Tomas watched, and seemed annoyed by what he saw. He shrank behind the front door, only his face and one shoulder revealed.

Eli attempted a neutral smile. Tomas was a snow pale, his face unshaven, his tongue protruding a little from his mouth. Dark curves were carved into the space beneath his bloodshot eyes. He wore just a vest and a stained, baggy pair of cords. There were no shoes or socks, not even slippers. Not like him. Tomas would wear a tie to bed. A threatening, urine-tinged smell drifted out from the house. Eli gestured towards the end of Bass Avenue, towards the outside world.

'Thought I'd buy you breakfast. You eaten yet?'

'No,' replied Tomas, with some regret, as if this was something that he kept meaning to do. He looked up, suddenly alarmed. 'But I couldn't possibly leave the house. Leave the house? Leave the house? Are you mad? There would be no house when I got back.' To demonstrate how comical this notion was, Tomas emitted a flat, rasping sound.

'Oh, right,' Eli said.

Tomas stared at him. 'You really wanted me to leave the house?'

'Yeah, well, I just thought if you were doing nothing…'

Tomas opened his mouth again to release the rasping sound. He leaned out briefly, looked around like a nervous animal, then whipped his head back in. 'Look. I can't give you anything. But you better come in.'

Eli shrugged his compliance.

'I can't give you anything, right?'

Eli shrugged again, wondering exactly what this meant.

'And when you come in you have to do exactly what I instruct. OK?'

'OK, sure.'

Too late to get another director, though people often start on little notice – directors get ill, after all. But this is the middle of filming. Still, not some arthouse shit. Bloody light romantic comedy. Tomas has story-boards done. Could borrow them. Bet he won't let you. The story will get out. Gone mad. Investors will hear. Probably know already. The whole fucking crew knows. Or they think he's giving Karin Goldman one. Or both.

Tomas beckoned Eli inside, then ordered him to stand still. He shut the splintered door bolted it, turned several locks, punched a number into a key-pad beside the door and made sure a golf club was propped up in a corner. He turned to face the dark hallway, rubbing his hands together. The windows, Eli noticed, were all covered over.

'Yes, it's dark,' Tomas said. 'But I can't let them see into the house. It's one of the few advantages I have. I can move things, confuse them.' He tapped Eli on the arm. 'Follow me and do what I do.'

Like a limbo dancer, Tomas Dalton squatted down on his legs and took pygmy steps towards the kitchen.

'Do what I'm doing,' he panted.

'Why?'

Tomas halted, but didn't look around. 'You agreed. You agreed to do what-ever I asked when you came in here. Look, I haven't got the…I'll explain when we get to the kitchen. Will you just hunker down like this? Please?'

Eli glanced around, as if checking for hidden cameras, then squatted down in formation behind Tomas. Like grim party-goers they shuffled along the wooden floor until Tomas halted. Then he pointed upwards.

'See?'

Eli looked. 'See what?'

'Lean back a little.'

Eli complied, expecting to be asked to confirm the existence of some phantom of Tomas's boiled brain. If the film goes tits up, go public. Only way to survive. Only way to show it wasn't your fault. No one will ever trust you with a penny otherwise. But still. Tomas. Fuck. What choice do you have? Tomas who went bonkers. Bloody divorce. Bloody Marta, showing up. Always a bit snooty, that one. Stuck-up posh, but won't admit it, the worst sort. The boys at school. Tossers. Oi, are you a Cockney? Say something common.

Eli peered into the blackness, but saw nothing save a strand of stray spider web glinting in whatever light crept in from the kitchen.

'Sorry, mate. Can't see anything.'

'Nothing? Nothing at all?' He seemed quite alarmed.

'Well. I see a bit of spider web or something.'

Tomas exhaled like a man who has been holding his breath for a long time. 'My God, you gave me a fright. I thought...I thought...'

Waving Eli along, he shuffled forward another yard, then stood, indicating Eli should do the same. He pointed: another strand now, about six inches off the ground, stretching the width of the hallway. 'Get to here, then jump. Understand?'

Eli nodded. The two men kangaroo-hopped into the kitchen. Breathless from these exertions, Tomas dropped onto a chair. He ignored his guest.

The kitchen was thick with odours. A large black wheelie bin slouched in one corner, its lid propped up by a bursting mound of crushed boxes, egg shells, black banana skins and potato peel already edged with green. It resembled a child eating with its mouth open. Carrier bags, stuffed with more rubbish, gathered around the bottom of the bin like hungry chicks. Eli put a hand to his mouth. The sink and kitchen cupboards seemed reasonably clean but the table was covered with a pile of heavy, greasy tools, pieces of wood and brown paper bags containing nails and screws of various lengths and colours. Sawdust sat in tidal mounds on the floor beneath.

'Yes, yes,' said Tomas. 'I know the place is a mess. Is the smell bad? I can't tell any more.'

'Pretty bad,' Eli gently replied. Tomas nodded.

'I just can't risk putting out any rubbish, can I? I have to think the way they do, and if I were them I would jump at the chance of a rubbish bin sitting outside the house. It would be perfect, say, to set fire to or even plant a bomb in, which I have no doubt they are capable of building. Not with actual explosives – though you never know – you do hear of fertilizer bombs and the like. I'm sure they can do damage.' He waved around the room. 'Which means my kitchen doesn't smell too wonderful, for which I apologise. I can't give you anything. Did I say that? No milk. Ran out of tea this morning. But of course, I can't risk going to the shops. You do understand?'

'Yes, yes.'

'They are watching. I know that sounds paranoid, but they are. Really. They wait until I'm at home so they can make nuisance calls. Then they wait until I go out so they can break in and destroy my collection. Still no idea how they are doing it.'

'What about the police?'

'Police haven't a clue.'

Eli took out a cigarette and lit it. He inhaled two big lungfuls of smoke while Tomas threw out a choking laugh.

'Sorry. Didn't sleep that well last night, you know. Spent most of the time setting up the trip-wires.'

Finding a dirty saucer to tip his ash into, Eli sat across from Tomas at the crowded kitchen table. He nodded towards the tools. 'What ya making?'

Tomas reached out and picked up one of the pieces of wood, cut thin enough to resemble a club, the top end clustered with bent, spiky nails. He made a weak attempt to swipe it before him, swordsman-like.

'Weapons. Going to make a few more like this and leave them all over the house. Risky, of course – they might get to them first – but at least I have the advantage of knowing where each one is.'

'They look nasty.'

'They are supposed to.'

Eli extinguished his cigarette, considering what to say next. He could think of nothing. Tomas gently fingered the bent nails on the club. He gently sang:

I am the woman who stabbed the child,
Weile, weile, wáile,
I am the woman who stabbed the child,
Down by the river Sáile.

Eli shifted in his chair, cleared his throat, looked around the kitchen, then back at Tomas. 'But ain't these just kids? Like, ten or something?'

Tomas looked at Eli as if he deserved pity. 'Take my word for it. They may be only ten or eleven, but they are capable of anything. *Anything.*' He gestured at the kitchen. 'I mean, have you ever seen me act this way before?' He put down the makeshift club, then picked it up again. 'These boys are deliberately trying to destroy me and I everything I value. Quite coldly. Quite calmly. I have no option but to defend myself. Only thing they understand. Or deserve. I don't care if they are children. They are *not* children, as far as I'm concerned.'

'Yeah, I know what you mean. But bloody hell, Tomas.'

The phone rang. Tomas gestured towards it, as if this was further evidence of the campaign against him. Yet he didn't move. Eli went to stand, but Tomas waved insistently to keep him sitting.

Beep beep. Beep beep.

With a groan, Tomas stood and glanced at the caller display. He grinned slightly, then sat again. The phone continued to ring like a crying child. He snatched it up as soon as the beeping was finished. He quickly dialled some numbers, then listened, made a *hmm* sound, half-smiled, then hung up.

'Don't answer the phone now. No point. Though that was Karin, believe it or not.'

'What did she want?'

'To come around. Come visit with you. It seems as if I'm back in the good books. God help me.'

Eli gently rocked back and forth on his chair. 'Well, you know. Maybe it would help with, you know, all this.'

'What?' Tomas was smiling. Ever so slightly. 'You can't stand the woman,' he said.

'I know, but I thought…'

Tomas shut his eyes and shook his head vigorously, serious now.

They sat in silence. Eli tentatively smirked. 'You'll get no argument from me on that one, mate. I am a bit worried about you though, I must say. But if you can tell that Karin's barking, that must mean you've hung on to some of your marbles. Ha? Ha?'

Eli smiled again, this time waving across the table to Tomas, encouraging him to do the same. But Tomas shook his head dismissively; such jollity was unseemly, like loud laughter a funeral.

'You have no need to *worry* about me.'

Eli grimaced. 'Mate, I didn't mean it like that. But, you know.' He tipped his head towards the table. 'Making weapons and all that? Bloody hell, Tomas. Bit over the top. Like, all this stuff you collect. Is it worth it? All this aggravation?'

'Yes. It is.'

'Why?'

'Impossible to explain. You either understand or you don't.'

Both men fell silent.

'This is a battle,' said Tomas eventually. 'It's them or me, because it's *me* they are attacking. I will win.'

'You think you can do that?'

'I will do that.'

'I don't know, mate. You can't *make* people be nice. Can't make them like you. Do you know what I mean? Look at the Yanks, they're always invading countries to make the world safe, or so they say, and still everybody bloody hates them.'

Tomas shook his head. 'Not the same thing.'

Eli looked around the room, as if searching for an escape route. 'Well, how long do you think this is going to take?'

'I have no idea.'

'But you have to leave the house some time.'

'Not necessarily.'

'What about work? Tomorrow we got the shoot in Grafton Street, Tomas. What are you going to do about that?'

Tomas didn't answer.

*

DEFINITE PANGS now, sharp crunches of pain in his stomach, like some clawed animal is inside and trying to chew its way out. *They took her away and they put her into jail, Weile, weile, wáile, They took her away and they put her into jail, Down by the river Sáile.* At first he ignored it as weakness, his mind playing tricks, the way smokers will justify going back to cigarettes. But after a dizzy spell he was forced to accept that he needed food, that he had no option but to briefly leave the house. Risky. Still, good chance they're not watching right now. Can't keep it up all day long. They have to eat, sleep, go home to their mammies. School. Went there yesterday. School today?

What day is it?

Tomas thought Thursday, though he wasn't entirely sure. Get a newspaper. Look it up in the shooting schedule. One lying about somewhere. Two days filming. Or three? Then a day off. Why? Something technical?

Thursday? Or Wednesday?

Must be what it was like for him. At the start. Though when was the start? Probably hid it for years, every day an act, a search for clues – when he'd get lost on the way home from work, when he'd meet someone he should know but didn't recognise. A fence in his brain he couldn't scramble over. He wouldn't have told anyone, not even Peg until she noticed something was wrong and badgered it out of him. And then she would have remained silent too, regarding sickness as an abominable shame, something you brought upon yourself through laziness or cowardice or all-around lack of moral fibre. She said nothing until Tomas's first year at film school, when it became impossible to hide. And even then there were people who never learned what Tom Dalton Senior died from, who never knew how rare and randomly cruel his end was. The *word* was never used. Daddy is just poorly, sitting in his chair – wearing the braces those little fuckers cut up – the newspaper lying ignored in his lap, a look of amazement frozen onto his face, as if he knows what is happening to him and feels simple astonishment at the bad luck of it all. Man of his age. Don't be annoying your father now. He's a bit poorly.

Predictably, Marta had been more interested in the philosophical aspects of the decline. When did he cease to be Tom Dalton? When did his selfhood evaporate? Tomas found this speculation irritating, even offensive. As long as any evidence of father remains, then he is still here. Obvious.

Tomas would have preferred to talk – though he never did – about how it had affected him and his mother. Tom Dalton did not just forget himself, but his son and wife also – he made Tomas and Peg Dalton less by not knowing them.

Sometimes Tom Senior shouts. Sometimes a bit of flame comes back into his eyes and he yells Hurry up! I haven't got all day, you stupid, stupid woman. His thick neck vibrates from the blood rushing through the engorged veins, and Peg winks at Tomas, almost pleased with this abuse.

Yet Tom remains in that chair. Like he is glued to it. Doesn't even manage to stand the day Tomas takes the mail-boat to England, just a dull, left-handed wave. Then back to the staring, to absorbing the surprise.

He didn't say much after Tomas left. He gradually lapsed into absolute silence and died. Peg found him slumped over in the chair, his eyes still open, his face still informed by shock.

That's all she said at the funeral. Over and over. He sat in that chair. Didn't utter a word. Then he died. Not a word to me. For months. Then he died.

Yet as Tomas imagined it, the scene was not so quiet. As Tomas imagined it, only the nerves controlling speech and facial expression had been gnawed away by the Parkinson's. Inside, unable to tell anyone, Tom Dalton knew what was happening, what was to come, and for a while his brain buzzed and popped like a city as it tried to avoid the disease. But eventually, it slowed down. Eventually, one by one, every thought, every image, every sensation which had combined to create the way of existence known as Tom Dalton Senior were slowly devoured. The lights of the city going out one by one, leaving senseless fragments. Breath on your face. Searching through rubble. Excited. A kiss.

What's a kiss?

Darkness.

They put the rope around her neck, Weile, weile, wáile, They put the rope around her neck, Down by the river Sáile.

Tomas stood up from the table, shook himself. Go to the shop. Feed yourself. Out loud he said, 'It's a Thursday.'

*

IT'S A Thursday. It's what? 11:32. Should be at school. If they're not, if they're watching the house. They could be getting hungry, a bit bored. Tomas calculated: if he drove – and the shop was only around the corner – he could get the expedition completed within ten minutes, even less. Not long enough even for them to do any major damage. His stomach gurgled again. I want tea.

He peeked through the front window. Nothing suspicious. One of the Nigerian kids kicking a football. The frizzy-haired woman out again, staring at nothing. She'll put people off. Must talk to her about the back garden, try anyway – might give her a fright, wake her up.

Still.

He didn't want to go out there, where it was open and air moved around. Strange foreign air, sucked in and exhaled by God knows who, with all their microbes and nasty microscopic malignancies – strange-eyed people staring, thinking, muttering to each other – they could attack, could do anything. Do they know? They know; they all know. They'll look the other way when you are mashed into the pavement.

No, stop, don't be silly.

Is it silly?

When they were potty-training Anna, that horrible transition from comfort to exposure. She hadn't liked it, had refused point-blank at first, and Tomas hadn't blamed her.

Christ, you old fool.

He forced himself to peer out the window again, more forensically now, staring at each section of the street, every inch of the tiny yard outside the house. Nothing, right, get up, get up, come on, chop chop. Tomas stood back and examined himself. Vest and trousers. Hardly in a state to be going out. He located shoes underneath the sofa, then moved towards the stairs to get a shirt in the bedroom. Should start sleeping upstairs again. Not very sanitary to be doing everything down here.

Have a bath when you get back.

Tomas put his right foot on the stairs, looked up, then retracted the foot and moved back to the corner of the lounge where his mother's playing cards had dwelled in their leather case.

Gone, of course – he'd already seen the ace of spades torn in half, stuck to the wall at the top of stairway. Almost as an act of duty, as a tired parent agrees to view the latest crude drawing by their child, Tomas turned back and mounted the steps – duck, jump, duck – knowing he would be unsurprised by what he saw – he expected nothing less than excellence from them now, the acme of venom. Each of the fifty-two cards torn in half, then glued, collage-style, to the wall, leading in a trail down the hallway and into Tomas's bedroom, where the leather case had been set on fire: the smell of burning still thick in the room, a circle of ash forever scarring the centre of his bed. This was communication. Boy, could these boys communicate. We are invisible, non-corporeal. We can enter your house any time we wish, even when you are here; when you are just yards away you will not see us, or smell the burning or hear our footfalls.

Tomas nodded, as if convinced of something, then trudged back down the stairs, shirt forgotten. He switched off the alarm and walked out of the house, shivering as the damp, misty air fell upon his bare shoulders. He left the door wide open. Tomas got in the Saab and drove to the shop, where he bought tea and coffee, milk, sugar, eggs, a roll of black plastic bags, mushrooms, jam, bread, cheese, pasta, a Yorkie and five King Edward cigars. He got back in the car, started up the engine but at first was unable to pull out, the tears so blurred his vision.

Marta wasn't impulsive. Wasn't in her nature. You'd already drifted far away, deep into the fog. It was her only option to leave – the hope that you would follow.

He had to wipe his eyes several times and wait for the shuddering to ease off. And when he finally moved towards home, his cheeks were still wet, as if he had sprung a leak which could never be completely fixed. Yet he could see well enough to drive. He could see the boys, who, as Tomas rounded the corner into Bass Avenue, stood in single file opposite his house, staring at the open door as if it were a thing of wonder, an ancient message yet to be decoded. Tomas slowed down a fraction, wanting to study them, to watch as they roamed in their little herd about these streets, eyes popping for new targets.

One of the twins must have heard the engine. He turned his head, just enough, then said something to the others. They glanced at Tomas, but their bodies betrayed indecision – they seemed to want to stay there, look at this wondrous open house some more.

Tomas squeezed the accelerator. *They pulled the rope and she got hung, Weile, weile, wáile, They pulled the rope and she got hung, Down by the river Sáile.*

The car zipped up Bass Avenue, the Swedish-engineered springs and shock absorbers letting it move smoothly over the cracks and bumps in the road's surface. Tomas wiped his eyes.

The twin looked up again – not at Tomas in particular, but at the front of the car, as if they were the one creature, something sniffing the air, gently stalking them on crouched legs, breaking into a gallop now – and this time he nudged the tall one, hard enough for him to look properly, to see the car was coming faster, that it was drifting towards their side of the road. Both turned away, half-dragging the second twin along the pavement, falling into a wild run, yet unable to resist glances behind as the engine roared and the car shot up in a silvery, unstoppable streak, bouncing onto the pavement just as they cornered into the alley, smashing into a black wheelie bin which toppled over like a felled tree. Empty tins of dog food clattered along the ground, each one carrying the face of a happy, waving mutt.

'Go on, run!' They heard the man yell after them in a voice that was almost happy, that had found purpose. The boys kept running and didn't look back.

And that was the end of the woman in the woods, Weile, weile, wáile, And that was the end of the baby too, Down by the river Sáile.

13

THE WINDOW in the bathroom was tightly screwed down. Definitely not getting in here.

Underfoot, a squelching sensation.

Tomas stepped back to see a tribe of tiny spiders scattering in all directions like a routed army, terrified by this god-like creature.

If not the windows, then how?

The phone rang.

He tramped over to the bedroom. Dizzy. Everything seemed to take ten times the effort it had before, burning up his precious supply of energy. Tomas sat heavily on the bed. When the ringing finished he dialled his voice-mail.

'It's me again.' Eli sounded breathless. In the background there was a crunching sound, footsteps on gravel.

'Look, Tomas. I'm not going to do this any more. If you've decided not to come in, not even talk to me about it. After all the years we've worked…well, that's, I dunno. But look what you're throwing away…I, I dunno.'

The crunching sound stopped.

'I'll wait here for another half-hour, all right? If you haven't contacted me by then I'll assume you're not coming and I'll send everyone home. I could get another director, but I don't know. Doesn't seem worth it. Money was tight anyway, I told you that.

'Tomas, why are you doing this to yourself, mate? You know the story will get out. You do. And like, you know, that will be it. Your career, mate.

The whole bloody thing gone. Thirty years of work. And for what? A few books or something?'He sighed.

'It's up to you. Film is in your hands now. All the people here who have jobs, who need the money, who have kids and all that. All the actors. And me. The dozy git you've been working with for years. Now I have to go back to the people who put up the money and say, Sorry about that. But the fucking director didn't feel like turning up today. He wants to sit in his house like a fucking...'

More sighs. A clank of metal as he deployed his lighter on a cigarette.

'It's ten forty-five now. I'll wait until quarter past eleven. Then I'll close it down.'

He hung up.

Tomas dropped the phone on the bed, yawned, looked out the window. No sign yet. They said between nine and ten. Bad enough to have to answer the door at all, damn it, come on, don't like this, too distracting.

He had been busy all night, had barely slept, even though he really needed to. But they'd want revenge after the car incident, that was obvious, so it made sense to halve the area he had to guard. He moved everything upstairs. All the rugs and furniture, pictures, coins, cameras, bolts, the sofa (nearly killed him, that one), the kettle, contents of the fridge, the television. Everything except for the kitchen table and some of the chairs which Tomas had never really cared for anyway.

Naturally, it took quite some time to get everything stuffed in and organised properly. But at about four in the morning, when he finally got a chance to sit down, a cup of tea in his hand, the TV blazing at the end of his bed, he saw the supermarket commercial. Shop online. Home delivery. Should have done that days ago.

It took him little more than twenty minutes with his laptop and credit card. Strangely distasteful. Tomas didn't trust the internet, a mammoth glob of human consciousness, but unformed and disorganised, like the mind of a baby. Everything without a context.

Afterwards, he considered what effect his actions were having on the outside world: on Anna and Marta, Eli, the film people, on Karin. Bad, bad. But no way to leave here. Can't back down. It is a vendetta. One they will pursue until there is nothing left. Death, inch by inch.

No option. An easy choice, really – beyond intellectual set-pieces, your life versus the livelihoods of others; who is worth more? What would a utilitarian say? Marta would love this. Must stay, no matter what, for me, yes, for Anna

— she doesn't know what I'm saving for her, for her grandparents, what they gave. We deserve survival. Explaining to Eli or anyone is pointless, undignified. Show some restraint. Daddy's word. His hand heavy on Tomas's shoulder, rain drumming on the umbrella above.

Whose funeral? An uncle, perhaps, or some withered Republican Mother had long admired. No other children there — this is unusual. Can't hear the priest either because a murder of crows is arguing nearby. He and Tom Senior standing, nothing to do but stare at death. He feels his father bend down. Hot breath on the back of his neck. Stale tobacco smell.

Do you see this now? Gently turning Tomas's head, he directs his gaze to the woman standing closet to the coffin. Slim and pale-faced, wearing a wide-brimmed hat. She is desperately beautiful.

That's the way to do it, son. With a bit of restraint. No making a big fuss. He leans in closer.

At my funeral now, when I'm gone, this is the sort of thing I want. No crying, all right? I'd hate that. You just do what your Mother does. She'll know.

Tomas nods, keen to please, yet also bewildered and fearful.

The doorbell rang. Tomas stood.

'At last,' he said.

*

'DO YOU need me to sign something?' Tomas said.

'What?' said the man.

He was small and wiry. His hands hovered around his mouth, as if he wasn't quite sure of what he wanted to say and might need to quickly stuff the words back in. His face carried a permanent look of anguish.

'For the food. Credit card slip.'

'What? I don't want any food. Are you the man in the house?'

'The man *in* the house. *In* the house? What rubbish are you talking?'

Tomas took in the caller's grubby grey suit, the uniform of lower middle management. Already reached the pinnacle of his drab career and getting nothing but impersonation and insolence.

Weak, moustached little man.

He straightened himself, then took a step backwards. He had a slight limp. 'I'm Ted Mulvihill.'

The words were delivered in a tone which seemed to assume that Tomas would find this news devastating.

'You're not here to deliver my groceries?'

Ted Mulvihill considered this for a moment. 'No. I'm Ted Mulvihill.'

'So?'

'Well, well,' he stuttered, hands over his face again. 'I'm, I'm.'

Tomas had the door half-closed before the name registered. Mulvihill and Doyle, Mulvihill and Doyle. He wrenched it open again and leaned out steeply until his face was inches away from Ted Mulvihill's.

'What are you? The father?'

'Of the twins, yes. Of the twins. And I've come around to have a word.'

'A word? A word? Ha!'

Tomas straightened up, allowing the dressing gown wrapped around him to fall open. Underneath he wore pyjama bottoms and a stained blue T-shirt. Several days' worth of beard clung to his chin. With great deliberation, he placed his right index finger on Ted Mulvihill's chest, then shoved.

'Hey,' called Ted as he staggered back, alarmed yet infuriatingly passive.

'Here's a word for you. Two words. Fuck off. I've nothing to say to scum like you.'

Ted Mulvihill blinked several times. He pointed at Tomas, but discreetly, with his arm bent, his finger barely extended, as if hoping no one would notice.

'My family are all upset. My wife is in bits. You tried to...you tried to run them over.' He shuddered slightly as he completed the accusation.

'Oh, don't be ridiculous.' Tomas inhaled deeply. He looked around, searching for something more worthy of his attention. The dressing gown hanging long from his shoulders gave him a tatty yet regal air.

'If I had intended to run them over, I would have done so. I was merely trying to get their attention – something I think *you* have failed to do.'

Ted Mulvihill shook his head furiously. 'Well, well. That's not what it looked like, oh no.'

He turned his body sideways-on to Tomas, making it more difficult to see his face. He talked at a spot on the ground equidistant between them.

'People saw it, you know. Your car going up on the pavement and crashing into a load of bins and that. The lads had to leap out of the way to save themselves. Covered in scrapes and bruises and all that, so they are. I...I wouldn't call it. No, it doesn't look good.'

Tomas squinted. 'Doesn't look good for who? What do you mean, you stupid little man?'

Ted Mulvihill looked up then; for just a second he squarely caught Tomas's gaze, a tongue of anger misting his eye. Then it was gone, and Ted looked down at the ground.

'Well, like. Not good for the guards or anything like that. This is serious. Attempted...'

'Oh, shut up!' Tomas placed his hands on his hips. 'I have the guards out here every other day because of the destruction and mayhem your brats are causing in my house. Destroying irreplaceable objects. Family heirlooms – things my mother and father gave me to me. Both dead now. Can't be re-placed. Are your parents dead?'

Ted Mulvihill said nothing.

'Are they? Dead?'

Still he didn't reply.

'Are you slow, man? Are you retarded in some way?'

'Now you've no call to be talking to me like that!'

'For God's sake!' Tomas lurched out of the doorway, causing Ted Mulvihill to involuntarily move backwards, then – remembering that he was there to represent family pride – stand his ground. Tomas produced his index finger and again shoved Ted in the chest.

'Your sons stabbed my daughter.' Almost a tone of victory.

Ted shook his head. 'I don't know anything about that. Don't you be mak-ing accusations—'

'They stabbed my daughter. She has a scar!'

'I'm going to get the guards, so.'

'Go ahead!' screamed Tomas, this time shoving Ted Mulvihill with both hands, causing him to spin off at an angle and collide with the half-open gate. Ted crashed to the ground, but quickly sprang up. He backed away steadily now, an arm and crooked finger outstretched.

Pathetic creature. Hard to believe he's their father. He didn't put them up to it. No brains, no balls.

'You can't be talking to me like this. It's not right. I'll send up me brother to you. He was in the army. You won't be shoving him around.' Ted Mulvihill retreated across Bass Avenue until he was swallowed by the alleyway leading to Beatha Road. 'I'm telling ya, the army!'

'I won't miss next time.'

Tomas watched him go. Then, with an imperial sweep, he gathered the dressing gown around him and turned back towards his house. The woman in number 16 was outside her home, frizzy hair standing up like an exclam-ation mark. She stared at Tomas without blinking. Tomas treated her to a long, theatrical bow.

*

The History of Things

WHERE ARE those bloody groceries?

Way past eleven now, almost half past. Website said between nine and ten. *Nine and ten.*

Tomas gazed out the window, saw nothing, sat back on the bed, then looked out the window again. Finally he switched on the television.

Bored now. Probably what they want. Waiting for me to lose concentration.

Sending the father out to complain. My God. Cheek.

Tomas flicked through the channels. CNN. MTV. Comedy Central. Disney. HBO. RTÉ. BBC. VH1. Sky Movies. Channel 4. National Geographic. He paused for perhaps twenty seconds on each. The sort of thing Anna used to do when she lived at home. Back then he found it annoying, yet today it gripped him in an immediate, dazzling fashion. Music. Pity. Rape. War. Laughter. Football. Bunnies. Remorse. Cowboys. A multiverse of event. Everything instant and forgettable. A culture obsessed with itself. On September 11th no one had told him about the attack on the Twin Towers, no calls or text messages. He was walking down Tottenham Court Road when he first saw it, a bank of unblinking TV sets in a shop window, a dozen planes silently gliding into a dozen silver buildings. But without commentary, Tomas wasn't aware what he was looking at and so assumed it was a scene from some controversial new disaster movie featuring, to his eye, some rather cheap-looking special effects. Later on, almost everyone seemed to have a story about how they had first heard of the attack. Tomas never told his.

He switched off the television and listened to the ambient sounds of the city creeping into the room. A light swish of wind, and behind that, plane engines, scraps of voice. Came here not just to escape Marta, but to escape everything: all this modern din I don't understand threatening to drown me out. Came because I knew no one would remember me, yet here I remember so much.

The phone rang.

*

'TOMAS, WHATEVER you are going through, please know that I've been to the same place. Similar places, anyway. So please ring me, OK? I don't know what's going on, but your friend Eli doesn't seem too happy today. We've been sent home, you probably know that. There's a rumour they are going to close down the production entirely. That couldn't be true, could it? The whole thing? I mean, crazy. We've got stuff in the can and now we give up? Anyway, what am I doing, chattering on? Look, all I'm ringing to say—'

Karin's voice was suddenly replaced by a dull beeping, like the monitor of someone close to death. Tomas gave a stiff smile. Not enough time to say what she was ringing to say.

He threw the phone on the bed and whispered *Fuck*, his lips curling around the word. Swearing compulsively now, a vulgar pleasure he couldn't get enough of. Like wiping your ass with silk. A line from something. What? One of those *Matrix* movies. Noisy, pointless trash. Must have been an industry do.

Tomas had been good at them, weaving his way through the crowd, smiling and nodding like yes, he really was delighted to be here. And mostly, he was. People were pleased to see him. How are you, Tomas, always-smiling Tomas?

'Fuck.'

Through the window he eyed the squad car growling up Bass Avenue and crunching to a halt outside. Taking their time. Two in uniform, getting out, stretching, chatting to a white-haired woman across the street, the other kicking a ball back to the Nigerian kids. Thank you, Sir, the boys rattle off, thank you, Sir.

Letting everyone have a good, long look.

They had threatened. Mister Dalton, I'm ringing to let you know that a warrant has been issued for your arrest. Now I know you've had some problems and I am aware of those so I'm sure we can sort it out. But if a serious complaint is made, an arrest warrant has to be issued. Which is why I'm ringing you. It would be better for all concerned if you made your way down to the station. Save us having to send a car up, do you get my drift?

Oh yes, I get the drift. Doubt if Mulvihill complained. Must have been the other one, Doyle. The tall one. Father in prison or some such. His mother, then, some long-legged slattern with sagging breasts and a permanent frown of complaint. Jaysus, he's a fuckin' loony, that man. Attacking my young fella. Never did anything on him.

Tomas felt the hotness around his neck and had to staunch an urge to wrench the window open and scream blue abuse at the guards. Screwed down though. Just as well. Send splinters everywhere and make an awful racket. Vulgar, screaming out the window. You'll never take me alive, copper. Like them. Not like a Dalton. All about restraint.

Should never have sold the house.

Tomas shrank back inside the room. They could look up at any second. Sit quietly until they go.

The doorbell rang. He remained still, hands folded into his lap. Restraint now. It will be over soon. Do what your mother does.

But Mother didn't do what was expected. And even though Tomas was a man by then – first year in film school – and even though he understood how exhausted she must be, having nursed her mute, puzzled husband, having kept her grief private while the being that was once Tom Dalton slowly dissolved before her, Tomas still thought she would do what Daddy instructed. Dressed in a black wool suit which made him itchy, Tomas had moved slowly and said little. He read a prayer, carried the coffin, marched to the graveyard and remained as solid as granite, all the while pretending not to hear while his blotchy-faced mother snorted and cried, arms extended to keep her aloft.

Like the town drunk.

He understood her grief, yet – as much to his own amazement as hers – could not forgive her for expressing it in public. An extravagant waste of something far too valuable to squander. Father had said.

Tomas had expected her to apologise, given time, to realise how she had let them down with that display. Yet it never came. Nothing came. She sat in his chair, looking much older. Sometimes crying, sometime spitting bitterness at him for his new life in England. She told him she wished for death now, and Tomas hid his disgust by not replying.

Probably told a lot of people. Dead within the year. Huge funeral, and all of them acting as if this was a complete shock, as if they didn't know about the drinking, about the pills. A neighbour found her, and although the body had gone to the hospital by the time Tomas arrived back in Dublin, the stink was still overpowering, a sickly-sweet pong of decay which filled the house, which made remaining there unendurable.

No choice, no. No money. Mother's family were all too old to be of any use, and Daddy's people lived miles away. Anyway, nobody offered. Sell the house to pay for college, for the future. What they would have wanted.

Tomas kept what he could. His father's braces. Her set of playing cards. Some other small things. But everything else had to go. Where would he have put it? Didn't have anywhere, except for the grotty bedsit in London.

No option. So how could that be betrayal?

Downstairs, the doorbell rang several times more. Tomas heard them try to open the letterbox, which he also had screwed shut. They shouted through the door. Mister Dalton, could you come out please? We know you are in there.

No they don't.

'Please go away,' whispered Tomas. 'Go away.'

*

'DELIVERY BETWEEN nine and ten, it said on the website.' Tomas pointed at his watch. 'It's a *quarter to one* now.'

The young man – he was no more than nineteen – nodded, then looked up and down the street to indicate that he didn't care about any of this, but also, Tomas fancied, to show off his haircut, which was long and very carefully dishevelled. Having glanced around, the man faced Tomas. He attempted to shrug, but the large cardboard box in his arms prevented this. Instead, he gently wiggled his elbows. He pointed with his chin towards the interior of the house.

'So, do you want me to…?'

'I'll take it,' said Tomas, wrenching the box from him.

The young man rubbed his shoulder, as if he had sustained an injury. 'Sure. Up to you.'

Tomas placed the box in the living room, tipped the young man a euro (which seemed to be too little, judging from the reaction) and sent him on his way. Then he stepped into the front yard for a quick recce. Guards gone, thank God. No sign of tampering. Gate closed. Seemed fine. The three boys from next door (how many children do they have?) were still playing, moving nimbly back and forth across the tarmac, dancing around and behind the ball. They passed it to each other in a well-defined triangle, within which each had his own small area to practise ball skills. Pass, dribble, pass, bounce, bounce, pass, chest, knee, head, pass.

For a moment – just a moment, because he really had no time to waste – Tomas remembered the optimistic feelings which had crowded upon him when he first arrived on Bass Avenue. He watched the boys, listening to the slight *umph* sound they made with each pass, and so didn't notice the fist coming towards the right side of his head.

A much louder *umph* arrived into Tomas's ear, leaving it soundless for some seconds as he sprawled into the railings, grabbing for handholds like a sailor in a storm. The ear came back to life, whizzing in complaint.

Panting and wild-eyed, Tomas turned to face former Corporal Marcus Mulvihill – known as Maxer to his friends because some years back he let it be known that he would bate anyone who considered calling him Marker, or worse still, Muccer. Marcus Doyle slowly rolled up the sleeves of his navy blue tracksuit, exposing faded turquoise tattoos. Slowly, Marcus arched his back until his arse was sufficiently protruding. He released a long, buzz-saw fart.

'Do you know what that is?' he said. 'That's the smell of justice.'

Marcus straightened up and relaxed for a moment, like a man somewhat relieved that this part of his routine had gone well. Hours of rehearsal bringing their reward. He placed his legs slightly apart and jabbed a thumb towards his chest.

'Marcus Mulvihill. Do ya know who I am?'

Marcus Mulvihill looked remarkably like his brother – close enough to be his twin – yet this physical resemblance was almost totally negated by the difference in personality. Even the way he rolled up his sleeves seemed designed to reveal how Marcus was an aggressive and malevolent being, someone others would call upon (for a few bob) to provide pain and blood. Perhaps because of some abnormality in the womb, or some childhood trauma, or the brutalising effect of years of army life, or perhaps because he was not a very nice person, violence made total sense to Marcus Mulvihill. He subscribed to it as a lifestyle choice in the way others are keen on yoga or vegetarianism. His commitment was such that Marcus even hoped his victims would love it also, that they would admire the dexterous cunning he employed for the first surprise attack, the way he would torture them mentally as well as physically. Because there was a moral dimension to the way Marcus Mulvihill handed out beatings. Wouldn't touch, say, a cripple or a blind fella or someone who didn't really deserve it. Marcus would always let them know why they had it coming so they could learn something from the experience.

'Do you know who I am?'

Tomas straightened up and gently probed the part of his face where the blow had landed. He looked back at his attacker. 'Well of course I know who you are. Do you get pleasure from asking pointless rhetorical questions?'

Marcus Mulvihill frowned. 'What kind of questions?'

'Rhetorical.'

Marcus kept the frown, disliking the tone of this exchange. Tomas flashed a memory of something he had seen once on television, though he had no idea what show or when or where.

Bits of life flaking away like a diseased scalp, detaching from the temporal context. At least it isn't a static process, like cells in the body, while some memories detach themselves, new ones form. This is new. When was the last time someone hit? School?

The television scene consisted of an English policeman interviewing a woman who had seen a flasher (though was it the interview he saw, or the policeman telling others about the interview?). He asked her, Was the man in a state of arousal? No, she said, I think it was a Ford Escort.

'You think this is fucking funny?'

Marcus Mulvihill unzipped the jacket of his tracksuit, did it with the air of one who has been professionally offended, whose methods, dedication, even integrity had been called into question. *Smiling* – this had never happened before. Especially embarrassing, now that he was representing the family. Fucking pervert. Think I'll kick him in the nuts. A lot.

The removal of the tracksuit top finally revealed one significant physical difference between the Mulvihill brothers: Marcus had a gym-built body, his arms so thickly landscaped with muscles it seemed scarcely credible they could move at all. Slowly, he stretched them.

'Fucking destroy you,' said Marcus, in a tone of voice which implied that he was genuinely hurt.

'We destroy our enemies when we make friends with them,' said Tomas, backing away along the railing. 'Abraham Lincoln said that.'

'What? Fuck. Stop talking like that.'

'It's the only way I know how to talk. I've led a rich life.'

The smile was still sitting on Tomas's face. The boys on the street had stopped playing football. They stood rigid, staring, not sure yet of the level of threat. The eldest bundled the other two towards the house, telling them not to look, but knowing they would because they had before, when they lived on the little farm in Kwara and the men came at night with their big sticks and asked Papa to come outside.

How strange this chilly, pale-skinned world must be to them. Tomas moved sideways towards the gate. He's about to lunge. Don't feel particularly alarmed. Strange. Almost enjoyed that punch. A pleasant jolt. Jumping into the sea on a boiling hot day.

'Where you think you're fucking going?' said Marcus, finally moving. Tomas dodged sideways – not near quickly enough – but a small patch of still-wet cobblestones came to his aid, causing Marcus to slip and half-fall, a staggering motion which rendered him awkward and rather stupid-looking. Tomas raced back into the house.

The History of Things

Despite the thick darkness in the hallway, Marcus chased without hesitation, ignoring the tiny stabs against his legs and arms. Felt like piano wire. You could lop a man's head off with that. As he skidded into the kitchen he quickly checked for ripped skin or blood, and righted himself just in time to see Tomas, crouched like a baseball player, that weird smile still sitting on his face and in his hands a long plank of wood, forested with nails. Marcus raised an arm as the plank came towards him and was briefly transported by the idea of just how *meaty* his limbs were, of how there was a distinct, chunky sound when the nails sank in, so deeply that the plank was now affixed to his arm, like some crude prosthetic. And while he was screaming and preparing to pull it from his flesh – while Tomas scrambled out of the house again – Maxer Mulvihill found pride in the fact that he had enough muscle development to support the weight of something as large as this.

The stick clattered to the floor, globs of Maxer's blood darkening the nails. Quickly – and this was another source of pleasure – he knew exactly what to do. Marcus shook his injured arm under some tap water, then took a wedge of kitchen towel and pressed it against the two holes, about six inches apart: as if he had been bitten by an giant vampire. He ran in pursuit.

Tomas waited in the Saab, doors locked, engine running. He could have pulled away, but he wanted Marcus to see first. Perhaps even follow a little, bounce off the car and shatter bones against the pavement.

Marcus reached the gate before realising where his quarry was. He shook his head, said something Tomas couldn't hear, then glared intimidatingly. In return, Tomas gave a pinched smile.

Fool. Too stupid even to beat up an old man like me. He's not behind any of this – boys are twice as clever. It's them, only them.

Marcus glared some more, then walked back and pulled the front door shut. He gestured and shouted and although Tomas couldn't hear, he guessed that Maxer was saying he had done this to prevent him returning to the house; Tomas had nowhere to go.

Marcus grimaced, one hand placed gingerly across his right forearm, the kitchen towel quickly turning a dark, sloppy red. Tomas brought his window down just an inch; just enough to be heard.

'Thanks for shutting my door. Idiot. And you should get that arm seen to.'
He shot off in the Saab, leaving behind the trails of his screaming laugh.

*

BLOODY DIFFICULT to find anywhere to park: somewhere close enough to keep an eye on the traffic moving in and out of Bass Avenue, yet not so close to be spotted by the Mulvihills or any other irate relations. He settled on a spot just off the far side of Clontarf Road, almost directly opposite Bass Avenue. Same sort of houses, yet here they seemed smothered with care, the red brick intact and scrubbed, the railings painted. Proper curtains. Even speed bumps.

He positioned the car at the side of the shop. It was a de facto grocery store, yet, perhaps for local marketing reasons, gave the impression that it was an off-license and sold nothing but alcohol, specifically cheap European brands of lager and cider. Posters, hastily scribbled in marker, filled up the front window, each one screaming a low-cost path to oblivion. Cans €1.30! Large Cider €2! Bottle Powers, €7.50!!

He bought a can of Coke, some Tayto, a box of cigars. In the car, he munched the crisps and studied the outside terrain, occasionally glancing in his rear view mirrors. He chuckled about Marcus Mulvihill closing the front door. Idiot. Did me a favour. Club worked well. Splat. Straight into his arm. Have to wait here though. Until dark.

Tomas tried sleeping, yet despite the weight in his eyelids couldn't keep them closed for more than a few seconds. They'll attack the house again. Where else will Marcus go but to the home of his brother, just one street across? Look what the bastard did to me. The twins will hear some mythic version of the battle, of how Uncle Maxer chased the bad man away, leaving the house alone and exposed, deserving of more punishment.

Go back.

No. He'll be waiting.

Shit. Shit. Shit.

Tomas watched the gloomy traffic creep along Clontarf Road, stared so intently that for a few seconds he didn't recognise the blue van – Swan Removals – with the bit of rust crusting around the left rear light, the short fat man at the wheel talking to the long thin man beside. Alfie pointed towards Bass Avenue, Dave glanced in the same direction. That's where we moved in your man, you know. The bloke from London. Film director. Oh yeah. Then they looked away and drove on. Tomas considered running after them, waving. But he wouldn't have made it in time.

Nearly forgotten them. Not so long ago though. What Karin said – all the different times existing in the same space. Me then. Peg and Tom Dalton, the Kellys, the O'Connors, Mrs Brady, the Conways, the Barrets, the Galvins, the staring woman, the Nigerian family, the Doyles, the Mulvihills. Me now. An article once. In *Nature*? Time travel is theoretically possible, if not practical. But it means the past doesn't die. It's there somewhere, just beyond our vision. Like ghosts. Mother and Father and me, still here.

We hated it.

Tomas laughed out loud, then glanced around to ensure no one was watching.

No. Mother loved Ireland. Just never said it. Ranted against the bishops and the politicians and the small-minded neighbours and the filthy state of the place and look at them, watching us, gossiping into their hands. But she was a patriot. They didn't deserve her. Your ma is weird. She loves the gunmen. No brothers and sisters, you're weird. No one wanted you.

Bastards, bastards.

Tomas stayed where he was and cursed his miserable cowardice.

*

JUST WAIT. Bit longer. Wait. Patience.

To keep his mind from clawing out of his skull, Tomas decided to come up with a plan. Something simple, which took advantage of his current situation, something which would work.

Of course he didn't think everything out: he didn't, for instance, decide what he would do once he had captured the boys. In the scene he imagined, he would interrupt them in the prosecution of their crimes (but before any more serious damage was done) and then be relieved to find the guards arriving only seconds later. Like in a film.

Relieved. Funny word to use. Maybe not. Relieved because those other urges were so inarguable – once he caught them, there was nothing else he could do, his life against theirs. Could hardly take them prisoner or bring them to the useless police or back to their trashy parents. No choice.

But you couldn't. Not really?

Eventually, the sky began to turn navy and each sound became more distinct as the daytime bustle died away. Driven by boredom, anxiety and a profound need to pee, Tomas got out of the Saab, locked it and made for the house, smartly crossing Clontarf Road, then pausing at the end of Bass Avenue to check for any sign of activity. Seemed to be deserted, though in the thinning light it was impossible to tell for sure. He chose to walk on the pavement opposite his house, and despite his scratchy need to get back there, found his step slowing. Such a milky coward. Everything could be destroyed and you're acting like this. Yet still he walked slowly, remaining on the far side, glancing up the alleyway and walking past his house to check it from several angles. Nothing, nothing, the whole street empty and bleached of sound. Tomas felt bloated, as if any number of his internal organs might burst with pressure.

Go on, go on.

He teetered on the edge of the pavement. In one breathless rush, he raced across the road, unlocked the front door and slammed it behind. He shot the bolts and set the alarm, checked the golf club was still in place, then switched on the hall lights. Slivers of fishing line lay on the floor from where Uncle Marcus had burst through. No sign of anything; not yet.

Where first? He doubted the sitting room: already been in there. Put the ants in the kitchen. Been upstairs too. The letters, the cards, the dollhouse. So where? Best start upstairs. Get to the loo.

Tomas bounded up the steps, unzipping as he went. His piss splashed thunderously into the toilet, the torrent of urine seeming to continue long after he felt his bladder had emptied, causing him to howl in frustration at being trapped in this manner, while the bones of his life were being ground down. But eventually it ceased and Tomas moved fervently from room to room.

Everything here: the secreted matches still in place, even most of the fishing wire. One broken in the hallway, but he could have done that himself. Nothing vandalised, though – pictures, objects, Harry Boland letters, all of it untouched. Tomas frowned. The bloated sensation was still there, as if some invisible fist was squeezing his insides.

Must be downstairs then.

'Oh.'

He had to hold onto the wall as he made his way, suddenly struck weak by the knowledge of what they had done.

Tomas staggered to the kitchen and felt a curious sense of disappointment. Not up to the usual standards – none of the vicious inventiveness he had witnessed before. Simply grab and throw. They were disturbed or didn't have much time.

He shook himself. Did you want it to be destroyed? What for? So you can suffer? Say boo-hoo, poor me. They wrecked the only thing Mammy gave me? Unhinging you, this.

The frame lay shattered on the ground, tiny shards of glass crunching under his feet. He shook the looser bits out, then gingerly extracted the scapula. Undamaged. But the obvious prize to go after, the heart of the matter. Like they already know all about Tomas Dalton and are working their way backwards, through his daughter, his marriage, his childhood, to this. Tomas sat down and stroked the cheap brown cloth with his thumb. As a boy he had imagined that this was the material monks' habits were made of. Deliberately rough, so they could offer up their suffering. Kept it under his pillow back then. He'd look at the picture of Saint Brigid – that was why Mammy gave it to him. Probably didn't have much time, and wanted to leave something the nuns wouldn't spot, seeing as she knew they would never meet again. Probably moved to some other convent after, to stir huge pots of boiling clothes along with all the other sluts and fallen women. Because Saint Brigid, she was like them. Her mother was a slave girl and she wasn't born with a daddy either. That was why she had to give Tomas up, for his own good because a girl like her couldn't be minding a child with all that sin and disgrace on her head.

He was three when he left. That's what he thinks he remembers. There are white stairs, his coat being buttoned. Shouting from somewhere. His mammy whispering, shakily, Be a good boy now. Make Mammy proud. That's all.

Later on, he imagined her free of the convents, living in her own nice flat and turning up one day, just like that. His parents would be delighted, they wouldn't mind: they might all live together. Later still, when he found this fantasy too unrealistic, he imagined she was watching over him, that she had discovered his circumstances and address, and every weekend or fortnight would come to Beatha Road to watch for a while, watch her tall son getting stronger and learning more each day. Going to be a film director. Well.

But the month after Peg Dalton died, Tomas had sold the house and moved to England and there was no way to tell his mammy about any of this.

She didn't want him to find her. Always known that. The decision was made, and couldn't be undone by some fake reunion; that story was lost.

Tomas never tried to make contact, though he had gone through a phase of collecting orphan tales. George Orwell's son, Richard. Lost two sets of parents by the time he was eight. President Niyazov of Turkmenistan. Driven insane by the childhood loss of his mother. He ordered that the month of April be named after her. And Tomas Dalton, the boy who doomed his mammy to an endless search of Bass Avenue, to wondering why her only treasure had vanished.

Never should have sold that house.

No. Mammy would have understood, wouldn't have wanted him to stay here with all their insect eyes. Parents both went mad, and him adopted. Bad seed. She would have known that anything was better than staying, even the galactic loneliness of the boat, the endless spread of a strange city.

Yet he had broken the link, and since then Tomas Dalton had failed to own anything in his life.

14

FOGGY, LIKE the street had been drowned in a sea of milk. It re-created Bass Avenue as a fairy tale place, the buildings reduced to lightly sketched outlines, all detail scrubbed away by this lumpy mist which seemed to have substance, which had the seductive nature of clouds. Come on, jump. We'll catch you.

Tomas didn't trust this weather. Didn't believe it. Shouldn't occur in Ireland. It was for *noir* films in Germany or LA or as a ponderous symbol of God in one of Marta's Bergman flicks. (Once he told her that in film, *everything* is a symbol of God. Even the camera; especially the camera. Her face had stalled – impressed, but unwilling to admit it.)

Fog didn't belong here. Handy, though; keep everything at a distance. If I can barely see them, then the gardaí can't see me.

Why do they bother? Obvious I'm not going to come out. Doing their job, can't be blamed for that, all be over soon, by this evening, with luck. Then turn yourself in. The weary outlaw. Surrender your will to the legal process. Laws, like houses, lean on one another. Edmund Burke? Can't remember reading Edmond Burke.

It was like some malicious individual had downloaded a virus into Tomas's brain, filling it with nonsense, disrupting the memory connections he wanted to maintain.

'Mister Dalton.'

A familiar, breathless voice from the far side of the front door.

Of course they'll bring him back now, the friendly, harmless one. Sly.

'Mister Dalton, it's Norbert, Norbert Clarke.'

What will he say? Can you lie, Norbert?

'Mister Dalton, I know you must be very upset at everything that's been happening to you and your family. It's stressful, it's unfair. It seems like the law can't protect you, and we should talk about those issues. But Mister Dalton, what you are doing now will not make things better. For your own sake, I beseech you to come down and talk to us. Just talk.'

Beseech? Ain't you fancy, Norbert.

There was some low muttering, then Norbert again.

'Mister Dalton, there is another reason why you should come out here.'

Yes.

'Do you remember the other day I said all this, you know, the vandalism seemed familiar?'

And you said it was nothing, just a random surge of impulses in your dull brain. But now it's something? Suddenly Norbert Clarke has a big break in the case? Yes, of course you do, and yes, I can't wait to hear what it is, let me run down there. Better yet, let's all go to the garda barracks for a nice cup of tea. Sweet, that he can't lie any better than this; insulting that they think I'd fall for it.

'It's come back to me what this reminds me of. I know I said before that I shouldn't have said that, but now I'm glad I did, because there is something.'

Yes, yes, yes.

'I don't want to go into details here, you know, shouting through your door, but I think this may be some sort of game.'

They are children – *of course* it's a bloody game.

'I can explain it all to you, Mister Dalton, if you just come out and talk to us, that's all.'

Stop it, Norbert, you're embarrassing.

'So, you know, I think we have a solution to all this. Or an explanation anyway. We just need you to come out here, Mister Dalton, really, you know, there's nothing to be…'

An explanation, could he have?

No, no, no, no, it's a trick, it's an *obvious* trick, just to get the door open.

Tomas slapped his hands over his ears, reducing Norbert's voice to a distant murmur. Concentrate, keep watch, be ready for the plan.

Eventually, the voices stopped. Tomas picked up the phone. Make some calls, apologise while there's still time. Afterwards, well.

*

A LONG gap at the start, then shuffling, throat-clearing. A few Errs and finally Hello. It's me. Well, you probably guessed that already. Anyway, it's, ehm. Not sure exactly what time it is. The morning. Quite foggy out there.

Ehm.

Been stuck in this house for so long now, but I'm going to resolve the problem today. One way or another. I just wanted to ring to say that I understand how upset you must have been about my behaviour. I won't try and justify. I mean, I had no option. I am fighting for my life in this house. But I understand your position, how upset you must have been. Losing the film, well. Can't have been easy, no. And obviously I'm aware that people have lost their jobs over this and that is terrible. It's appalling. But I had no choice. It's just that I greatly, oh, I suppose I greatly regret all this. For all the people on the film. And for you, Eli. Especially you because we have worked for so many years together and I do genuinely have great respect and admiration for what you.

Beep. Beep. Beep.

Tomas stopped talking, then glared at the phone as if it had said something impertinent.

Where did it cut off? The bit about respect? Ring back and add that in?

No, silly, sound crazy. Doesn't matter now. Probably never see him again anyway. Just as well. Exposed him to debt, legal action. Eli will get out of it, it's what he's good at.

But won't forgive. Why should he?

Outside, the fog had become threadbare. From his bedroom window, Tomas could make out the cracked roofs of the houses across the street, and – he only noticed this for the first time – see halfway down the laneway to Beatha Road. Can easily spot the boys sneaking up to attack. Excellent.

Guards being a nuisance today.

They had stopped banging on the door, but clearly had no intention of leaving – nice and visible, where all the neighbours could see, talking into phones and their car radio. They kicked ball with the Nigerian kids and stopped to chat with some of the old women waddling past, veiny hands clutching worn shopping bags.

Tomas picked up the phone again. Anna: work or home?

He didn't answer the question. Instead, his gaze drifted back to the street. The guards, big smiles halving their red faces, spoke to a man with his arm in a sling. The man kept his head at a sideways incline, like a politician forced to listen carefully to constituents' concerns, no matter how ridiculous.

Tomas stemmed another urge to shout out the window.

Uncle Marcus and the gardaí all pulling together, the police and the thug. I am the outsider here.

The guards went back to playing football, but Marcus Mulvihill remained where he was, leaning against a graffiti-splattered chunk of wall on the far side of Bass Avenue, awkwardly smoking a cigarette with his injured arm. Out here, waiting for you. The police won't stop me.

*

RING HER at home. Leave a message. Yes, avoiding her, but not weak – fallible, human, perfectly understandable, what with all you've been through. Why face all those heavy sighs, those judgment-shaped questions?

Anyway, it was efficient. The time limit enforced by the answering machine imposed a pleasurable need to be brief, to be slightly formal but totally to the point in a way neither he nor Anna was used to.

Tomas reached for the phone, but it rang before he touched it. His hand retreated, waited for the ringing to cease, then dialled his voicemail. Like eavesdropping on the world. Being here but not.

'Tomas. Hi. Ah, sorry to ring you at home like this, but, ah, it's Clara, um. Really sorry about, you know, everything. I hope you're OK? You must be upset, and, and I was enjoying working with you. Well, maybe we will again. Anyway, I'm sorry to bother you, I mean, I don't know if you're even in contact with her, but if you are talking to Karin, could you say a really huge thank you to her? I mean, I don't know why she did it, but it was really, really sweet of her. So could you just say thanks for me? She'll know what for. Oh yeah, and say thanks from Peg too. You know Peg in make-up? Anyway, that's all. Bye, bye, bye.'

He hung up, frowning slightly. An act of kindness from Karin. Probably some extravagant present. But not that surprising, she has that in her. She can see others. She saw me.

Eli closed down the film then.

Tomas nodded slowly, then picked up the phone again.

As he dialled, he sipped tea. Marcus Mulvihill had finally vacated his perch across the street. Probably gone for lunch, or to the pub or the bookies. The gardaí were still there, draped over the squad car, the Nigerian kids having gone inside. Tomas cleared his throat and waited for the *beep* on Anna's machine.

Anna. Anna.

I was going to say…but I've forgotten. Completely gone out of my head.

How is your scar? Your face. Your beautiful face. Happened because of me, and I will carry that. And I am truly, truly sorry for being remiss. I mean, as your father. I…oh, shit. I always feel as if there is something we have to discuss. I don't mean, you know, the lesbian decision or whatever you want to call it. It's not that at all. It's something else, but I don't know what and it seems like I have to guess and you won't forgive me unless I do.

There is so little time. It just flies away.

He hung up the phone, and for a while sat with his hands covering his face.

*

THE GARDAÍ will go shortly: bound to. Hardly going to waste resources on two of them out there indefinitely. Why not kick down the front door and grab me? Because I'm innocent, moral pressure is all they have. They'll go when the hours tick into overtime, then the boys will come. Probably hiding out there already, skulking.

Tomas set about thinking of how best to protect the collection for the period he planned to be out of the house. Won't be long, a few minutes. Yet still. He walked around the upstairs landing, then back into his bedroom. He looked at the phone, considered who else to call.

As if in response, it rang.

Who's this? Fuck it, fuck it, who is this? Why call, what's the point?

Calm, calm.

Nothing to lose now.

He pressed the button and neutrally chimed hello. The sound of crowds, footsteps, a mush of chatter, a voice mangled by a tannoy asking to come to the courtesy telephone in the. Rustling. Breath.

'Hello? Hello?' She sounded surprised.

'Hello.'

'Tomas?'

'Yes, Karin. How are you?'

'I'm, I'm fine. I guess. How are you?'

More crowd sounds, tannoy announcements.

'Are you in the airport?' He heard sniffing, scraping.

'Yes. I have a plane.' She said the words quietly, as if ashamed.

'So they closed down the film?'

'Yes. They did. Just like that. I dunno. I mean, Tomas, what the hell happened? Oh, don't bother. I let you down far more anyway.'

Tomas didn't reply at first, letting the aural mush of the airport swell between them. 'Clara rang me.'

'Yeah?'

'She asked me to pass on her thanks to you. From her and Peg. What did you do for them?'

Karin shushed, as if these were events which had happened years ago. 'You know, the film ended abruptly. It's these kids' livelihoods. I remember what that was like. Clara has a baby. It was nothing, nothing. A few bucks.'

The tannoy reminded travellers not to smoke in the airport.

'So you're headed back to New York?'

'Yeah. My agent got me some off-off-Broadway number. You know, something with integrity that won't make any money.'

Tomas smiled gently. 'You never had leukaemia, did you?'

There was another rise in background chatter, the sound of fumbling. 'Karin?'

Some sniffs, then, 'No. No, I didn't. How did you know?'

'My father-in-law had it. He wasted away, had no strength. You ate far too much for a sick person, and anyway, she...it doesn't really matter now.'

'No, Tomas. It does. I lied to you. Well, I didn't actually lie, technically. You asked and I didn't say anything. But do you hear that? That's the way my mind works, that's how I convince myself.'

She sighed, and Tomas could see her astride a mound of neat, fashionable suitcases. Sunglasses on, perhaps an unlit cigarette perched between her fingers. She would be wearing something long and dramatic, a leather coat, and would have situated herself in a part of the airport where her fellow travellers would have to negotiate their way around her. Karin would seem not to notice, feeding on their inconvenience. Look at me. I'm still alive.

'I told you about my divorces and all that messiness and the publicity and after the second, I guess I had a breakdown. Next thing I knew I was booking myself into hospitals and claiming to have cancer. I'd steal the empty pill boxes and carry them around in my bag. I was flying up the coast because all the hospitals in LA knew what I was doing. It was just, it was crazy.' She sighed again. 'Eventually I got into a programme and I got therapy. Munchausen's Syndrome. It's quite common. And I got over it, but I never got out of the habit of carrying the pill boxes around. I don't know why. Sort of comfort, I guess. And then you asked me, and I so wanted you to like me, and I couldn't resist. It just...man, I blew that, didn't I?'

Tomas didn't reply. The gardaí had got in their car and were preparing to drive off. No sign of the uncle. What time? Nearly three. On their way back from school. All be over by six.

'I'm hardly in a position to judge,' he said. 'You wouldn't be flying home now if it wasn't for me.'

'That's completely different, Tomas. What's happening to you isn't your fault.'

'Well, thank you. You're about the only other person in the world who sees it that way at the moment.'

'You're welcome.' Her voice had taken on a soft, viscous quality, and now Tomas wanted to end the conversation. She had a plane to catch, he had his plan to carry out. Anything else was a waste of time.

'Do you think you might get over to New York some time?'

'I don't know.' There was a time when he would have made some vague commitment to show no hard feelings, to struggle against the idea that everything ends. Maybe. You never know. But you do, you do. 'I'm afraid I can't see past my current situation and I have to resolve that first. You better go and catch your plane, Karin.'

'Yeah, OK.'

'Take care of yourself.'

'Yes.'

He hung up. The garda car was gone. Tomas yawned, stretched and wondered at his sudden sense of ennui, as if what happened with Karin was a regular occurrence, as if he had grown quite bored with proving and reproving the thesis that eventually, all people disappoint one another.

*

IT WON'T be any safer in the attic. They'll guess. But it's only a few seconds I need. Might puzzle them, might even fool the fuckers into thinking I've moved everything out of the house in the dead of night. Keep them occupied long enough to get back.

Still, though. Everything? Up there? Everything? No, tired.

Don't be such a wimp, move it. Just take a look.

He lugged the stepladder upstairs while fighting a cotton sleepiness. Could go to bed now, pass straight out. He yawned and shook himself, concentrated on placing the ladder squarely underneath the hatch, which suddenly seemed much further away, the distant ceiling lightly burned into his vision, like a ghost image on television. Sheets of black darted in and out of his peripheral vision as he made his careful ascent. Time slowed to a series of still images.

The step. Your veined hand. A bent knee. Don't look down. Be able to see all the way to the bottom of the stairs from here. Jesus, dizzy.

The phone rang. Tomas froze, his body jolted by the noise.

A wall. A doorway. Your hand.

Ignore it. Enough conversation for one day.

His palms were wet, kept slipping off the aluminium steps.

The step. Your hand.

Blurry.

Concentrate, think. Who will that be? Karin again? No, long gone now. Anna? Perhaps, probably got the message, worried, Dad, you're not like yourself. Is there a self to be like? Is this what appearing sane requires? A Platonic template of Tomas Dalton which has to be approximated at all times, or everyone starts to get worried. Tomas has to be Tomas and isn't allowed be anyone else. Bet it's Marta. Heard you rang Anna, meaning: you didn't ring me. What did you mean by what you said? Are you within your Platonic template today? The punishment which the wise suffer who refuse to take part in the government is to live under the government of worse men, quoth Plato.

How do you know? How do you know? Where does this come from?

A step. Your hand.

Hotness sizzling his neck and face, Tomas neared the hatch, his eyes closed to counter the dizziness. Sharp stabs in his chest from every breath. At the top, he briefly opened his eyes, but this only brought on the sensation that the ladder was slowly tipping sideways. He swung an arm now, feeling for the flat wooden surface above, banging it with the palm of his hand and crying with the effort because he wished the telephone would stop and he knew he must be falling now because he couldn't see and the muscles in his hand had turned to water and now he couldn't feel anything, his entire body free of sensation, and even though his eyes were still closed he still had a sense of something spinning away, of an orange patchwork of light and shadow.

Good God. Good God.

*

THE TATTERED uniforms of Tayto, Jonny Onion Rings, Refreshers, Smarties, chocolate buttons, chewing gum in a variety of colour-coded flavours. Coke and Club Orange. An empty ten box of Silk Cut Purple. Matches. Tomas sifted through the rubbish congealed around the rusty water tank. Had a few picnics for themselves. Up here like rats, gobbling, sniggering, waiting.

The attic was thin and dirty, sectioned by shadowed wooden triangles. Sparkling dust waltzed in the thick air. The roof tiles coughed. In the far corners, where the light from the weak bulb could not penetrate, strange noises leaked from unidentifiable black shapes.

Like an archaeologist, he examined the naked blockwork. Curling letters on the wall. Red and black, mostly. They're no artists. *Beatha Road Rules, Man Utd Rules. Shit. Fuck. Out of me bin.* Matchstick pictures of women with huge breasts or men with monumental erections. Innocent, in their ugly way. Tomas leaned against the water tank, relieved that at least this mystery had been revealed to him.

Should have thought of it. Why would she help them? Unless she wasn't aware? No. Ridiculous.

He took long, mountain climber steps towards the wall which separated his house and number 16, where several of the blocks had been removed. It was easy to squeeze into the adjoining attic, though without the benefit of a light fitting on this side, it was almost impossible to proceed. Straddling the wall, Tomas produced the small torch he had put into his pocket. A few boxes. More graffiti, in blue this time. *Celtic rocks.* The hatch on this side had not even been closed properly.

'Right. Right.'

*

QUICK CHECK for the guards or the uncle. Excited now. Finally, some luck, shame there's no one to tell.

And as he staggered out the front door, there she was, saving him the bother of having to extract her from her house (banging on the windows, going around the back, setting fire to a newspaper and stuffing it through her letterbox – he'd collated a list as he'd thundered down the stairs). As usual, staring brutally, her head rotating robot-like to the left and following Tomas as he exited his own gate and walked to hers.

'Hello,' Tomas said. He shivered.

The woman said nothing. Her hair and eyebrows were unusually thick, yet despite this she was quite beautiful, her features creamy and nymph-like.

She continued staring while Tomas came closer, until his nose was almost touching hers.

'That's a great act.'

No reply. No expression.

Tomas pointed upwards.

'I've been in the attic. I know. Been in *your* attic.'

Nothing.

'I suppose you thought I was stupid, not realising this sooner. Perhaps I was, but I'm sorry, I'm used to dealing with civilised human beings. You do know what that means, don't you? Civilised?'

The woman blinked. Tomas took a step backwards, then gestured towards the houses.

'What's in this for you? Why would you let those brats? Are you scared of them? Is that it? You do know what they have been doing to me? The destruction in my house, attacking my daughter. You've seen the guards banging on my door as if I'm the criminal. Their maniac uncle tried to kill me…I, I don't know.'

He folded his arms. The woman still stared, yet she had softened her expression, as if she didn't understand what Tomas was saying, yet didn't want to cause any offence. Her head was tipped at a slight angle now, her mouth stretched slightly into what could be construed as a smile. Several of her teeth were missing.

'Look, why don't you drop the lunatic act and tell me what's going on? Have they threatened you? Why have you been so hostile towards me? From the first day you were looking at me as if I had offended you. Do you know me?'

His anger rinsed away, another wave of tiredness broke over Tomas.

Not going to say anything. At least you know. Go home, get off the street. Get on with the plan.

He had already taken a step backwards when the woman held out a hand towards him, palm upwards, like an American Indian saying How. She jabbed the palm in Tomas's direction several times before retreating into her house, leaving the door open. Tomas remained where he was, suddenly aware of his heart kicking, of sheets of sweat forming along his back.

Eventually, the woman re-emerged from the house. Against her breast she clutched a curling school copybook. She took two steps towards him, then, with great deliberation, tongue extended with the effort, flicked through the book until she found a page. She turned and showed it to Tomas.

On it was written: I'm Deaf.

15

HE SPENT nearly an hour in her plain front room, a negative version of his, shaved of any adornment. Peach-coloured walls, spotted grey carpet and two red leatherette chairs which sagged uniformly in the middle, like grinning twins. There was a smell of cats, though Tomas didn't see any.

The woman – whose name could have been Alma or Agnes – didn't speak, didn't make any sound. She didn't offer him tea or apologise about the mess. She merely sat, bolt still on her leatherette seat, face set in its default expression.

If she understood what he was saying, she nodded studiously, or pointed to one of the words in her copybook, written, it appeared, many years before by people who were dead or long gone. A phrasebook for a noisy world which Alma or Agnes would never hear.

As far as Tomas could ascertain, the woman was born and had lived in this house all her life. Both her parents were dead, though there was a sister or perhaps niece who visited once a week. The woman was born deaf but never learned sign language, possibly because she was brain-damaged also. She lived entirely in the lower portion of the house, refusing to even look up the stairs. Perhaps it was where her parents died. Perhaps she found the bodies.

It took some time to explain that the boys were using her attic to get into Tomas's house, by climbing up a drainpipe and in an upstairs window, judging from the scuffmarks. Then she was mutely horrified – hands cupped to her mouth, her eyes wild, her breath coming in short, grating gulps. Tomas had to calm her down, give reassurance that it wouldn't happen again, even though he wanted it, just one more time.

She was reluctant to let him go, hanging onto his hands like a lover, moving her mouth to pronounce silent words Tomas had no hope of understanding.

How long since anyone had visited this place, apart from the sister or niece? Probably in and out. Does a clean-up, brings some food, shouts a few platitudes. Poor woman. Poor woman. No contact other than me, and the boys, squealing giggles at how clever they are, creeping into the home of the woman who can't hear them. Evil little bastards.

Fingering the scapula tucked beneath his shirt, Tomas quickly opened his front door, went upstairs, located an empty picture frame, a blank sheet of paper, a marker and some gaffer tape. He brought all of it into his bedroom. He looked out at the alley. Nothing. Nothing yet.

On the paper he wrote, in large, bold, letters (hopefully one of them can read):

Mid pleasures and palaces though we may roam,
Be it ever so humble, there's no place like home.
In this house, I CAN hear you. I can see you too.

He placed the paper inside the frame, then taped the frame across the hatch to the attic, glass side up. That will startle them. For vital seconds they will stay there, puzzling on what to do next. He knows how we're getting in. *I can see you too.* What does that mean? They'll panic. They'll run. They'll be scared.

Greatly satisfied with this work, Tomas remained by the window and waited.

*

ONE OF the old women tottered up the road and stopped in front of her house.

The phone rang. Tomas ignored it.

The old woman aimed her bloodshot eyes at Tomas's home, as if insulted by its existence. Then she commenced the painful and awkward procedures involved in opening her front door.

*

A HALF-HOUR later, Marcus Mulvihill appeared in the alley. He halted about twenty feet back from where it emerged into Bass Avenue, where he thought he couldn't be seen. The arm was out of the sling now. Like a nervous bird he moved his head from side to side, then edged further up. He kneeled and carefully studied Tomas's house, as if searching for some structural defect. He lit a cigarette, smoked it, then strolled back to Beatha Road.

*

TOMAS MADE tea and a sandwich which he didn't eat because the ham – delivered only the day before – had become stiff. Wasn't hungry anyway. Still, should complain.

The phone rang again. Tomas didn't move.

*

THE MAN in the wagon-wheels house came out to wash his car.

Always washing that car.

He carried an orange plastic bucket. He poured water over the bonnet and massaged it vigorously with a polka dot cloth. But soon he had a coughing fit and retreated back inside.

*

A SQUAD car gently swooshed past, radio crackling, the garda's reddening arms draped out of the window. They stared at the house as they went by, but didn't stop.

Bored now, Tomas checked his voicemail. Marta. Voice a bit croaky. Must have a cold. Tomas. Pause. Please ring me back. Sniff. I know we parted on bad terms in Dublin but we can't just leave it like this. And I've heard about the film. That's terrible. Sniff.

Eli told her? Fuck, fuck, interfering bastard.

And yes, Tomas. I am worried about you. Stuck in that house by yourself. With those boys. But at least now you have no reason not to come to London for a visit. Just for a few days, just to get some distance on your predicament? We could go to the Lake District if you like. Or I could come over to you. We could visit Galway. I've always wanted to see the west of – that's not important. Anna wants to talk to you as well. I don't understand any of this, but she thinks these boys could be playing some sort of game? I don't know if that makes any sense to—

He threw the phone at the wall with as much force as he could rally, but it left his hand awkwardly. It tumbled against a chair and came to rest beneath it, the small green light still flashing like an accusation.

These people will do anything. They are talking to each other – Eli, Anna, Marta, the gardaí, all sharing information about the film, conniving over what's the best story to get the mad old man out of the house – didn't work with Norbert, but he might buy it from a family member – you can mention it, Marta, but best not explain because, after all, he did throw you out of his house the last time you met; best to have the story coming from Anna, his beloved, only daughter, the straight-talking one, the one he trusts, the one he feels guilty about because of that scar on her face. Believe anything from her, he will.

Throwing a lot of phones lately.

Never liked them, not the modern ones anyway, with their menus and their games and cameras and Bluetooth GPRS 3G function button rubbish. Always left him in a mild state of panic, a sense that he *just about* understood what was going on here, that inevitably he would be bewildered. Ring me. The pen digging into the soft flesh of his hand. Beautiful pain.

It struck him that he wasn't angry, but appalled – behind all the deception, people can care for me. Even now.

*

TOMAS LAY back on the bed, just to rest for a minute, then awoke with a jangling start. He dreamed he was shouting at Mother. Peggy, be strong, he yelled. Daddy wanted you to be strong. Don't disappoint me! But she was deaf.

*

THE GRUBBY couple with the dreadlocks ambled past, not holding hands this time, swinging stained brown paper bags which seemed to contain take-away food.

The phone, now resting in its cradle, rang again. Tomas ignored it.

The couple wasn't speaking, possibly due to tiredness or because of an argument. To Tomas it seemed they were silently calculating how much time there was left.

*

HE SAW them moving in the shadows of the alley, scrabbling on hands and knees, pausing, checking behind, scrabbling forward again; small monkeys, rightly scared of the big world.

Tomas held up his arms and half-smiled.

'Finally.'

He stood and carefully stretched, watching them twitch their heads about and signal to each other. They cocked their noses in the air, then slunk back and huddled around the orange tip of a cigarette.

Tomas left the bedroom and moved towards the stairs, making a final check on the frame taped across the attic hatch. As he descended to the ground floor, he slipped on his long white raincoat.

Wee bit of a flaw. They might notice, they might wonder – fog gone, brightened up now, much too nice for a coat like this.

No, boys don't twig such things. Too busy smoking, too busy being pleased with their cleverness.

At the front door, Tomas turned off the alarm and picked up a long club dotted with bent nails. He held the club tenderly, then placed it under the raincoat. He put the door on the latch and left the house.

Don't look at them, don't look at anyone – eyes forward; children from next door with the football, ignore (they do play a lot of football). Look at the pavement, no, no, looks suspicious, walk rapidly, smartly, clickity-click go the heels upon the cracked pavement. Don't worry lads, be back soon.

He wanted to turn and look now, was surprised by how much. You've fallen into my trap this time.

This is all you are now, what they have reduced you to.

Tomas counted as he walked – one hundred and forty-three steps to the end of Bass Avenue, but nearly another seventy before he could find a way across the riot of Clontarf Road, cars screaming at him from both sides, their grills like bared fangs. And on the other side he had to duck behind a mucky Hiace van (*I've made you all up* daubed into the dust), heart thumping, the screaming cars far too close, the exhaust fumes attacking his throat.

Was that him? Was that him?

Two hundred and thirty-one. Two hundred and thirty-two. Two hundred and thirty-three. Two hundred and thirty-four.

Shit, shit, too much time, they'll be in the house. In the attic, even, puzzling over the sign. *I can hear you.* What the fuck does that mean? Quick, lads, let's leg it. Next time we'll dig a tunnel and he'll never catch us.

Moving from behind the van meant walking past the shop, where he had just seen (had he?) Marcus Mulvihill's pugnacious frame emerge, swinging his shoulders like he was dancing with some invisible partner; like he was looking for someone to say, Isn't that a little strange, the way you walk? What, pal? You starting? Shit, shit, shit.

Tomas hunkered down and peered along the pavement. Grubby white trainers. Could be him. Or did he wear boots? Old, lost their shape but had a hint of their former shine? Two hundred and forty-seven. Two hundred and forty-eight. Two hundred and forty-nine. They'll be in the house. Definitely be in the attic. The right trainer seemed to slide along the pavement as Marcus moved. If I wait, he'll walk straight past.

Hang on. Idiot. They'll be in the house.

Tomas leapt to his feet and strode out to meet Ted Mulvihill, the hunched, moustached rat of a father to those twins. Two hundred and fifty-three, two hundred and fifty-four.

'Ah!' Ted cried. 'My brother is looking for you!'

'He knows where I am,' Tomas drawled, swooping close enough to invite a collision of shoulders, if that's what he wanted. Wormy little man. Two hundred and fifty-nine. Two sixty. Two sixty-one. Two sixty-two. Get the car keys out, slippery from sweat, use both hands, let the club fall, doesn't matter if Mulvihill is looking, let him look, open the door, grab the club, get behind the wheel and gun the fucker down to the corner. Two seventy, two seventy-one. Seventy-two, seventy-three, seventy-four, come on, come on, push out, out, go, blow your horn, roar across the road and into Bass Avenue. Eighty-two. Eighty-three. Eighty-four.

Tomas scrambled out of the car, dragging the club behind him, scratching his arm on some of the protruding nails. Front door still closed, must have gone in the back. No one, Nigerian kids gone in. Good, no sign of the deaf woman. Ninety-eight, ninety-nine, a hundred.

I'm bleeding.

What next? Three hundred or four hundred? Shit.

The boys came over the side door at number 16, their eyes white and wide as they hit the ground and split in different directions around him. Tomas went to swipe at one, grab at another, but the attempt was half-done in both cases. They swept past, heading for the alley, Tomas in screaming pursuit now, ignoring the pains in his chest and legs, encouraged that he could at least keep them in sight – they were slowed by their panic, the twins partic- ularly uncoordinated as they crashed into the walls of the alley and each other. One of them slipped to the floor but scampered away just as Tomas reached him, club swinging. Too high. It clattered into the wooden fence, launching a tremor in each direction, again partially unbalancing the twin as he caught up with his brother, bounced into him, then back against the fence, then forward into the tall one, who staggered with the impact, coming to a skidding halt on his hands and knees in the tatty open area halfway along. The twins dodged around but turned once they were past to confirm that he would get up, that the man wouldn't reach him in time, swinging the club low now, extended out, just enough to smack the boy in the left thigh as he stood, the black nail skewering the scant meat on his upper leg and causing him to scream in a way the twins had never heard before, a way that brought their childhood to a crashing end.

The man was half-roaring, half-singing in some sort of ecstasy, dancing around the tall boy, who couldn't move, who could do no more than cry and hold his trembling leg.

'Yes! Yes!'

The man pointed at the twins to confirm their defeat also. They huddled together, four wide eyes, their power leaked away. The man beckoned at them to come closer, to position themselves behind the tall boy as if to pose for a photograph. They moved, but not too close, not within range of that bat.

They looked at Doyler, still unable to control the shudders as he examined the damage to his leg. Jeans ripped badly, but on the thigh little more than a nasty scratch – the nail didn't penetrate, even though it felt that way. Really sore, and everything else cocked. Like at Granny's funeral, at the end when he felt all weird because those priests were standing around praying and sprinkling holy water and it was a bit like they were scared, you know? Really scared of what happened to me gran 'cos she was breathing, she was breathing only the day before and she only had about three teeth and she smelled a bit but she was all right. She was breathing, breathing. Oh Jesus, God, please. I'm sorry, I'm sorry, I'm sorry.

The man hefted up the club, spun it over his head and grinned. He has lovely teeth. The twins were crying, arms enfolded around each other, their sobs in rhythm with Doyler's, who even now did all the talking, begging the man to stop please, Mister. Please, Mister. We didn't mean. We're sorry, we are. Please, Mister. Let me get me mammy. I want me mammy. Please, Mister, I want me ma, ma, ma, Ma Banana.

*

'WHAT DID you say?'

Doyler's eyes tumbled in their sockets, searching for the correct answer.

'I'm sorry? We're very sorry?' Doyler breathed urgently through his mouth, panting out the words.

'What did you say about your mother?'

Rapidly, the boy swiped a hand across his red and shuddering face, spreading the snot and tears to the outposts of his cheekbones.

'I want me ma?'

Tomas yelled, 'What did you call her?'

Doyler's hand came back up. 'I called her ma,' his voice cracked. 'Ma Banana. It's what we call her.'

'Jesus Christ.'

The spiky club clattered to the ground. The boys scrambled backwards from where it landed, as if the weapon was capable of continuing the attack on its own. Hands to his mouth, Tomas took a step away, then approached the boys again.

This is it – of course, of course – this is it. Look at him, coming back here and into that big house with the money from our letters, our letters. His mother cheated at them cards, she did, she robbed us and left us stuck in this kip of a place in this kip of a house and now he comes back and thinks he's one of us? He's not and we'll let him know he's not.

'Ma Banana? Ma Banana? You're sure?'

Too contorted by tears to produce any sound, the boys nodded in unison. Tomas stepped away again, a hand pressed to his forehead.

'No. She'd be too young.' He pointed. 'What ages are you? Ten? Eleven? Your mother is how old? Thirty? Forty? Fifty?'

They didn't answer, didn't even attempt.

'OK, OK.'

He was calm and sane now – weird: as if he had never meant to batter them with that stick, as if this was a guessing game.

'Your grandmother. What did you call *her*?'

Doyler nodded frantically while trying to re-engage his voice box. 'Same,' he eventually managed.

'Why?'

The boy swallowed rapidly, but this time couldn't get any purchase on his spasming throat. The pleading hand came back up.

'Why?'

'M-M-Moore Street.'

'She had a stall there?'

Doyler nodded, grateful for this assistance.

'Jesus Christ.'

Tomas smiled then – actually smiled. Yet this only increased the boys' tremors. They'd seen it in millions of films. If a bloke smiles at a time like this, then he's a real psycho.

'So that's what this was about. The letters.'

Three blotchy faces stared up at him, then glanced at each other for clues.

'The letters? The Harry Boland letters?'

More puzzled looks, transforming into alarm now – the wrong answer could go badly. But to lie risked being caught out, risked him picking up that club again.

Tomas leaned against the wall opposite, then slid down onto his hunkers.

'My mother, Peg Dalton, she won these letters from your grandmother. In a card game. You know, the ones you stuck the nail through. Years ago. Before you were born. Before I was born.'

Cautiously, they nodded no.

'But you have heard your parents speak about this? Your parents encouraged you to attack my house, didn't they?'

Doyler opened his mouth, but only a dull squeak emerged.

'His ma killed him,' one of the twins finally offered. 'She said never to go near your house. Didn't she, Doyler? We're cousins. She's our auntie. Ma Banana was our granny too.'

Doyler nodded.

Tomas frowned, then laughed a bit. Psychos always laugh.

Suddenly he was on his feet again, striding back and forth within a tight rectangle. He pointed at Doyler.

'What *exactly* did your mother say?'

'Just, you know. Don't be annoying the English man. Stay away from him.'

'The English man? The *English* man? And she has never mentioned any letters? A card game? She doesn't know who I am?'

'No, Mister.'

No, no, no, no? How can it be no?

But they did put a nail through one of the letters. Should have destroyed all of them, if that's what it was. Or stolen them. Tomas stopped walking.

'So this is just a coincidence? That's what you're saying?'

The boys shrugged cautiously, hoping this might be the right answer.

He stared at each of them in turn.

You're disappointed.

Why?

'Then why, why did you do all that to me?' The question was posed gently, with genuine curiosity.

The boys looked at the ground and shrugged again.

'Come on, there must be a reason.'

'Dunno,' murmured one of the twins.

'Yes?'

He flicked his eyes towards Tomas, assessing the risk. ''Cos, like, you're posh and that. Just for the laugh, you know? Wind you up, you know?' He looked directly at him now. 'I dunno. Bored. There's this game we—'

'Game, game, game. That's all anyone can say.' Tomas pointed towards the alley. 'So stabbing my daughter, that was a game?'

'We didn't mean to, Mister. Really. We only meant to give her a fright and that. But she turned her head this way and, like...'

The twin fell silent, thumped by his brother. Tomas stood, and in response they scrambled backwards some more, arms thrown up.

'Jesus,' he whispered. 'I wanted there to be a reason, for this to make sense. Stupid, stupid. Like a fucking film. If my mother hadn't won them, your life...it would have been quite...'

He let his head dip forward, half-laughed again.

'And I come back here. I come home. And the only people who have a connection are these little thugs. These little...but it's not...'

Tomas was mumbling now, didn't seem to be talking to them.

'No explanation, no end. A game? Hardly that. No aim here, nothing to achieve. Coincidence and aimless spite, that's all this is. Messy and unpunctuated and pointless. That's it? Why did you do it? Dunno. The answer to everything. Dunno.'

He could have been laughing, but it was hard to see with him bent over and the hair flopping into his eyes. Just the sort of thing psychos do. The boys huddled together more tightly, and when they saw that the man was indeed crying, his whole body gripped by each sob, they couldn't help but do the same. It is frightening when adults act this way, when it seems as if there is nothing in the world but tears.

*

HE LEFT them there, still shaking. They'd wait until he was gone, then scamper home, probably giggling by then, convincing each other that this had been some sort of victory.

Tomas staggered down the alley.

Would you have hurt them?

Really hurt them?

He stopped walking, instructed by some barely remembered instinct. Tomas crouched, then crawled forward until he could peek around the corner and towards his house. Gardaí there again, one of them furtively smoking a cigarette, the other making a murmured phone call. They exchanged a few words with the Nigerian kids, then laboriously turned the squad car around and sped off. Tomas listened for the crunch of gravel and the slight screech as they turned onto Clontarf Road.

Evening now, yet Bass Avenue seemed brighter, as if he hadn't been here for years and his memory had tricked him into thinking of it as a dark place. It sparkled, the gap in the evening clouds large enough to project sheer blasts of orange sunlight along the cracked street. It smoothed off the sharp edges, made everything comfortably worn. And there were people. For once, the silence was punctured by voices – the Nigerian kids shouting, the man from the wagon-wheel house sloshing water over his red car, the deaf woman looking around and trying to smile, the crusty couple, squatting cross-legged on the edge of the pavement, arms thrown around each other, squinting into the sunlight, leaning over for the odd softly taken kiss.

You don't belong here.

Hardly matters now. Make some trivial amends.

He crossed the road, nodding in response to the greeting yelled by the kids. He climbed the stairs, ignored the ringing phone, took the three remaining Harry Boland letters off the wall, then left the house. He opened the boot of his car and carefully placed the letters inside.

Neat that there are three left, one each, a lot of money, for boys their age, for their families. Cousins. Would be theirs already, only for.

Tomas shut the boot. He turned to speak to his deaf neighbour, to let her know it was all over, but she had gone back indoors. And it was in that moment that he saw the glass from his front window hurtling towards him, followed by a fireball with the face of a demon.

16

WHAT HAPPENED next?

Is there a next? Is that how it works? An orderly queue of occurrence, A + B = C. No, never was, like what Karin said – when was that? – all the time in the same space. A temporal washing machine, the events packed into a tight drum, but spinning so hard they mix and twist in endless combinations – the illusion of infinity. Heat. Breathless. Hard tarmac, a stinging scrape on the arm. Soft black skin, sweat. Heat. Smell of burning, then curry, then some other thick, sweet scent. Heat. Soap. Head stroked. Bed. Goodnight. Silence. Daddy, speak, please, Daddy, come back to us, will you? Heat. Sigh. Heat. No responsibility. Tomas scooped up and taken care of, a rotation of concerned faces dissolving past. Neighbour. Uniform. Breathe into this, Mister Dalton. Heat. That's fine, that's good. Tomas, I'm worried about you. Already have the fella. Don't worry about that other thing either. Them charges will go away.

Go away where? Can you escape the washing machine?

Tomas opened his eyes and lay still, his facial muscles unwilling to move. Later on, he managed a stiff nod for his visitors, while for some he even rose to a half-formed smile. But he didn't speak, not for what felt like several days, though it was in fact just hours. He was cosseted within a comprehension-free fog, safe for a while from ramifications. He nodded from within the womb. Rest here, Mister Dalton. Take your time. So he did, eyes sometimes closed, sometimes open, not entirely listening as Karin wandered through a story about James, you know, the guy you had chauffeuring me? *Fantastic*

214

Dublin accent. So he's deaf, OK? Can't hear a goddamn thing but the guy refuses to wear his hearing aid, you know? And that is stupid, yeah – hey and probably not too safe either – but he's *such* a lovely guy. In his sixties, with this fat little face and a great smile and he's showing me pictures of his kids but the thing was that he couldn't hear most of what I said to him, especially if I'm in the back of the car shouting up. Not a word. But he never tried to avoid that, you know? He'd point to his head and shout back at me, The hearing isn't too good, and then we'd spend like the next twenty minutes with him trying to figure out what I was asking. And he never gave up – not once. Every time he kept going until he understood me. Or thought he understood me because to be candid I got pretty tired with it sometimes. I ended up visiting a few places I had no intention of going to, I can tell you. Still – I dunno – there was just something about James I really admired. I liked the way he refused to wear the hearing aid, as if he was saying, Yeah, OK, there's a bit of me that doesn't work. That's me. But there's a lot of other good things still here. You know? And hey, I've always wanted to be able to say *Home, James*.

'What are you doing here?'

These were the first words Tomas spoke. He sat up, resting on one shaky elbow. He shovelled back his madly waving hair and eyed Karin Goldman suspiciously.

'How are you here?' She gestured towards the plaid wallpaper which surrounded them. The room was decorated in a series of patterned garish colours, each competing with the others in an effort to be the most vivid. The walls seemed to shimmer, as if not completely solid. 'Mister Kuku told me.'

'Who?'

She patted his hand. 'Your neighbour, silly.'

The hand remained on his.

'Oh, yeah. You may not have heard this one yet. And it is a little weird. I mean, if I was some spiritual type I might even think there was something *in* this, you know? But I guess it was just good luck.' She indicated with her head. 'Your house. Obviously there's…not much left. But the weird thing is that one of Mister Kuku's kids – how many does he have? – is out in the back garden when he hears a ringing sound. And it's, like, your phone – the phone from your house – the explosion must have thrown it out there. But it's still working. Isn't that weird?'

Tomas frowned. His lips vibrated slightly. 'Who was ringing?'

She nudged him. 'Me, of course! My God, I've been meaning to ring since I spoke to you from the airport, but to be honest I was pretty embarrassed. But when Mister Kuku told me what happened, I came right over. I think he was relieved because he didn't know who to contact. Isn't that weird?'

'Coincidence.'

'Yeah,' she glumly conceded. 'I suppose.'

*

KARIN TOOK over then, and he was content to submit. Tomas had received no great physical injuries – he had apparently refused to go to hospital – yet still he felt reduced by the experience, the echo of the explosion still humming in his head, like the remnant of the Big Bang.

She brought him tea, strong and sweet, hardly contained by the fragile china cup. The cup was embossed with a string of elephants, each slightly different from the last, each with its trunk curled around the tail of the elephant in front. They seemed to smile as they marched, reminding Tomas of *The Jungle Book*. He sipped and smiled. In thanks, he gestured with the cup towards Mister Kuku, who stood in the hallway, seemingly too shy to enter his own living room. Mister Kuku grinned, bowed and backed away.

Karin perched on the edge of the sofa and watched him. She had been packed and ready to go, resigned to fleeing from the lies she had spewed up. That Tomas knew about her deception only made her desire to get out more intense. Never see Ireland again. Really.

But then, the plane was delayed by fog – did you see that? Wow, it was something – and at first she was furious, then scared, then after a while, when her breathing had slowed and the sweats had eased off, it was like, you know, a *sign* or a second chance or something. *Something.*

After booking back into the Shelbourne, she had marched around the streets, throwing the pill bottles away, one in every bin she found, so even if she panicked it would be impossible to relocate them all. Do you know how many there were? Forty-three. Just weird. Well, all gone now. Most of them, anyway. One or two, she hung onto.

And here's something – I did it because of you. For the first time in, oh, I dunno. For the first time, I cared what somebody else thought of me. And I felt, you know, ashamed.

She stood up awkwardly, hands clasped in front of her. She swayed in her high-heeled sandals.

So that's it.

He nodded, slowly.

She asked, Can you stand?

Think so.

Good. Then you're coming home with me.

*

DARK COVERED the street when they left Mister Kuku's house, so Tomas was spared having to see how the fire had devoured his home until the following morning, when, after a death-like sleep and a gigantic, meaty breakfast in the Shelbourne, Karin instructed James to drive them back to Bass Avenue. Tomas stared at the cindered shell while Karin chatted to one of the gardaí loitering around, a woman carrying a toolbox so large it seemed inconceivable she could even pick it up. Wow, Karin said. Forensics. Cool job.

The house looked like it had been emptied rather than burned down, as if every piece of his collection had been moved, along with every stick of furniture, the windows, the paint on the walls, even the roof. Then, for good measure, soot had been smeared over what was left, a face wearing too much make-up.

Karin and the forensics officer joined him. The garda was short and dumpy and combed her shoulder-length hair in such a way that Tomas suspected she was trying to hide her face. They exchanged nods. Karin discreetly took his hand and squeezed.

'Can't believe it,' he said.

The garda hmmed, as if she couldn't believe it either, though this could hardly have been true, her working day filled with little else but the burned and the maimed.

'It's amazing what a fire will do. This one seemed to have a lot of fuel, though. You had a lot of combustibles in the house? Paper and wood?'

'I suppose.'

'The signs are there. There's a lot of ash.'

'Everything gone,' said Tomas.

'Pretty much,' said the garda.

Karin squeezed his hand again. He looked at her, smiled then. 'Actually, not everything.'

'No?'

'The letters – the three remaining Harry Boland letters – I had just put them in the boot of the car.'

She released his hand. 'Now that *is* weird.'

*

A DETECTIVE, wearing scruffy jeans and a stud in his nose, said they would need him to make a statement, though there was no rush. Already have the guy. Confessed after an hour. Easy. Hard man at first, then he starts crying like a girl. Mulvihill? Marcus Mulvihill? Uncle of those boys you were having the bother with.

Yes, said Tomas. I see.

Not the boys then. Wouldn't have been so vulgar.

Good.

What exactly did he do?

Simple. Filled up your chip pan with oil and left it on. Probably left some damp curtains nearby. Eventually – whoosh – the whole thing went up. Simple. You'd be amazed.

The detective began retreating to his car. You'll come down to the station, so?

I will, said Tomas.

*

NORBERT CLARKE shuffled into the right side of Tomas's peripheral vision and remained there, preparing to be ignored, or worse.

Tomas turned, smiled, waved him over.

Norbert approached cautiously, like a much-kicked dog being allowed near the fireplace. He bobbed his head at Karin and Tomas in turn.

'All over now,' Tomas said.

'Yes, yes.'

'And they have the chap already?'

'The uncle, it seems. Yes.'

They looked at the collapsed remains of the house, still emitting the occasional hiss and crackle.

Norbert turned to face Tomas, then back to the house again. He began speaking, quite quickly, as if he feared interruption. He told them about *Hi Jinx II*, which is a game, you know? A computer game, very realistic. Rated for over-eighteens, but that means nothing, of course, every ten-year-old in the country has it. There was a bit of a stink in the papers when it first came out because it encourages delinquency, but to be honest, compared to some of the other games it is quite mild. I mean, for swearing and violence and that. Quaint by comparison.

But the thing about *Hi Jinx II* is that it isn't just a racing game or a shooting game; it has a story. It's about a group of young boys who carry out pranks on a man who lives alone in a big house. You can play it from the point of view of the man, where you get points if you catch the intruders, but most of them like to play as one of the boys, where you get points for carrying out various pranks and not getting caught.

Tomas and Karin said nothing.

Now, naturally, this could just be a coincidence. But it wasn't just the game that was bugging me, it was the sort of pranks they were carrying out, that's what was familiar. And yesterday when I checked it, well.

He counted on his fingers. There's a prank where they rewire a doorbell so that it gives off a shock. The game shows them how to do this, it's all incredibly detailed. There's injecting urine into milk bottles, smearing faeces on the front door, throwing freshly painted rocks through windows, grinding up an ornament into dust. They get more and more points for each prank and there's a help section they can go to where it gives detailed instructions on how to carry out each prank, how not to get paint on your clothes or inhale the smell from the faeces. I didn't have time to check all the pranks, but I bet all you experienced can be found in that game.

He nodded at the pile of charred timbers and sooty bricks.

Apart from, er, this last bit.

Norbert stretched out his arms, like he was waiting to be crucified.

So you see? That's where they got all this from. It was a game they were trying out in real life.

Tomas frowned. In what way is that a story?

Well, at the start of the game the boys kick their football into the man's garden – Crabby Crinkle, he's called.

Tomas smiled.

Crabby Crinkle punctures the ball and gives it back. Same thing happens with a Frisbee. Crabby Crinkle glues metal weights to the Frisbee so it won't fly and gives it back. Eventually the boys vow revenge on Crabby Crinkle. They try to play pranks on him, but he also leaves traps for them. The story ends either with the boys getting caught or Crabby Crinkle moving out.

That's kinda sick, Karin said. Do these kids not know the difference between fantasy and reality?

Tomas shook his head. There was a story to this? They wanted to see could if they make me move out?

Yes, I suppose so, Norbert said. I don't know if that makes you feel any better, or…

The three of them stood in silence.

Eventually, Tomas smiled. Actually, it does make me feel better. He turned to Norbert. Could you do me a favour?

Yes?

I have three framed letters in my car. I want to give one each to the boys. Doesn't matter who gets which one. Just one each. Could you pass them on?

Sure, sure. Norbert opened his mouth to say something, then seemed to change his mind. OK. Sure. I'm actually going around there shortly.

Tomas paused.

No. I'll bring them up to the station. I want to write a little note, explaining where they came from. The history of the things.

*

'I SUPPOSE I should confess to something.'

'Yes?'

'I lied to you too. My daughter is a lesbian.'

Karin smirks. 'Why, that's great!'

Tomas smiles too, even though he feels terrified – the guards, the fire brigade, all the comforting uniforms gone, the dusty remnants of his house swirling around. The blackened windows resemble empty eye sockets, the house a skullish tomb, half-eaten by nature.

She roots in her bag, hands him a brown plastic pill box.

'Here. Try this.'

Like a mourner at a funeral, Tomas walks into the shadow of the house, then hunkers down. Gently, he scoops some of the ash into the container and replaces the clear plastic stopper.

Karin watches, and once again resists an urge to hug Tomas lavishly. Doesn't like that sort of thing. Too reserved, too proud, too brave. Doesn't realise how brave he's been, risking everything to protect the memory of his family, their time on earth.

Because what else is there? Wish I'd done the same; wish I hadn't been so quick to dump my past.

Tomas returns to her side. He badly needs a haircut, thinks Karin.

'I suppose it's more compact,' he says. 'Everything melted together now.'

He slips the pill box into his pocket and takes her hand. They say nothing for several minutes.

Daddy squeezes his hand just a little too hard as they walk by. He knows he'd get a clip around the ear if he tried looking in a window of the posh houses, yet he wants to; he suspects Daddy wants to as well. There's the quality now.

'How are you feeling?' she asks.

'Bit nervous.'

You're shaking.

Karin says nothing, inviting more. Tomas's voice is croaky, like splintering wood. 'You know, everything I am was in that house. All the things that reminded me of my life.' He taps his forehead. 'Now all I have is my crappy brain and half the time that's no use.'

He swallows, then looks away.

A light wind skips up Bass Avenue, wrinkling the surface of the puddles left behind by the fire hoses. Wavelets appear on the puddles.

The deaf woman stands in the open doorway of her house, waiting to be noticed. A thin smile stretches her face. She makes a gesture somewhat like a salute, and holds it for so long it seems to become painful. Tomas nods several times, until she retreats inside.

Karin hmms, then asks, 'Is that so bad?'

Anna's hand is small and fat and slippery inside his. She keeps twisting and pointing. Is that where you lived, Daddy? What did you play? Did you have television? Was it the olden days?

Tomas shrugs. She leans up and deposits a peck on his cheek.

'I'll help you remember. Two heads are better than one.'

Tomas smiles to cover his desperation. What Karin offers is insane, a crazy risk. Barely know the woman, hardly the most stable, either – have me clawing the walls within days, all that talktalktalk. No, nonsense.

What else is there? Everything gone now.

Tomas is unaware of how much he will need to remember in the future. The move to New York. How he hated it. Anna's baby (donor sperm). Her wedding in Amsterdam (to Hazel, a gym instructor). Hazel's nervous breakdown. The move back to London. The stiff reconciliation with Eli. Marta's death in a car accident. The award he won for the TV series; the award Karin won for acting in the TV series. His heart murmur. Karin's emphysema.

Things first to be experienced, then salted away for later examination, to discover that only a tattered part remains in memory.

The stout woman moves in short, uncertain spurts along the footpath. Is this the right street even? Silly looking here, how will you know what he looks like? Go home, you silly old fool.

Karin and Tomas hold hands and look at number 17, Bass Avenue. Gently, she nudges him.

'Perhaps you should ring your wife? You know, let her know what's going on?'

Tomas nods, grins slightly. 'Yes, yes, I must. She had been ringing me, threatening to come over again, actually. But I never rang her back.'

Unseen by him, Karin pretends to gag.

They watch the remains of the house, in no hurry to leave.

'I won't lie,' Tomas says. 'I may never say I love you.'

She smiles gently; generously.

'That's OK. That's fine. Let's see what happens.'

Also by Sean Moncrieff

Non-fiction:
Star Raving Rules
God: A User's Guide

Fiction:
Dublin